SNOW-COMING MOON

Also by Stan Evans,
published by Horsdal & Schubart

OUTLAW GOLD

SNOW-COMING MOON

Stan Evans

Horsdal & Schubart

Horsdal & Schubart Publishers Ltd.
Victoria, BC, Canada

Cover painting by Jim Wispinski, Victoria, BC.

We acknowledge the support of the Canada Council for the Arts for our publishing program.

This book is set in American Garamond.

Printed and bound in Canada by Hignell Printing Ltd., Winnipeg.

Canadian Cataloguing in Publication Data

Evans, Stan, 1931-
  Snow-coming moon

  ISBN 0-920663-52-4

  1. Frontier and pioneer life—British Columbia—Fiction. 2. Chilcotin
River Region (B.C.)—History—Fiction. I. Title.
PS8559.V36S66 1997   C813'.54   C97-910141-7
PR9199.3.E93S66 1997

Printed and bound in Canada

For Kim, Nicholas,
Laura and
David

ACKNOWLEDGEMENTS

Many of the characters in this book are historical figures, and the areas described exist, but *Snow-Coming Moon* is a work of fiction, as are some events and place names. Incidents which I describe as taking place in Waddy Flats occurred elsewhere, and I have altered the names of many actual characters.

In 1993, Judge Anthony Sarich was appointed to examine the breakdown of trust between native peoples and British Columbia's justice system. Judge Sarich found that the roots of twentieth-century discontent could be traced directly to the questionable justice meted out to Chilcotin leaders in 1864. In his report, Judge Sarich wrote:"Whatever the correct version [of the Chilcotin War], that episode of history has left a deep wound in the body of Chilcotin society. It is time to heal that wound. Since that trial and the hangings occurred before British Columbia joined Confederation, it is appropriate that Victoria grant a posthumous pardon to those chiefs, and so I recommend."

Preparation of this manuscript involved much research, and I thank the staff members of the B.C. Archives and Records Service, in Victoria, for their courtesy and assistance.

Stan Evans
Victoria, 1997

CHAPTER ONE

Mrs. WILBUR WAS so tired of life and so tired of her shiftless husband that sometimes she could hardly hold her head up. But she had no business taking their butter churn back to Decker's store and telling him they couldn't make any more payments on it — that was her husband's job. Wilbur kept putting it off because taking it back would make him look useless and foolish in front of his neighbours. As if they didn't already know. Sick of waiting she returned the butter churn herself.

When she dragged it into the store, the men jawboning around Decker's stove took their caps off, to show respect, even though she was a no-account woman with a no-account husband. Looking queer, wearing a shapeless home-made frock and a cloth bonnet and a pair of men's brogans laced with bits of string, she went right on past the barrels of apples and the sacks of grain and the bolts of cloth, until she'd toted that butter churn clear across the store, to where Decker was standing behind his counter.

"Here you are. I brought it back 'cos we can't afford it no more," she cried in her harsh, cracked voice. "Wilbur paid you five dollars up front and we got five dollars still owin', so you ain't losin' nothin'."

"Mrs. Wilbur," Decker said quietly. "Don't trouble yourself. I'd be obliged if you'd keep on using the churn until things get better."

"Things won't never get no better," she snapped, her eyes colourless and blank. "Wilbur s'pose to bring the churn back weeks ago, but he's too proud. He'd rather daydream and loaf in here, jawbonin' and carryin' on, pretending everythin's all right, while everybody with a lick of sense knows the town's falling apart round our ears."

"Now Agnes, this ain't proper," Wilbur said, grinning like a fool as he came forward from his place by the stove and went across the creaking floorboards to touch her arm.

"You go outside, husband," she said, with an angry twist of her body. "You schemed us into the poorhouse, but we won't be makin' no more butter. That's owning up. I'm owning up fer the both of us."

"Hit's not decent," Wilbur said, tall and clumsy, his sunken cheeks yellow beneath a straw hat. "Talkin' our business in front of the whole town."

"Will you keep on percasternatin' till them savages come runnin' out of the hills and kilt every last one of us?" she rasped. "Schemed us into the poorhouse is what you done, bringin' us to this hell hole of a place! What will it take? How much is I suppose to take before you does what's decent and takes us away to a town what ain't just a dumpin' ground fer no-good failures?"

"It's all right, Mrs. Wilbur," Decker said. "It's no trouble at all."

"I can't take no more," she cried. "Don't nobody understand it? Waddy Flats is finished!"

Wilbur had hardly a scrap of pride, but to be disgraced in front of his neighbours was more than his flesh could bear. So he slapped his wife's face and seized her wrist and in a minute they were tugging and wrestling like a pair of wild animals.

Decker's throat was drawn so tight he could hardly breathe, watching that man hit his wife until ribbons of blood and snot and tears dripped off her face and down her frock. Wilbur kept hitting her too, until the stuffing went out of her as if somebody had slashed a sack of oats with a knife. And then she had to cry.

There wasn't a thing Decker could do. If there's one thing a fellow can't do, it's to get between a man and his wife.

Wilbur pulled her outside, her crying, with that cloth bonnet twisted over her face and her ugly brogans scratching and clacking on the bare floorboards, the witnesses silent and ashamed, shuffling and staring at their feet, as Wilbur put her on a small, lop-eared, rough-coated mule, and led her off home.

Sombre and thoughtful, Decker closed the store. With the sawtooth edge of the treetops blurring in the fading light he walked to the corral and watched his horses. A young woman came riding along his fence line wearing high polished boots and a black divided skirt, and a tweed jacket over a ruffled white silk blouse. She was mounted on a black blood-mare that stood fourteen hands and he saw that the horse's legs and belly were white with salt and the woman's boots and saddle-flaps were wet because she'd been riding on the beach. She was beautiful, in her black hat with a wide flat brim and her long black hair woven into french braids that lay gathered against the long white column of her neck. Going past she turned towards Decker and touched her hat with her fingers. At her passing, an eagle on the top of a Douglas fir dropped down and swooped low across the land, before it flapped and circled up again and landed in the same tree. Over against the western shore and along the marshy verge of the inlet, flights of waterfowl were racing the sunset in the last golden glow beneath a few thin clouds as the girl disappeared down a trail into the jackpines.

Decker drifted across to the pig hole and scratched Sally with a stick until she grunted with pleasure. Sally was a Berkshire and many of Decker's hopes were riding on her. Last time she'd farrowed, Sally dropped twelve piglets. Being clumsy and inexperienced at mothering she squashed three before they were a week old, and bears ate most of the rest. Now Sally was in farrow again.

Bears were a problem at Waddy Flats. Black bears, brown bears. Grizzlies were the worst. There was nothing grizzlies liked better than a nice fat pig, although grizzlies would eat anything when they were hungry. It wasn't safe to go walking, sometimes, unless you were packing a gun. Decker had more or less given up on guns since a maniac shot Montgomery with a Winchester repeating rifle. With his best friend gone, Decker got tired of city living and pre-empted land at Waddy Flats. Sometimes, though, when he'd spent the best part of a week sweating with an axe and a cross-cut saw falling a single Douglas fir and trying to burn it, he thought the place would never be more than a tree ranch. No sooner had he felled one tree than three alders and a crop of thistles were poking out of the earth to take its place.

Bushrat was Decker's hired man.

There were few men who knew more about ranching than Bushrat. He'd said as much himself, when he walked out of the woods one day with everything he owned in a gunny sack; a short, heavy, angry old squirt with thick black eyebrows and a white beard and a few licks of white hair sticking up from his head like strands of barbed wire.

"You Decker?" he'd said when he came stumping up onto Decker's porch in overalls and a straw hat and carved riding boots with holes in the toes.

"Who wants to know?"

"I'm Bushrat Wright. I guess you heard about me?"

"I can't say I have," Decker said.

"The reason you ain't, I guess, is 'cos you're a stranger in this country. Ask around all you want. Seek high and low you won't find a man who don't call Bushrat Wright a straight shooter. You'd know that without me having to tell you, if you weren't a greenhorn."

"I'm green, all right," Decker allowed. "It hardly seems five minutes since I built my barn and drove pickets into the ground for that corral."

"What you doin' buildin' a barn in the first place? Ain't you supposed to be a lawman."

"Lawman hell. I'm a two-bit constable."

"Lawman or not, you need to build another rocking chair like the one you're sitting on so's you can entertain company," Bushrat said. "And if you ever expect to amount to anythin' serious, you need to get yerself a hired man."

"Who says so?"

"I do. You needs a man with local knowledge."

"Hands with local knowledge are mighty scarce," Decker conceded. "A fellow who's any use at all would be building roads for Trotter."

"Did you say Trotter, cousin?" Bushrat, said, stamping his foot and glaring. "Is you buddies with that bird?"

"No."

"Man's a idiot. Fired me fer no reason," Bushrat declared, sitting down on the porch step and fanning his face with his hat. "Seen me talking on duty. All's I done was, I laid down my shovel fer a minute to cut me a chaw. What's he do? He gives me my time. Trotter's sorry now, I reckon, but I ain't never going back, nossir."

Decker needed a hired man, and Bushrat needed a job, although he was too proud and ornery to come right out and beg for one. Decker was wondering whether it was worth making room for a cantankerous old desperado who looked angry enough to bite somebody. He said, "I'll tell you something. If I knew a fellow who could ride fence and rope steers, I might make room for him."

"Most fellers would, but I'm lookin' fer a grubstake, is all. I got my eye on a prospect," Bushrat said, playing hard to get. "There's gold nuggets in there big as eggs, just waitin'..."

Words failed Bushrat for a moment and he frowned at the surrounding trees, his eyebrows jumping up and down on his forehead like a couple of black moths. "Lookit them soapberry bushes popping up where you cleared them firs," he jeered. "Soapberries is fine hog food. You point a hog at one, he's looking at his dinner. All you needs is a bred pig and you got a passel of land clearers on the hoof afore you can turn around."

"Wouldn't surprise me to hear that you're a pig fancier yourself."

"I always fancied pigs," Bushrat returned philosophically. "Specially one that's being turned slow over a fire with a apple in its mouth."

"Think you could make a pig hole in the floor of my barn if you put your mind to it?"

"I could, but first I'd have to put my mind to it. Pigs like nothing better than a nice pile of warm manure to roll in come winter. If I put my mind to it, I'd have one dug and waitin' fer occupation in no time," Bushrat said, studying the arthritic knuckles of his hands. "But what I need at the minute is a grubstake. Groceries and a shovel. A hundred dollars buys you a tenth share. Worth a million, probably."

"If it's worth a million now it'll be worth a million later. Park yourself here for a spell. For starters, you can clear some of the rocks off this place and drag 'em over here in a stone boat."

"What for?"

"To make room for grass to grow. And I need rocks to build a chimney with."

"Stone boatin' and masonry? I done plenty of that too, in my younger days," Bushrat said modestly. "Carpentry too, not to mention railroadin', muleskinnin', and fightin' in foreign wars just fer the hell of it. Only thing I never done is been a sailor. If you could find a feller with skills like mine, why, he'd be worth his weight in gold."

"Not to me, he wouldn't. I might go as high as free board, plus ten dollars cash every month, for a real top hand."

"What kinda man would be swayed from his heart's desire by ten bucks?" Bushrat said as he admired the view. "Why, I'd pay you ten bucks a month fer the privilege of settin' on this porch every night, and watching the sun light up them pretty mountains like that, 'cos hit's a view I'll never get tired of, and I've seen some views. The snag is, I ain't got ten bucks."

Decker focussed his eyes on the edge of the barn while Bushrat wrestled with weighty ideas.

"You done hired yourself a top hand," Bushrat said at last, slapping his knee. "It's just temp'ry, till I goes back to prospectin'. Right now, though, I'm drier'n a salt codfish inside a hot oven. You got any mountain dew in yer cabin?"

First: Bushrat knew as much about digging pig holes as a peacock knows about higher mathematics. Second: he'd rather contemplate the beauties of nature than clear rocks with a stone boat. But he was a fair hand at stuffing firewood into Decker's stove, and a half-decent cook. What Bushrat excelled at was cutting chaws and spitting tobacco juice.

Governor James Douglas had twisted Decker's arm mightily or he never would have moved here in the first place. Before he arrived, it had been a landscape unmodified by human design where nobody spoke English and only the stars were familiar to him.

"I need a constable to establish a British presence on the Chilcotin coast," Douglas had said. "And you're the only man I know reckless enough to go."

"Except you."

"I've already got a job."

"And a wife."

"If you had a wife, Decker, I wouldn't let you go."

But the job paid fifty dollars a month. Decker and Douglas visited Colonel Moody in the land commissioner's office and gazed together at a map that showed an area the size of Belgium without a single township marked on it. Decker stabbed the map with his finger and signed on the dotted line.

That done, Decker purchased one little Highland bull, three cows, two cocks, fifteen hens, two sacks of seed potatoes, two gelded quarterhorses, three thousand board feet of sawn lumber, kegs of nails, miscellaneous tools, and many rolls of number eight wire. Douglas arranged for the Crown to pay Decker's moving expenses so he hired a steam tug, and had the whole outfit towed up to Bute Inlet.

A calendar in the tug's wheelhouse showed the date — May 15, 1862 — when they reached Decker's section. His land — one thousand feet of low bank waterfront and undulating bench country — was heavily treed, except for fifty acres of bunch-grass meadow bordering the inlet.

Decker landed his supplies on the beach. Four-legged creatures were shoved off the barge and left to swim ashore, or drown. By the time the steam tug puffed down the inlet on its way back to civilization, Decker's little bull had sampled the silverweed and verbena and gumweed growing along the shoreline, didn't like any of it, and chased his harem into the high country.

Decker watered his horses at the creek and rode the chestnut down among the trees to a stand of cottonwoods overlooking a long curve of the inlet and knew it for the place where he wanted his house to stand. Before tackling a house he built a barn big enough to stable himself and the two horses. Rats and fleas and bedbugs promptly moved into it and poultry were soon roosting in the rafters. Things were messy until Decker stretched canvas over his sleeping quarters. Days, he felled trees and cleared trails and put up fences. Nights, he listened to wolves and drew the plans for a two-roomed shack that would have to serve as a jail, gold commissioner's office, and, as it turned out, a store for general merchandise.

Then Alfred Waddington transformed Decker's remote wilderness into Waddy Flats. Against everybody's advice, that stubborn, misguided Englishman talked Governor Douglas into granting him a charter for a toll road. Now, Waddington was determined to build his road from Bute Inlet across the mountains as a shortcut to the interior. Land bordering the north side of Decker's ranch became a townsite with a grid of three streets and seven cross streets (only one street had been cleared). Decker had no sooner finished building his shack than he needed an extension; he added another room, hung up a shingle with 'Decker's Store' written on it, and brought in groceries and other supplies from Victoria. Soon, steamboats were discharging men and equipment on a wharf at the mouth of the Homathko River. Roadbuilders were sleeping in a bunkhouse, practically in Decker's back yard. Decker slid sideways from being a lawman with a ranch, to a rancher with a store. Sodbusters with names like MacCormack and Wilbur and Strongitharm and Quirk pre-empted land, and built log cabins.

In no time at all, Decker's store was the unofficial town hall. Decker was the town constable, unelected mayor, and honorary surgeon. He gave Bushrat Wright a deputy's badge. Bushrat went around bragging that when Waddington got finished building his road, Waddy Flats would have a permanent population of, why, thirty people. But there wasn't a dern thing to stop Waddy Flats from growing as big as San Francisco. Bigger.

Decker leaned against a fence and looked up at the slivered April moon, hooked into the mountaintops. Bushrat came out of the house carrying two coffee mugs and gave one to Decker. After a while Bushrat said, "Did you see that little sweetheart ride on by just now?"

Decker did not answer.

"The worst fool things I got into was mostly done without thinkin'," Bushrat said. "I just let 'er rip and ended up to here in cow shit. You hear what I'm sayin'?"

Decker nodded.

"And that's what's givin' me wrinkles."

"Are you talking about Mrs. Trotter?"

"Hell yes. The one who just tapped her hat at you. Isabel. That pretty girl shouldn't be ridin' alone."

"Why?"

"'Cos hit's as sure as the world that there's fellers aplenty might commit a foolishness agin her, without thinkin' overmuch till it was too late, or I ain't a certified goddam bronc-buster."

CHAPTER TWO

ONE-EAR BROWN WAS dozing on his bunk when his anchored sloop rolled on a rising tide. Tucking a pistol inside his belt he went on deck. A blue heron soared above and flapped around a bend into the upper reaches of the tree-lined river. The air was dark ahead, but astern, across a mile of salt marsh, surf made a white fringe along a yellow beach. Above the sounds of loose tackle banging in the rigging and the slow gurgle of water flowing along the hull, One-Ear heard a familiar thumping noise. He took four quick angry strides and delivered a kick to a tarpaulin that was writhing on the forward deck. There was an enraged howl as one edge of the tarpaulin peeled back to reveal Gridger, entangled in the coils of rope he'd been using as a pillow. Sitting up, Gridger banged his head against the main boom and fell back, groaning.

"Quit hollerin'," One-Ear said. "A blow to the head can't hurt a fool."

"I ain't nobody's fool!"

"You're a danged fool is what you are. Don't you know better'n to turn in on watch?"

"I weren't turned in nohow," Gridger said, clenching his fists. He was about to swing a punch when he found himself staring into the muzzle of One-Ear's pistol.

"You ain't got no more brains than a dishrag! Won't you never learn? While you was funnin' yourself, we could have been ambushed."

"Nobody's gonna ambush this turkey. Besides, I been doin' some ambushin' myself," Gridger leered, and yanked more of the tarpaulin aside to uncover Missy, a naked Cowichan girl about fourteen years old, with tiny high breasts and a little fuzz of black pubic hair. She stared up at One-Ear without the least trace of expression on her broad brown face.

Gridger was a skinny man of thirty who had no chin at all; his face just fell off at his bottom lip and ran in a wedge to his adam's apple. He put on filthy woollen longjohns, scratched himself all over, ran fingers through his lank blonde hair and touched the swelling bruise on his skull.

"We got work to do. Grab that towrope and get over the side with it," One-Ear said, as Missy skipped aft and went below.

"I'm hungry. What about some grub?"

"You ain't earned no grub."

"That ain't been proved yet," Gridger muttered, but when One-Ear took a sudden menacing step towards him he grabbed the sloop's heavy towline and went over the side into the ice-fed river. Shivering and cursing, he waded ashore and took the strain while One-Ear cranked the anchor up with the windlass.

One-Ear Brown was wearing a baggy cloth cap and canvas trousers rolled up to his knees above his bare feet. When he looked, Missy was watching him from the cabin doorway. She gazed shyly at the deck with her shoulders drooping and long strands of oily black hair falling over her face. "Don't you go sampling none of my liquor or I'll heave you overboard!" One-Ear yelled.

Tears sprang into Missy's eyes and she slammed the cabin door. Grinning malevolently, One-Ear unfastened a long pole that was lashed upright to the main shrouds and plunged it into the water. When the pole bottomed, he threw his weight on it and walked aft, shoving, with his bare feet braced against cleats nailed crosswise along the decks. With Gridger heaving on the towline, the bootleggers worked their sloop upstream.

Three hundred feet above, Douglas firs waved their topmost branches in the wind, but at water level the sails shook languidly and the air was heavy with the stink of rotting vegetation. Shafts of April sunlight dappled the moss-draped trees. Odours of decay rose from the ooze and Gridger's feet sank ankle deep with every step.

Panting and slithering, Gridger slapped at insects. "By crikey!" he yelled as he tripped over an arching root and fell face down. "If muck was gold I'd have a fortune sticking to my skivvies."

"Oh aye," One-Ear retorted. "And if sheep climbed trees and ate maple leaves this backwater would make a dandy ranch."

Gridger gritted his teeth and kept heaving. Half a mile later he fell to his knees for the twentieth time. "Dern, I'm beat," he panted, and made the towline fast to a tree root before sitting in the mud with his hands clasped around his knees and his head drooping.

"What you think you're doing?"

"Readin' a dern newspaper."

"Keep pullin'. We ain't got all day."

"I already pulled me guts out."

"You ain't pulled your guts out, you wore 'em out last night."

Gridger was regretting there wasn't an axe handy, because he might have split One-Ear in two with it, right then and there, as payment for all the back-talk and slights he was enduring, until he bethought himself that he couldn't read a compass, and with One-Ear dead, he'd be lost among these remote dern islands. Vexed, he reached down for a handful of mud and threw it at a little frog that was taking its ease on a piece of driftwood.

It was mid-afternoon when One-Ear dropped his anchor again and the sloop swung to rest in the middle of the river across from a sheltered meadow where, years earlier, the meandering river had washed the trees off a two-acre patch. A single moss-covered Indian longhouse stood partly concealed beneath overhanging maple and cottonwood trees. Half a dozen cracked and weathered totem poles frowned down in the silence, and there was an overpowering stink of fish coming from the splits of salmon that were drying on lattices in the sunlight.

"Where's them dern Injuns at?" One-Ear said, puzzled, as Gridger clambered aboard. "And what's them there things?"

Gridger turned to look. Dozens of shiny black crows were feeding quietly on large dark bundles that were draped across the lower branches of trees.

"This don't look so promising," Gridger said. "Mebbe we should clear off, seeing as how there ain't no customers."

"I'll do the thinking on this ship," One-Ear snapped. "Quit yapping and get out from under my feet, damn you."

One-Ear sat on the cabin top. For five minutes, he brooded and fumed, wondering why he wasn't surrounded by jubilant Indians, anxious to trade skins for liquor, and wondering also where he could get himself a new mate, and the sooner the better. Somebody with strength and brains who wouldn't cut and run at the first sign of trouble. The trouble was, nobody with those qualifications would work for a bootlegger — he'd be bootlegging on his own.

Grinding his teeth, One-Ear waded ashore, followed reluctantly by Gridger, and five yards into the long grass they almost tripped over a corpse.

"Holy God on the mountain!" One-Ear cried, yanking the pistol from his belt.

Gridger stood by, his eyes as large as goose eggs, while One-Ear examined the body. It was a full grown human being — male or female, they couldn't tell. The body had been covered with a Hudson's Bay blanket which scavenging animals had ripped off to gnaw at the flesh. Bones lay scattered and maggots were crawling inside the red-boned skull. Five more of the unburied dead were scattered beneath bushes. Other corpses rotted on platforms in the trees, eight feet above the ground.

"Jesus," Gridger murmured. "My Jesus."

"Haidas murdered 'em, I reckon. Don't worry, Gridge. Them killers is long gone."

Gridger opened his mouth to venture an opinion but before any words came out he thought better of it. In his present foul mood, One-Ear would seize on anything he said and turn words around until they made Gridger look stupid. All the same, he knew the natives hadn't been murdered; they had perished from disease. The conjecture made Gridger tremble.

The longhouse was a low rectangular shed, full of mysterious shadows. One-Ear didn't want Gridger to see that he was nervous so he straightened his shoulders and barged inside where more bodies were staring up from the disorder of their blankets and small unseen animals moved in the dark. Hearing their faint scutterings, One-Ear's nerve snapped and he backed into the sunlight. When his heart stopped pounding, he shouted, "Over here. Gimme a hand."

Gridger was sitting on a fallen tree, gnawing a piece of dried salmon with the decayed black stumps of his teeth. "What do you want?" he said, wincing from the pain of toothache.

"You're a lazy swine!" One-Ear yelled. "Help me to collect these here blankets, then let's clear off from this cursed boneyard."

"Dead men's blankets! Hell fire and damnation, I ain't collecting no .... How much is a dern blanket worth, anyhow?"

"Ten marten skins apiece."

"Ten marten skins is nothin'. 'Tain't enough ter tempt me, anyhow. If you needs 'em so bad, Charlie, get 'em yourself, and good luck ter you. I ain't so greedy, myself."

"What's the matter? You scared of ghosts?"

"I ain't scared of nothin' or nobody!"

"Ah, you're full of wind," One-Ear scoffed, and re-entered the long-house, where he found six blankets and stowed them in the sloop's forward hold.

The bootleggers were stuffing sacks with dried salmon when Gridger heard a scratching sound, and stiffened.

"What's eatin' you now?" One-Ear said unpleasantly. "Is these the first dead men you seen?"

"Something moved over there," Gridger said, peering across the meadow.

"Scared by a bunch a dead Injuns, ain't yer?"

"Shut up and listen," Gridger hissed, as he sidled through a patch of bushes. An old woman wearing a dog-hair cloak was lying face-down beside a fallen tree. Matted hair covered her head like a white shawl. One-Ear came up and nudged the body with his toe, saying, "Here's a mystery. This one ain't been dead long."

The woman rolled over, moaning, and reached for Gridger's ankle.

Her face was covered with blisters. Where she had raked herself with fingernails to relieve the intolerable itch of smallpox, red and yellow liquid matter was drying into crusty scabs.

CHAPTER THREE

Decker AND BUSHRAT were burning slash on a bonfire in their yard. Half a mile away, Wilbur was locking the door of his house. He stood outside for a moment, his shoulders bowed and his eyes blank with grief, until with a sudden angry jerk of his wrist he withdrew the key from its lock and heaved it into the weeds.

"That's hit," Bushrat said, as the Wilburs appeared, taking their final walk down Waddington Street. "I never figured Wilbur would actually do nothin' though. Boil that feller down to his bones and you won't get enough starch to stiffen a ladies' hanky."

Decker's eyes were focussed on the *Nonpareil* — a red-sailed schooner moored at the wharf. He said, "Go easy on the poor devil."

"Wilbur ain't nothin' but the cause of his own misery."

"What the hell. Come on, we'll give 'em a sendoff, anyhow."

In the evening breeze, wavelets were flooding the bay with blue and white. Wilbur came up the dirt road, cowed and sagging in overalls and boots, his cheeks so hollow that he seemed to be sucking them in. His wife followed two paces behind, ashen-faced, in that same shapeless old frock and those ugly brogans and a rag bonnet. She it was who counted out the money for their fares from a mixed bundle of sixpences and pennies, and silver dollars that she took out of a knotted handkerchief, slowly, one coin at a time and handed over to the schooner's mate.

Gridger said, "They didn't tell nobody they was leavin' today, did they?"

"They're embarrassed and don't want a fuss," Decker said, as MacCormack and Strongitharm showed up with Quirk. "I don't blame them."

Quirk tried to lighten the proceedings with a joke about saving a place beside Decker's stove, for when Wilbur got homesick and came back.

"Who's he tryin' to fool?" Bushrat whispered. "Them Wilburs is through with Waddy Flats forever."

Wilbur shuffled aboard without speaking, carrying a few sacks and string-wrapped cardboard boxes. He turned when he reached the deck of the schooner. With one last look at a break in the wilderness where the roof of his house showed among the trees, he stumbled below to the passenger cabin.

Ten of Trotter's roadworkers arrived at the last moment and went aboard before the *Nonpareil*'s gangplank was taken in. Sail was raised, mooring lines were released, and deckhands poled their ship into the ebbing stream. Red canvas bellied in the wind. Picking up speed, the schooner held a steady course down the channel until a sloop, coming in on the wrong side of the inlet, sailed too close. Sharp words were exchanged between the two skippers as the *Nonpareil* went hard to starboard. A collision narrowly averted, the *Nonpareil* sliced a curving white arc towards the Strait of Georgia.

"That's another bunch of Trotter's men quit and gone," Bushrat remarked as MacCormack and Strongitharm and Quirk left the wharf, shaking their heads. "If Trotter ain't careful, he won't have nobody left workin' on the road."

Decker and Bushrat waited until the sloop came into the wharf. Gridger, standing in the bows, heaved a line. Decker caught it and hooked it over a bollard.

"You see what that schooner done?" One-Ear barked, as he warped his boat alongside. "Dern near run me down, he did, and I calls that a deliberate hoggin' of the high seas."

Decker said, "What brings you here?"

"That's my business."

"It'll be my business too, if I find you selling rotgut to Indians," Decker replied mildly. "I'll be keeping an eye on you, my lad, so watch your step."

"I ain't sellin' liquor to nobody. I wouldn't even be here in the first place, except we needs somebody to yank Gridger's teeth."

"What's wrong with yanking 'em yourself?"

"I done one tooth, but the coward won't let me touch no more."

"He doesn't trust you any more than I do."

"I don't care who yer trusts and who yer don't trust, mister bloody Decker. You ain't the boss of me."

"I'll be your lord, master and high executioner if I find any drunks wandering the streets tonight. And here's something else. We found a dead European on the beach."

"When?"

"A week ago."

"Anybody special?"

"We won't know, until we find his head. It's struck on a war lance, I guess. If you are dumb enough to go selling liquor to Indians on my territory you'd better be careful who you deal with, otherwise your head might be the next one to go missing."

"Folks that messes with me better reckon on this, first," One-Ear said, patting the revolver at his hip. Scowling, he sat in the sternsheets with Missy and Gridger. Scratching themselves and drinking, the bootleggers watched the lawmen walk up the dirt road and disappear into the trees behind a rough shack that marked the beginning of Waddington Street.

From its rock-bound entrance to the sea, the harbour was fringed by Douglas firs and cedars. Here and there, rough cabins clung to the craggy foreshore. Fires glowed where Homathkos and Euclataws and Chilcotins — sometime enemies brought together by the recent coming of white men — had built temporary lodges and, for the moment, dwelt uneasily side by side along the river. The beat of Indian drums drifted down the inlet, along with the smell of woodsmoke.

Gridger opened his jaws and mumbled, "Take a look at this, Charlie. I think one of these chompers is coming looser."

One-Ear got a whiff of Gridger's foul breath and reeled back. "Shut yer dern face afore the stink puts me under," he cried with loathing. "Whyn't you take the pliers to 'em yourself, and be done with it?"

"There's use in a few of 'em yet."

"Aaaaaagh! Yer dern mouth makes me sick," One-Ear said, as he gazed upriver. Speaking half to himself, he said, "Them blankets that we took off them dead Injuns. I bet them Chilcotins'll give us something for 'em."

Gridger raised his shoulders, sighed, and took another drink. To entertain himself, Gridger imagined tearing One-Ear's gums off with hot pincers, until he knew what it felt like to be the second mate of a bootlegger's sloop, with aching teeth and limited prospects.

***

Clarence Trotter left his dining-room table abruptly and sat in an armchair beside the fire. Agitated, his right knee jerking nervously up and down like a blacksmith's hammer, he shouted, "Those damned Indians and their drums are driving me mad! Will they never stop their blasted noise?"

Isabel, seated at the long walnut table, flinched at the violence of his words but remained silent.

"What's the matter with you?" he cried. "Have you lost your voice?"

"Forget the drums, Clarence. Put the drums out of your mind..."

"How can I? Indians are pounding 'em outside my damned house from morning till night!" Trotter said as, with another forceful movement, he flung himself out of his armchair. Hurrying past the table on his way out of the room he brushed a lamp to the floor with his elbow. The glass chimney smashed, spreading its jagged shards across the carpet, and the flame went out. "Clean that mess up before I cut myself," he bellowed. "What else are you good for?"

Isabel stared at the tablecloth as Trotter's footsteps faded along the corridor. Downcast, she pushed back her chair and rose from the table, a slim beautiful woman in a creamy silk dress. Taking a candle from the mantelpiece she lit it with a taper at the fire, went into the corridor and opened the panelled wooden doors of a closet. When she reached inside for a broom, one of Trotter's attaché cases, balanced on an upper shelf with some loosely piled books, fell down and burst open, disgorging a litter across the floor. Kneeling in the candlelight, Isabel saw pictures of naked women in dissolute poses; cartoon books with titles like *Lady Helen's Rape*, and items of inscrutable intention made of moulded rubber. She imagined Trotter ducking into dingy back-alley shops with his collar turned up and his hat brim pulled down, and forking over greasy coins for these abominable goods.

Trotter came into the corridor followed by Byron McEachren, his foreman. Still kneeling, she bowed her body over the filth on the floor as the two men went past to the dining room. Trotter slammed the door on her.

She overheard Trotter say, "Watch where you put your feet. That useless woman of mine just made a mess and there's glass on the floor."

Gathering the pornography and tidying the closet, she heard Trotter moving about and pouring drinks.

"Vicious savages," Trotter said, as glasses chinked. "Listen to their blasted racket. We should shoot a few as an example to the others. It's the only one thing to be done with 'em."

"Decker won't stand for it."

"Are we supposed to stand still and do nothing while they drive us mad with their perpetual din, or work themselves into a state where they rise up and murder us all?"

"If peace and quiet is all you're after, we can give them jobs as packers. Or we could give 'em some food, that's what they're asking for."

"And I'm asking you to keep a civil tongue in your head when you speak to me."

"No offense, Mr. Trotter," McEachren said calmly. "But if they do cut loose, my head'll be on the chopping block, same as yours."

"The Chilcotins will get no more concessions and no more jobs. Let 'em ask till they're blue in the face, I'm done with 'em. I gave 'em work last year, and what did they do?"

"I know what they did. I was there."

"I hope you remember it all. Remember that I hired Chilcotins as packers, once. Instead of bending their backs and carrying my supplies, they looted store houses, dropped their packs by the side of the road, and then went fishing." Trotter drove a tightly clenched fist into his other palm and added fiercely, "There'll be no tears shed if we shoot every last one and heave 'em into the sea."

"There's no need for shooting. Smallpox and liquor is killing 'em quick enough."

"Hah! But not quick enough for me!"

"Mebbe so, Mr. Trotter. But murder's a hanging matter."

"It's a hanging matter if you're fool enough to get caught," Trotter was declaring, when Isabel went upstairs to her bedroom along the cold, dark corridors hung with portraits of people unknown to her.

At midnight, somebody knocked on the back door of the house. McEachren opened it. Hayes, the stable hand, was standing on the step holding his hat.

McEachren let him in and Trotter said, "What the hell do you want?"

"Begging your pardon, Mr. Trotter, but I believe somebody's broke into the storage shed."

"Thieving sons of bitches! They need teaching a lesson and I'm the man to do it," Trotter said, as he unlocked a gun cabinet and took out three shotguns. "They think they own this country, but I'll teach 'em who's boss here."

The three men went outside and gravel was crunching under their feet when Isabel got out of bed. Below her window a dozen Indians, huddled in blankets, were beating drums and chanting. When Trotter and the others appeared, there was at first an outcry as angry natives surrounded them, shaking their fists and demanding work, until Trotter pointed a shotgun over their heads and fired both barrels. The uproar died as the Indians fled, and the three white men went swinging into the long shadows on their secret business.

Isabel knew that Trotter kept secrets from her because he was a man; men were fated to keep secrets from women, not always successfully. She knew that he was mad with anger and up to no good, probably, and this frightened her a little. But it was not only Trotter's secrecy which kept her off balance; it was his boastful, foolish posturing — a feckless vanity which added to the horror of her existence. Isabel ran downstairs, threw a long red cape over her white nightgown, and went outside.

The night was cold and quiet now. Down by the river, Indians were moving to their lodges. She heard voices behind the house and went across to where a light showed inside the barred windows of the storage shed. Inside, McEachren and Hayes were restraining a naked Indian boy. The boy seemed unusually dark-skinned, until she saw that he was actually covered with soot. A few puzzled moments passed before she realized that he had entered by climbing down the chimney. With Trotter slapping and kicking him, the boy was dragged over to the cold fireplace and shoved screaming up the chimney. Trotter collected an armful of loose packing straw and some bits of paper, and set a match to them in the hearth. Isabel pounded on the door but it was locked and smoke was pouring from the chimney when the screaming boy climbed out, slid down the roof, and tumbled to the ground. Wailing, he ran into the forest. When Trotter shouted Isabel's name she fled down the hill to Waddy Flats, looking for Decker.

Decker's store was closed, and his houselights were out. There was a movement in the shadows and a man called Schnurr appeared. "What's the matter?" he said. "Something wrong?"

"They've been torturing a boy up there!"

"Torture!"

"They set fire to him but I've no time to explain," Isabel cried. "Somebody has to do something!"

"That's the law's business. I ain't getting mixed up in it. Last time I seen Decker was at the wharf, a while back that was. I seen him waving the Wilburs off."

Gusty winds were buffeting One-Ear's sloop when Isabel's footsteps sounded on the wharf. "Decker?" Isabel called timidly. "Is anybody here?"

"Who's askin'?" said One-Ear, coming out of his cabin. "Oh, it's you, lady. What do you want?"

"Have you seen Decker?"

"Not lately. Anything I can do?"

"I need a constable."

"Decker'll likely be coming back this way in a few minutes," One-Ear lied. "Step aboard and wait fer him here in my cabin, where it's warm. "

"I understand that you ... I wouldn't mind a drop of whisky," Isabel said, shivering with cold and nervousness as she pulled the red cloak tightly around herself.

"Ah, whisky! Sure, I'd like a drop of whisky myself."

"They told me, people in the town," she said uncertainly. "They say you have it sometimes. For sale, I mean."

"That's right pleasant of people, spreading tales about a fellow. Putting rumours round what's liable to run him into difficulties with the justices and all, and me a law-abiding fellow, generally speaking."

"But you might have some? Something surplus to your own personal needs that you might want to sell?"

"Oh, personal needs," One-Ear said. "We better not go into that."

"Look," she snapped, impatience rising in her voice. "I don't care if you're a bootlegger or what you do but it's cold, waiting here."

One-Ear folded his arms. Dim light, falling through the cabin doorway, revealed his flat, unsmiling eyes and bared teeth. He thought, Now there's a woman! With a woman like that aboard, there was no telling where things might lead.

"Come aboard and wait here," One-Ear hissed. "I might rustle up a drop of private stock."

"I don't want to come down. All I want is a small bottle of brandy, whisky, anything you've got."

One-Ear moved his feet and seconds passed before he said, "It's here, but you got to come get it your ownself. I ain't bringing none fer nobody."

Shivering in the April night, she moved closer to the edge of the wharf and put her hand on the ladder.

There, he thought, excited. I've got her.

"'Tain't far, a few steps. Careful, 'cos we don't want a young lady slippin' and fallin' and hurtin' herself," One-Ear said. "Then into my cabin, all sociable, and we'll sit right friendly. Won't nobody ever know you been here, unless you tells 'em."

"I prefer brandy. You have brandy?"

"Whisky, but it's the real stuff, bottled in the Old Country," he lied again. "I got a private cache here that goes down smooth as oysters."

"My husband," she fibbed unconvincingly. "He'll be along in a few minutes."

"Good. Your husband's welcome to a social drink too, only, if I got to supply the both of you with booze I might have to close the bar early."

"It's understood that I'll pay? I don't want..."

"Now don't fret, lady. This here is a friendly boat."

Isabel turned her back to the sloop and saw Schnurr, watching her from fifty yards away. His presence reassured her somehow. She put one foot on the ladder, hesitated, and began to descend. When her feet touched the deck, One-Ear seized her and with one rough, powerful movement of his arm swept her into his cabin. Her mouth opened but her little gasp of dismay and shock was drowned by the noise of the door banging shut. In a moment she had been slammed onto a seatlocker up against the forward bulkhead with her legs under the cabin table.

The sloop's greasy cabin, its walls and ceiling black with lamp soot, absorbed most of the light from a single dirty globe, swinging in its gimbals. In the reeking dark, ropes of various dimensions were coiled haphazardly like snakes in a basket. Two oak barrels were lashed to the foot of the mast, and spare sails lay bundled in a corner. Gridger stood with his back against the door, while One-Ear rummaged in a cupboard and brought out a cobwebby bottle and three pewter mugs. With a sudden prodigious sweep he cleared a cribbage board and a deck of playing cards off the table to make room. "Here," he said, extracting the cork with his teeth and filling the mugs. One-Ear shoved one towards her and said slyly, "Medicine for what ails thee."

He's dangerous, she thought. I'd better humour him, and clear off.

In the half-dark, her tongue came out of her mouth. "This is no good," she said, licking her red lips. "I wouldn't mind buying a bottle to take away but I shouldn't drink with you."

"Why not?

"Just sell me a bottle, please."

"I can't on account it's unlawful fer to sell booze without a licence. Why, if the law come down on me I could lose my boat," One-Ear said as he sipped whisky from the pewter mug in his fist. "My," he said, "that's smooth stuff, that's slippery stuff all the way down to yer belly."

Isabel pushed the mug away.

"It's all right, drink it. We won't tell her husband nothing, will we, Gridge?"

"Why should I care what you tell my husband?"

"I don't need to explain," One-Ear chuckled. "A young lady, locked in a cabin with a couple of sailormen."

Gridger inched towards her and said, "Here. Let me give you a hand to take that nice red coat off. Why, it could be a while afore your husband comes, so we might as well get comfortable."

Gridger was reaching for the ornate gold-coloured buttons at Isabel's neck when One-Ear grabbed his greasy hair and yanked him backwards. Yelping with pain and shock, Gridger slithered up against the barrels.

"Dern ignorant ruffian," One-Ear said lightly. "Gridge there, he don't know the difference atween a lady's coat, and a lady's cape."

One-Ear's yellow cat's eyes reflected darkness and light. They winked out as he turned his head. "Gridge," he murmured, "I believe there's a matter that needs your attention out on deck. A matter of trimmin' them port and starb'd lamp wicks."

"'Tain't nothin' as won't wait," Gridger whined. "I done all I'm doin' on deck tonight."

At ease with himself, One-Ear smiled. He cocked his head to one side and tried to discern Isabel's features. "Dern," he said. "That's pretty."

Gridger made a snuffling noise at the back of his throat.

Light from the gimballed lamp cast wavering beams into the black recesses of the cabin. One-Ear unbuckled his belt and withdrew it through the loops of his trousers. Isabel tried to get up but One-Ear put a hand on her shoulder and pressed her back against the bulkhead. "Gridge, this is how we does it with the quality," One-Ear said, as Isabel let out a tiny wail. "This here gal. I got a hunch there's more to this here gal than Trotter ever figured."

CHAPTER FOUR

ISABEL WOKE UP in a strange bed. In a sleepy, disordered moment between dream and reality she imagined herself back in her children's dormitory. Outside, in a brick-walled playground, orphans were beating drums and screaming at each other. She rolled over and saw a grey circle of porthole light a few inches from her eyes. With her face up close to the glass she looked out at the river, and at Indians with painted faces passing back and forth in dugout canoes.

Gridger, coming into the cabin, squatted on his heels and grasped a heavy barrel. Straightening up with his body leaning backwards to counteract the weight of his load, he wagged his chinless face and said, "Just bide there quietly, lady. Me and Charlie'll be done with these rascals in a minute. We'll soon sail away from this danged hullabaloo."

Grinning, he staggered out and kicked the door shut with his heel.

Isabel found her red cape in the darkness and tried to open the cabin door, but it was locked. She held the cape tightly around herself and sat on the edge of the bunk, her head bent a little, looking at her bare toes, and waiting.

Missy's guttural voice sounded above the clamour.

"I found one of your gold buttons," Missy said, emerging from her own dark place to press a shiny gold disk into Isabel's palm. "Get out now," she said urgently. "Go back to Trotter before they hurt you more."

"How can I?" she was saying, as a bolt grated in the door and One-Ear came in. Without speaking, he tore Isabel's cape off and went out with it immediately. The next time Isabel looked through the porthole, the cape was across the shoulders of an Indian man.

That night, the sloop was aground on a sandbank. Gridger — a bandage of dirty cotton fabric wrapped around his face and over the top of his head — was on deck putting a match to the wick of an oil lamp. He adjusted the flame, suspended the lamp from the main boom, and sat beside the tiller in a cone of light, holding his aching jaw in his hand.

Isabel, inside the cabin with One-Ear lying beside her, watched Gridger through the open door. There he was, unkempt and miserable, the butt of One-Ear's endless sarcasm and malice. When Isabel moved, One-Ear muttered in his sleep and rolled over. Fearing to waken him and hardly daring to breathe, she clambered across his naked body, went outside, and closed the cabin door.

"Eh?" Gridger said, peering blindly into the shadows. "Who's that?"

"It's me."

"Well, don't try nothin' fancy."

"You're hurting," Isabel said sympathetically. "I know what a toothache feels like."

"I guess your husband must have give up on you," Gridger muttered. "Unless you been tellin' us lies and he don't know you ran away."

"Listen," she said, her mouth bruised and her eyes hot beneath a tangle of uncombed hair. "Don't let that man treat you like a slave. Stand up to him."

"I ain't no slave," said Gridger, admiring her as she stood before him half-naked in one of One-Ear's thin buckskin shirts. "And I don't see you doin' no standin' up agin him neither."

"He treats us like slaves, both of us, but we can fool him. Trotter's generous. Let me go and he'll give you money, as much as you want. You'll never be at One-Ear's beck and call again."

For a moment, Gridger considered the matter seriously. He'd give anything to quit One-Ear's bootlegging racket. But what would he do, afterwards? Where would he end up?

"Generous!" Gridger said, as his surge of hope died. "Everybody knows Trotter's ruined. Things ain't so happy between you and him neither, or you'd still be tight as a tick in that big house of yours, instead of slinking down to a wharf at night and carrying on with the likes of us."

"It's not true," she said angrily. "I was looking for Decker!" But what Gridger said was true, in a way — all this slinking about, begging strangers to let her get on with her own life — she was now and always had been somebody's prisoner. "Just let me go, please," she said woodenly.

"So's you can tell the world we kidnapped yer?"

"You've nothing to be afraid of. I'll tell Decker that it was One-Ear's doing."

"Yer laid yer flowers out and One-Ear, he watered 'em," Gridger said, with a lascivious wink. "That's what yer wanted all the time, ain't it?"

"All I wanted was ... I was ... coming here .... It's all been a dreadful mistake, I just wasn't thinking properly. Please, just let me go."

"'Tain't my call," Gridger said. "One-Ear'd kill me, sure, if he woke up and found you'd given us the slip. The world ain't big enough. Have you seen him when he's angry? Why, I could tell you things would make yer head spin."

"Be a sport, a gentleman. I know you're a gentleman. What's the matter with you?" she said, tenderly. "Don't you want to help me? It's that tooth, isn't it?"

"Tobacco juice generally takes out the worst of the sting, but this back chomper is .... I been spittin' yeller, and blood."

"That means it's septic. Have a drink, that'll help."

"I know your game. You'd like ter make me drunk, then hop over the side, but I ain't drinkin' nothin' till Charlie takes the watch."

"Decker will find out, he'll hunt you down."

"Aaaah, quit yer noise. I got my own troubles and don't need none of yours, lady."

News of the Indian boy's torture had travelled everywhere and Indians were rioting beneath the distant trees. Shrill voices echoed over the throbbing beat of drums and the hoot of wooden whistles.

Isabel went back into the cabin. One-Ear was still fast asleep when she came out again, pitying Gridger and hating him at the same time, holding a bottle of liquor behind her back.

"Alcohol's the best for that mouth of yours," she said, moving a little closer. "I know a girl who got blood poisoning because they neglected a bad tooth. One tooth and she was dead in twenty-four hours. Dead and buried, the poor little thing. Alcohol might have saved her but she was too young, the doctor wouldn't give her any." She put her head on one side and added, "Go on. One swig won't make you drunk," and showed him the bottle she had been holding behind her back.

Gridger shook his head.

She thought of hitting him with the bottle but couldn't, and placed it within easy reach of his hand. A freshening wind set loose stays and halyards banging against the spars.

"Whisky's good," she said, "but laudanum is better. Laudanum, that's what you need. If I had some I'd share it with you. A little tap and the tooth's out. The pain's gone forever."

"Eh? What's that?"

"Laudanum. For pain."

Gridger closed his eyes as jolts of agony rocked him. "We got another one like you. Missy. Come aboard like you she did, looking. A woman aboard ship is nothing but a fuss and a bother. Put a dern woman on a ship and what you get is nothin' but bad luck," he said, groaning as he touched his swollen face. "I got a mind to pull it meself, with pliers."

"Don't. Not when it's septic."

"If I took this bandage off you'd see how swollen it is. My mouth is like a rotten tomato."

"That's because it's full of poison. Dangerous. Have a drink, man."

Fires burned on the shore. Over to port, moonlight reflected off a widening channel of water. Across the starboard rail, sand and rocks stretched uninterruptedly between the sloop and a desolation of forest. Timbers creaked inside the cabin where One-Ear was beginning to stir in his bunk.

"If you don't want a drink I'll have one myself," Isabel said, and reached for the bottle fully resolved to club him with it.

He seized her wrist. Squeezing hard he shoved his face up to hers and said, "No, yer don't."

Isabel released the bottle. Standing, she leaned across the gunwale and the hem of her buckskin shirt rose six inches. Gridger's eyes narrowed as he saw her long legs and the smooth surmounting globes. He had forgotten his toothache when the cabin door banged open.

"Belay that!" One-Ear shouted, as Isabel vaulted over the side of the sloop and down onto the smooth sand. She ran ten yards before a blast of wind knocked her flat and set the cabin door banging. One-Ear was swept to the floor by the main boom swinging loosely through its quadrant. Isabel picked herself up and ran towards the tree-fringed shore, until her foot struck a piece of driftwood and she fell again. Dazed, with blood between her toes, she got up and kept running. Trees obscured the moon and she felt herself going the wrong way. Confused, she stopped and saw two lines of rippled silver where the river divided around a rock.

A man with a face like a bear swam out of the river and walked towards her on two legs. It was an Indian wearing a carved and painted wooden mask. She turned away and fell into the arms of a man wearing a raven mask. Wailing, she freed herself and ran, with the bear and the raven and a man with red wings flapping along beside her. Isabel fell again and her hands fastened around a stone the size of her fist. Rising with the stone in her hand she flailed wildly, without effect, until the Indians pried the stone from her hand and carried her away.

CHAPTER FIVE

ONE-EAR AND GRIDGER ran out of liquor. They spent anxious hours placating the Indians with lies and promises backed up by revolvers until the tide rose and they worked the sloop across to the Waddy Flats wharf, a trip made necessary because Gridger was bound and determined to have Decker see to his teeth and there wasn't a thing One-Ear could do about it short of killing him.

Sitting on deck with the rag bandage wrapped around his face, waiting for Decker to open his store, Gridger was trying to distract himself by splicing two hanks of rope together. One-Ear, irritated beyond endurance by his tortured groans, found a pair of pliers and fetched a bottle of straight liquor. Lighting a cigar he blew smoke at his partner and said, "Your mouth stinks worse'n a camel with foot rot."

"It's a lie! If anybody don't like it they can stay upwind, and the hell with 'em," Gridger hollered, but this angry outburst exercised his jaw and brought on another acute throbbing spasm.

One-Ear waved the pliers and said unsympathetically, "It's no lie. That chomper's coming out now, 'cos I'm tired of your whinin'."

Gridger threw the rope down, folded the marlin-spike blade of his knife into its handle, and drank a mouthful of liquor. One-Ear peeked inside Gridger's mouth, and said, "Dern. Looks like a bunch of raw liver in there. Take another mouthful of that booze, swill it around, and spit it out so's I can see what you got."

Gridger complied. One-Ear tapped a black-green tooth with the pliers, experimentally, and had started to say "Is that the one?" when Gridger sucked in a huge draught of air, shuddered, and fell backwards holding both hands to his face.

Trembling, Gridger said, "I got to let Decker have at it."

"He ain't no sawbones," One-Ear shouted. "He's a lawman, is what he is, and I don't want no lawman near us."

"Maybe Decker ain't no sawbones, but he's a horse doctor, and that's good enough for me."

"You ain't goin' into town, nossir," One-Ear shouted. "You'll start blabbin' yer mouth off, tellin' everybody what we done to Trotter's woman."

"Shoot me then," Gridger said defiantly. "Backshoot me with both barrels and put me out of this misery. I'm gonna see Decker. If that don't bring ease I'll fill my pockets with rocks and go swimmin' in deep water."

One-Ear was ready to strangle Gridger. Why am I straining myself for this bothersome fool? he thought, as they left Missy guarding the sloop and went ashore past a few sorry native lodges built of sticks and brushwood. Next came Waddington Street — a narrow strip of mud and manure with nothing much on it, except Decker's store, Cuthbert's smithy, and Schnurr's lodging house.

Trotter's mansion (dubbed the Slough of Despond because the carpenters who built it all contracted dysentery), stood on a lofty point above the Bute Inlet wagon road.

When the bootleggers neared the lodging house, an apparition detached itself from the shadows of a doorway, and waved them down. It was Schnurr, a fat, black-bearded man in a brown greatcoat and a woollen balaclava helmet with loose earflaps.

"Morning," Schnurr said with a mocking half bow. "You gents ain't got no liquid supplies along with you, I suppose?"

"No," One-Ear said, in a tone intended to discourage further conversation.

"Pity, 'cos I run out. I was just about to come down to your sloop, and do a bit of business," Schnurr replied, unabashed. "Step inside, rest yer bones."

"We're in a hurry."

Gridger, now that his ordeal was near, did not relish the idea of immediate dental surgery, and mumbled, "We got five minutes."

Schnurr's lodging house was a vile-smelling shed, roofed with sewn-together bits of sailcloth. Erected in a surge of optimism which had yet to be fulfilled, its teetering walls were built of driftwood shored up by baulks of rough lumber. Sailcloth screens, suspended from roof beams, divided the dark interior into six-by-eight cubicles. Schnurr's wife, Klymtedza, a pigtailed Nuxalt woman, dressed in a cotton flour sack, her bare head and arms protruding through slits, a sleeping infant slung in another sack-like bag across her broad back, was boiling potatoes at an open fire. The only patrons were a bearded man and his partner, who was stretched out, groaning, on a rubber ground sheet.

"Prospectors. They come in, aiming to ship out, and just missed the *Nonpareil*," Schnurr muttered. "Terrible sick that feller is, won't eat, all he wants is water. Let's hope he ain't got nothing catching."

Hampered by darkness, One-Ear and Gridger picked their way across a tamped-earth floor. Schnurr, darting ahead, led them to a small private chamber with a stout locked door. He ushered them in, fumbled in the dark for a candle, lit it with a match, and placed it on the upended steamer trunk which served as his table. In the poor, flickering light, Schnurr hurled his woollen hat onto a four-poster bed, which took up most of the space in the room, and ran fingers through his short grey-black hair until every strand stood upright. He knelt and crawled under the bed. Emerging with a small cardboard box in his hand, he looked in his overcoat like a huge burrowing animal. "Sit, make yourselves comfy!" he cried, as he lowered his thick hindquarters onto his creaking bed, and liberated a great quantity of dust from its tattered eiderdown. There being no chairs in the room, One-Ear stood with his arms folded.

One-Ear didn't like the set-up at all. He didn't trust Schnurr at the best of times, and especially not now, because the fat man's lips were pulled tight, as if he were trying to stop himself from laughing.

Gridger, blind and dumb to everything in his misery, sat on the floor, holding his head, with the pain of his jaw leaking out of his eyes.

Schnurr removed a small item from the cardboard box and made an ostentatious display of stowing it in an overcoat pocket. "You don't think much of old Schnurr, nor his accommodations neither, but all the same it's a palace for lonely travellers," he said, giggling. "This is the place a fellow seeks out if he has no roof of his own to sleep under, and the snow coming down."

"And maybe it'll be snowing outside before you stop jawing and state your business," One-Ear jeered.

"Oh, clever!" said Schnurr, giving One-Ear a doubtful look. "But listen. Did you hear the latest? Indians took a feller's head off. Then Trotter grabbed one of the Chilcotin boys, and lit a fire up his ass."

"Is that why you dragged us in here?" One-Ear snapped. "You think I'm interested in yer dern gossip?"

"Business ain't gossip," Schnurr returned. "The Wilburs has quit already. Esau Knox and MacCormack will go next. Now that Trotter's put the cat among the pigeons, others will get the wind up, and follow."

"So what?"

"Waddy Flats won't be nothing but a ghost town for a while. There'll be abandoned farms and gear, waiting to be snatched up by them plucky fellows that stick it out, and waits for others to come here and join 'em."

"What's the use of a farm, if you can't sell your crops?" One-Ear replied, but a faint gleam of avarice had appeared in his eyes. "Decker has the only cash money in town, and he only buys to keep the town running."

Schnurr tapped his forehead and said with a chuckle, "Never mind, you'll see."

One-Ear gave a disgusted snort and reached for the door handle.

"Just a second, my friend. I saw a little business go your way the other night," Schnurr said coyly. "A special piece of business, wearing a red cape."

"Hear that, Gridge? He's been spyin' on us."

"And now the gal that was wearing that cape is gone missing," Schnurr said. "People are wondering what's happened to her? Whether she's lost, or stolen?"

Klymtedza's baby woke up and began to wail. One-Ear cocked his head to listen. When the baby quietened he said malevolently, "What do you want?"

"I don't want nothing much, old pal," Schnurr said, washing his hands with invisible water. "Just remember to bring a bottle or two, next time you're passing."

"Do you think you can squeeze me, you slimy dog?" One-Ear said, glowering at Schnurr and grinding his teeth together. "Do you think I'm soft and bendable, like them fellers rentin' yer stinkin' squats?"

"Gratitude is special..." Schnurr was bleating, when One-Ear rammed the barrel of a pistol into his fat stomach with enough force to make the lodging-house keeper gasp.

One-Ear reached into Schnurr's pocket and extracted the contents, which included a gold-coloured button. "Talk," One-Ear said, giving him another couple of prods with the pistol. "Talk, and make it quick."

"I was only trying to be amusing, Charlie!"

"Where'd you get this button?"

"Honest to God, Charlie. I don't know..."

"Gridge. Gimme your knife," One-Ear said. "Let's see how amusin' Schnurr is without no thumbs."

"I don't know the fellow's real name," Schnurr said with a terrified gurgling wail, lifting an arm to point vaguely outdoors. "An outcast he is. Jesuits had him for a while, so now he's Mark, or Michael, or something. You'll find him along the shore."

Klymtedza opened the door and stood with the baby cradled in her arms. Confused, unable to speak English, she looked from face to face.

One-Ear took Schnurr by the throat and said in a fierce whisper, "You know me, so remember. Watch what comes out of your mouth, in future."

Shoving Klymtedza out of the way, he went past the dying man and out into the dust of the street. His destination was not far: one hundred yards along the shore to Decker's store. Two saddled mules and a horse were already tossing their heads at the hitching rail outside when the bootleggers climbed the steps. Two men in overalls were crouched on wooden benches by Decker's stove. Their mumbling ceased and they stopped whittling and spitting long enough to survey the newcomers, and remark Gridger's bandaged face. Shrugging disinterestedly, they turned their faces away.

Decker — the man to call if you fell into farm machinery and were bleeding to death — was standing with his arms folded behind his counter among boxes of crackers, pyramids of tinned sardines, barrels of flour. Snowshoes and sides of bacon dangled from hooks in the ceiling.

Esau Knox was standing slightly apart from the men by the stove. He cleared his throat and said, "It's as plain as a rat on a plate. There just ain't enough white men here to hold the lid down on Injuns. There won't never be, now that Trotter's took leave of his senses and set fire to one of 'em. If them devils takes it into their heads to murder the whole bunch of us, there's no way to stop 'em."

"Esau," Decker said. "Just a minute..."

"Are you an Injun lover?" Esau shouted, jutting his chin. "Come on, Injun lover. Tell us straight, how come you're always stickin' up fer them fellers?"

To his disgust, Decker felt drawn to defend himself against a fool. "I'm not an Indian lover and I'm not a settler lover," Decker said mildly. "I'm a man who keeps his eyes and ears open."

"And I say we're sittin' on a powder keg with the fuse lit. Fellers were getting their heads lopped off even before Trotter went mad," Esau ranted. "Who can us fellers depend on if there's a war? The governor? Don't make me laugh. The governor and his buddies are too busy enjoyin' themselves in Victoria to care about a bunch of back country sodbusters."

"Hellfire, we can depend on ourselves, can't we? Are we supposed to pack up and leave Waddy Flats at the first sign of trouble?" Decker replied, raising his voice to overcome murmurs in the background. "We're the government here. Us. You and me. But we've got to include Indians in our plans. We can't ride roughshod and expect them to sit back and do nothing."

"Hear that? Decker wants us to include Injuns. Well, I'm through. If you fellers is smart like I think you are, you'll quit too, before them sneaking black wolves cut your throats."

Esau stalked out of the store with his shoulders hunched and his head down, and unhitched his mule.

One-Ear leaned against the counter and said, "Did he say something about Trotter burnin' somebody?"

Nobody replied.

"What's the matter, cousins, somebody corraled your voices?"

"It's all rumour, until I find Trotter and hear his side of things," Decker replied. "The town's full of rumours."

One-Ear tried to catch the eyes of the other men, but they all turned away. He said. "If you ain't too busy, I'll take a box of cigars and two ounces of Gridger's plug."

Decker moved behind his counter. "It'd be lonely and miserable on your spread, without tobacco."

Quirk, sitting quietly in the shadows said, "Be miserable with it, if One-Ear didn't have that home-brew business keeping him busy."

One-Ear whirled around and said fiercely, "Who was that talkin'?"

Quirk was watching Esau Knox through the window.

"Speaking of miserable," Decker interceded, "what's wrong with Gridger? I haven't seen a longer face in here since Blacky Scrimgeour got stomped and we had a collection to help his widow."

"You ain't man enough to call me One-Ear to my face," One-Ear said, glaring at Quirk as he tilted his floppy cap to cover that missing organ.

"'Tain't nothing, just a bit of a toothache, Mr. Decker," Gridger said. "I be in yer debt if'n you'd peek at it."

"Take that bandage off your face," Decker said, lifting a steaming iron kettle off the stove and carrying it behind his counter.

Bushrat, resuming an interrupted discussion, said conversationally, "Course, you never know how them things go. I knew a feller fell down a cliff, and called it prospectin'."

When the chuckles died, Quirk said, "I know a feller who rustled a hoss and called it farmin'. The only furrows he made was with his heels, when they put a rope around his neck and drug him up to the cross beam."

Bushrat looked at One-Ear and said innocently, "I don't suppose nobody knows nothin' more about them smallpox epidemics?"

One-Ear said, "You talking to me?"

"I'm talking general."

"I don't know nothing about no epidemics," One-Ear said and bit the end off his cigar. Taking deliberate aim, he spat it onto the floor at

Quirk's feet and said, "What I'm seein' right now, is a gallon of shit in a quart sack."

Quirk went outside, mounted his horse, and rode off whistling.

Gridger had removed his bandage when Decker brought him a hot, folded hand towel. Decker said, "Hold this against your face while you're waiting."

"What is it?" Gridger asked ungraciously.

"A bread poultice. It might help, some."

"If anybody needs diversion, ten more of Trotter's men just quit, so there's jobs going on the road gang," Bushrat said. "Trouble is, the pay's irregular. 'Tain't enough that Trotter's boys are quitting and he's torturin' boys. His wife's run off as well, so he'll be feeling the cold at night."

MacCormack said knowingly, "That's if Trotter's got a wife."

One-Ear said, "What's that?"

"That floozy, Isabel," MacCormack answered, his mouth sternly righteous. "She's livin' under his roof as bold as brass, but who's to say whether they're man and wife?"

"Hold it, Mack. I'll not tolerate that kind of talk in here," Decker said in a flat voice.

MacCormack reddened. "That's the limit," he said huffily. "I'm through with talking and I'm through with Waddy Flats. If anybody wants two good mules and a stump puller, they know where I'll be until the *Nonpareil* takes me away from here." MacCormack went out.

Irritated, Decker fiddled with mechanical paraphernalia on the counter, and put several grains of brown powder into a silver tablespoon. He held the tablespoon over a candle flame and said, "Over here, Gridger. Stick this tube in your mouth. You eat some of this smoke, and your troubles will be over."

Busy getting things ready to pull the tooth, Decker thought, Damn these men and their vicious chatter. They came to his store, drawn by a common urge for companionship, but all they did was bicker and spread idle rumour. He wondered how many of the rumours were true; whether in fact Trotter had tortured a Chilcotin boy, and whether Isabel had run away from home.

Suddenly, he remembered coming across Isabel walking her mare along a narrow trail above the beach. Sandhill cranes were standing in the shallows. A flock of dowdy little seabirds wheeling and crying in the heat haze above were turning parrot-yellow where the sun burnished their feathers, and falling to earth like drops of gold. Blind to all of that, she was staring out to sea with an expression of desolation. He spoke her name and raised his hat. Taken by surprise

Isabel stopped walking and stared at him for a moment, before looking back through a break in the bushes at the ruffled wavelets brushing against the shores. The mare was trembling. Isabel put her face against the mare's face and whispered softly to her, then turned and moved closer to Decker with the reins in her hand and smiled at him. They were close enough for him to feel her warm breath on his face. Still without speaking she lifted the reins over the mare's head, put her foot into its stirrup, went smoothly up into the saddle and rode off.

Gridger was in an opium daze and his eyes had glazed over. He was sitting in a chair, smiling foolishly, when Decker came out from behind the counter with a pair of pliers in one hand and a wooden wedge in the other. He said, "Bushrat, put Gridger's head in an armlock. Hold him still while I get to work."

"Eh, what's that?" Gridger said drowsily. "This ain't gonna hurt, is it?"

"Gridge, old fellow, I won't tell a lie," said Decker, brandishing the pliers. "This is going to hurt you one helluva lot more than it hurts me, but in this life you get what you pay for, and this time there'll be no charge for my services."

"Why?"

"You're a guinea pig," said Decker. "I've lopped off a few arms and legs in my time, and doctored plenty of critters, but the finer points of dentistry elude me."

Gridger opened his mouth to say something, whereupon Decker shoved the wooden wedge into the good side of his mouth to keep his jaws wide.

"Close your eyes and pray to Saint Barbara, Gridger," Decker said, as his patient started to writhe.

"Saint Barbara?" Bushrat enquired. "Who's that?"

"Patron saint of bombardiers and armourers. He'll think there's bombs going off inside his head, before I'm done with him."

***

It was nearly midnight when One-Ear and Gridger worked their sloop across the inlet. Five hundred yards away, single-skin drums thudded. Trees fringed red with flame showed where Indians had lit bonfires along the sandy beach. Fat bellied clouds, silvered by moonlight, drifted in from the west. The sound of drumming grew louder as the bootleggers crept up a ridge and looked down from a crest to see men in painted wooden masks dancing in circles. Bare-headed women wailed lamentations as a man wearing a red cape dragged a limp human body into the swiftly ebbing tide.

When Gridger saw the dead man, his heart began to pound and he forgot the pain of his recently extracted teeth. "Is that dead feller one of them that bought our blankets?" he said in a shocked whisper. "D'ye think he caught somethin' from 'em?"

"Quiet!" One-Ear hissed. "They got ears like bats."

Wails turned to screams as the man in the red cape released his burden to the sea, and allowed it to float away.

Gridger's mouth was dry and his eyes felt too large for their sockets. "Christ," he whispered. "They ... they's dyin' of pox! We killed 'em, Charlie!"

Gridger's words brought a shadow of malevolence to One-Ear's face. With his hatred of Gridger reinflamed, the bootlegger continued his search along the beach.

They found the Indian outcast a mile away, smoking a stone pipe in the doorway of a canvas tepee surrounded by flying bugs immolating themselves on the glass chimney of his lamp. His family sat coughing inside, surrounded by food-baskets, wooden boxes, blankets and moth-eaten skins. Smoke from a fire in the middle of the tepee's floor was adding another layer of soot to the inside walls before dissipating into the moonlight through the vent flaps.

One-Ear waved Isabel's gold button under the outcast's nose. "Found it, you say?" One-Ear said sharply. "Found it, but didn't know no better than to try and sell it to Schnurr?"

The outcast's guttural voice shook when he said, "I know nothing."

"You're a lying dog. Do you know who I am?"

The outcast blinked his watery eyes.

"Charlie Brown. Call me One-Ear if you dare, but not to my face. I need answers. If I don't get 'em, it'll be the worse for you," he said, knowing that threats alone were useless. What could be worse than this outcast life?

One-Ear continued violently, "That button belongs to my woman. You wanted her, eh? Fancied white meat, had your fun, and killed her after?"

Something moved in the outcast's liquid black eyes.

"Had your way with her and left her for dead, eh? Then you ran away, like a coward."

"It no me."

"Why did you do it, eh? For her lovely white ass?"

"I find button."

"Where did you find it?"

"On beach."

"Liar! Kill yer own wife," One-Ear said. "Kill as many Injuns as you want, but touch a white women and it's a hanging matter. We'll take a rope and stretch your rotten neck."

The outcast said with a spark of emotion, "Klatsassan. He say kill nobody."

"Eh? What's that?"

"We listen to Klatsassan, me and them," he said, pointing upriver to the main encampment.

"Klatsassan and his Injuns won't give outcasts nothin'," Gridger said contemptuously. "They hate you worse'n they hate King George."

"Everything different soon," the outcast insisted. "Klatsassan say that by and by, everybody live together in same lodge. Klatsassan is like bird. He fly above ground, look down, see everything."

"Where's Klatsassan now, eh? Tell me where he is. I'd like to talk to him, I would."

"Klatsassan coming soon, to parley with great white chief."

"That's me," One-Ear said in his hard voice. "I'm the great white chief, and don't you forget it."

A skinny dog came up to sniff One-Ear's ankle, before his kick sent it yelping away. Scowling, One-Ear went inside the tepee followed by Gridger.

"Horny devil," Gridger said. "One wife ain't good enough for him."

The outcast's number one wife was an old woman of thirty-five, with no teeth. His number two wife was about thirteen. Gridger jabbered at her, without result, and said, "It's got me beat, she don't speak no English."

"Uska chal?" One-Ear said, and the sad-faced girl murmured a soft reply, but her nervous glance kept straying to a pile of skins lying in the shadows.

"She's a Cowichan from Maple Bay. Now she's tired of her husband, and tired of this tepee."

Gridger, his greasy overalls shining like silver in the light of the oil lamp, said, "Ain't we all. I'm sick and tired of this tepee, myself, so what's keepin' us?"

"Shut up!" One-Ear said, and stood beside the fire, listening, with his head slightly cocked to one side. With a sudden movement he reached out and snatched a wolf skin off the pile lying on the ground. Isabel, wide-eyed with fright, stared up at him.

"Here she is," One-Ear said with gloating satisfaction. "The one I been looking for."

CHAPTER SIX

W HEN DECKER OPENED his front door and went outside, Old Tsulas woke up and crawled from under the porch where he had been sleeping. The ancient caretaker stood yawning and stretching, half-naked in a steeple-shaped hat and a dog-hair cape that was a little too short to conceal his buttocks. The shy old man closed his eyes while Decker wished him the time of day. After standing with his eyes closed for another minute, Old Tsulas whispered a few words. Decker thanked him and handed over two ounces of loose tobacco. In return, Old Tsulas would keep moochers away from the store, and maintain the peace for another week.

It was too early for customers and Waddington Street was deserted. Old Tsulas crawled back under the porch. Decker went into the house, filled his coffee cup, and sat on the back steps watching the sun rise over the mountains.

Over in the corral, the chestnut horse was dozing on three legs and the bay had his nose between the rails. Sally was teaching her piglets how to wallow in a mudhole. Bushrat came stumping around from the back of the barn, buttoning up the bib of his overalls as he went past the hens scratching and clucking in the red dust.

"You heard the latest?" Bushrat said. "Trotter's wife's gone after all. Cleared right off, she did, with just the clothes she stood up in."

"Who says so?" Decker asked, remembering her astride that mare above a beach.

"Frank Hayes. He's the feller that's swamping up at Trotter's house."

"What did he have to say about the other rumours?"

"Which ones?"

"About the Chilcotin chiefs getting fed up with One-Ear. There's that other deal too, about Trotter setting fire to some boy. I was talking to Old Tsulas, earlier. He says it was somebody called Piell."

"Hayes told me there's nothing to it. Nobody burned nobody."

"Well, Hayes better rein in his tongue about Isabel," Decker said. "You too. There's too much loose talk about that woman. A reputation's all a woman has."

"Eh?"

"A man can lose his name and make it up again, but a woman can't." Bushrat was taken aback. "Dern," he said. "I don't mean nothin'."

Decker knew that he was being hard. He hated to admit it, but Isabel had made a big impression on him. He knew what it was — it was sex, an absurd yearning for a woman half his age. It was shameful, ridiculous. He said, "I'll ride over to Trotter's place. Get to the bottom of things."

"Talkin' about reputations, One-Ear better watch out," Bushrat said, as he took a clasp-knife out of his pocket and opened the blade to clean his fingernails.

Decker cleared his throat and said innocently, "That was a mighty fine breakfast you us did yesterday. New recipe?"

Bushrat gave him a suspicious look. "Now what?" he said.

"Nothing. It's just, I was sitting here listening to my stomach rumble, and I got to figuring."

"Oh yeah?"

"I got to figuring that you must have been talking to somebody's cook, stealing trade secrets," Decker said, quite pleasantly. "I was in the Poodle Dog once. It's a ritzy French beanery in San Francisco. They've got this deal. Any time you order grub worth more than a dollar, you can have it flambé."

"Flam Bay?"

"When the cook has fixed your dinner, he pours cognac over it, and sets it afire as a finishing touch. Flambé cooking. Blue flames shooting all over. Scared the dickens out of me the first time I saw it. I thought the building was afire, until somebody told me it was just a French cook fixing somebody's dollar steak," Decker sucked his teeth noisily. "Maybe you come by your skill naturally? There might be some French blood in you. There might be some kind of race thing that kicks in when you grab a skillet."

Bushrat said fiercely, "Are you complaining 'cos the dern eggs was a bit scorched?"

"No way. Only a fool would argue with his cook."

Bushrat brooded for a moment, before his face broadened into a smile. "Pity somebody didn't tell Clarence Trotter that, a long time ago. It would've saved him a whole heap of trouble," he said, hooking thumbs into his side pockets and shoving his overalls down to ease the pressure on his crotch. "Mind you, if a man can't even run a wife, how can you expect him to run a road gang?"

"That's gossip," Decker murmured.

"'Tain't neither. Facts are facts, boss. The whole town's talkin' about how she run off and left him. Mind you, I wouldn't blame her."

"Give that topic a rest, will you?"

"Well, the thing is, if you know how a man treats his wife, it gives you a idea how he treats the world, don't it?" Bushrat persisted. "Trotter probably does have a special hatred fer Injuns, though. He's hated 'em since the first time he tangled with 'em. See," he continued, "a bunch of Chilcotins had been wintering in the upper canyons. When spring rolled around they dug themselves outta the snow to find the country full of white men..."

This was one of Bushrat's favourite yarns, and Decker had heard it before, but that was all right. He could half-listen to Bushrat and at the same time he could try to think of a way to hold Waddy Flats together. He knew that talking sense to panicked men was like trying to walk on air, but if he didn't do it, there'd be no town left.

"...country full of white men," Bushrat was saying. "It was Trotter's road gang, the first white men them Chilcotins had ever laid eyes on. Soon there were dozens of 'em parked outside of Trotter's grub shack, cadgin' grub and askin' fer work. Trotter needed packers so he made up these loads, seventy-five pounds apiece. Trouble was, them Chilcotin fellers wouldn't pick 'em up. 'Feed us first,' they said, 'we're weak from hunger.'

"Trotter being ignorant, he tells his cook to feed 'em all. See, he don't know no better. It happens that Trotter's cook was an old hand and he's up to Injun games, so he tries to warn his boss, but it's no use, Trotter won't listen to nobody, unless they says what he wants to hear. The cook ain't gonna waste his breath trying to educate a idiot, so he does like he's told and quits arguing. Soon, them Indian boys was gorging themselves on Cariboo strawberries and spuds."

"You're clerking in a store, now," Decker said mildly. "I wish you'd call 'em beans and potatoes."

Bushrat grinned. "Well, you know, us white fellows, we lives inside of our wages. A Indian's different, he lives inside of his stomach, has no meal time 'cept all the time. Once his stomach is full, that fellow has been paid, it's five o'clock on Saturday night, quitting time. He ain't gonna work until he's hungry again. But Trotter don't understand that, he thinks he's been gypped. 'Get off yer duffs you idle bunch of clowns,' he's shouting, 'Yer've had your dinners so get yer feet out of the trough and let's go.' But it ain't no use, it's a waste of time. Them

Indians won't move. So Trotter gets mad, goes home spitting bullets. Well, next morning, it's the same dern thing all over again. There's Trotter, pleading with them Injuns to hump them loads up the trail. Now they say, 'We're hungry again, too weak to pick up them loads, could we just have a little tiny snack?' He falls for it. The Indians get a bowl of meal and some bannock apiece to get 'em started. Trotter don't have the savvy to realize that a spoonful of meal and a pinch of bannock will take an Indian from here to the north pole. Then, in any case, the Indians figured that the fish had started biting so they went fishing and never did no work fer Trotter at all. The whole gang got two free dinners out of him, Trotter got nothing except aggravation. He had to hire white men as packers, and pay 'em bigger wages."

"It's a sad tale, but Trotter was only out a few dinners."

"He's out more'n that. See, Trotter's got a heart so small you could pack it in a grass seed, and the loss of them dinners weighed heavy on his mind," Bushrat said. "But Trotter bides his time. A month ago, Injuns showed up at his house. This time, they really was starvin', they was just skin and bone. They'd been out of grub for a couple of months, except for what roots they could find, and a few squirrels. They're really down to bedrock when they show up at Trotter's, askin' for jobs, and food. But he don't give 'em nothin'. Instead, he orders 'em to get out of his sight, to clear off of his land."

"Well, them Indians is puzzled. Here they'd been thinkin' that it was their own land they was standing on. This was the first time they'd been told they couldn't walk over their own ground. There was a few hotheads among that bunch too, so what they done, they said they was gonna sit outside Trotter's house, and keep on drummin' and carryin' on, until they drove him mad, or got jobs, which ever come first."

Sally picked herself out of the mud and trotted out of sight, smartly, followed by her offspring, and both horses had cocked their ears before the lawmen heard heavy animals moving invisibly in the trees beyond the corral. By the time Decker had brought his rifle out of the house, the woods were quiet again. Decker leaned his rifle within easy reach beside the door, thinking about Isabel, and wondering what was really going on.

Bushrat said, "Just a minute, boss. Did you say that the kid they burned up at Trotter's place was called Piell?"

"That's what Old Tsulas told me."

"Jesus. It better not be. Piell is Klatsassan's oldest son."

Decker was mulling this information over when Bushrat interrupted his thoughts by saying, "Klatsassan ain't a man to be trifled with. He was made a war chief under Alexis, when the Chilcotin nation was warring with the Bella Coola Nuxalts, years ago."

"Who won?"

"Klatsassan won, handily. Them Bella Coolas lost a hundred braves and Klatsassan took twenty slaves. I suspicion the Bella Coolas'll be licking their wounds for years."

Dry branches snapped and bushes swayed, under the trees behind Decker's corral.

"We should find Klatsassan and talk to him, right away, just in case," Decker said. "I should ride over and talk with MacCormack as well."

"MacCormack's made up his mind to quit and won't be no loss."

"He'll be a big loss," Decker returned. "If people head south at the first hint of trouble, what'll happen to Waddy Flats? It's the easiest thing in the world to say, 'Let's get outta town.' Once a man says it, whether he means it or not, another man hears it, and whispering starts. In a minute we've got folks in hysterics and things that people have worked their hearts out for are washed down the drain."

"Talk to Klatsassan, sure, but don't waste your time on MacCormack, boss, 'cos there's no grit in him. MacCormack talks good, but at crunch time he'll be hidin' somewhere quiet, where you can't find him. He's like one of them dern signposts. Knows how to point fellers the right way, but don't never go nowheres hisself."

There was more rustling in the trees, and Decker's little Highland bull came trotting into the yard, followed by five cows and three little calves. The Highlander hated fences, and this was the first time Decker had seen his cattle and their calves lately. The Highlander had a rack of sharp curving horns nearly four feet across and his long shaggy trailing brown coat of hair was all tangled up with weeds and mud and blackberry stalks.

"Wild and woolly and hard to curry and never to be combed below the knees," Bushrat chortled, as the Highlander stopped fifteen feet short of Decker's store, lowered his head, snorted, and pawed the ground with his nigh forefoot, while he made up his mind who to charge.

Bushrat didn't hesitate. He walked straight up to the bull, grabbed its horns, and tried to wrestle it over on its side, but the little fellow was rank and angry and uncooperative.

"Hop over to the barn, boss, and fetch me the twister that's hanging inside the door," Bushrat said, gasping a little as the Highlander raised his matted head and put three feet of air between Bushrat's feet and the ground. With Bushrat hanging on, the bull shot across the yard, heading for Bute Inlet, then he changed his mind and charged at the barn. Bushrat's boots left the odd scrape in the dust where the Highlander had nodded his shaggy head.

"Whoa, you scruffy son of a bitch, whoa!" Bushrat cried, trying to steer the bull by yanking on its horns before he was pinned to the side of the barn.

The twister was three feet of yew wood, with a short loop of soft wire at one end. Decker came out of the barn with it, hollering and waving his hat with the idea of deflecting the Highlander before Bushrat was converted into pressed meat. But with Bushrat hanging on like a burr in front the Highlander couldn't see what was lying ahead, and kept coming. Decker managed to hook the wire around the bull's nose and twisted it tight. The bull dug his hooves into the dirt and came to a stiff-legged stop. Bushrat did a flying arc to the ground and landed with a thump. Decker, hanging on to the twister, opened the corral gate and led the Highlander inside. Limping, Bushrat helped Decker to shoo the rest of the herd in behind him.

Breathing hard, Bushrat brushed himself off, sat on the fence, and wiped the sweat off his forehead with the back of his hand. Sunlight reflected off his bald spots because his hat was in the dust, being investigated by a hungry little pig.

"Like I was saying," Decker said. "I'd like to have that talk with Klatsassan."

"You can do the talking for both of us," Bushrat gasped. "I've had all the bull I can handle, fer a spell."

***

Isabel rolled off a sack of straw and sat on an upturned barrel for a minute, rubbing the deep shadows under her eyes with her fingers and remembering last night. It had been another of One-Ear's noisy, disgusting parties.

One-Ear's shack stank of unwashed flesh and old boots and rotten food. Dusty cobwebs draped the window. Dead insects had mummified on the window sill, alongside a collection of empty jars and bottles. A cracked teapot and several unwashed pewter dishes stood on a home-made three-legged table. Nails, bits of hardware, and rusting tools overflowed from boxes and sacks. Winter clothing dangled from pegs driven into cracks between the wall timbers. A small pile of kindling and bits of loose straw burst from mattresses were heaped dangerously close to the smouldering woodstove.

Loathing One-Ear from the depths of her heart, she went out of the shack to cool her aching head in a rainwater butt. Brushing aside the floating green scum, she drank too deeply. Her stomach heaved and she fell to her knees, vomiting.

Missy was in a nearby field, planting potatoes. She stopped work and frowned, as Isabel reentered the cabin.

Isabel knew that she ought to run away, but she was still getting over the beating that One-Ear had given her the last time she'd tried it. She poked about the filthy cabin, looking for coffee, and found a bottle full of dark-coloured liquid. She removed the cork, sniffed and wrinkled her nose. "My Jesus," she said, after tasting a mouthful of the foul liquid and spitting it right out onto the floor. Groaning and retching, she lay on the sack of straw and closed her eyes.

Waving cedar branches, swishing across the roof of the shack with a sound like scuttering rodents, woke Isabel an hour later. She drank more water at the rain butt and weaved across a clearing to One-Ear's barn. She was wearing loose overalls and a pair of men's boots and when she leaned inside the barn door, the overalls gaped open to reveal her white breasts and belly. Unaware of this, Isabel rocked her head slowly from side to side, and raised her shoulders a few times, trying to ease her aches, but she only made herself dizzy.

Gridger was busy at a workbench in a corner of the barn, shaping metal with a hacksaw.

Isabel said, "What was in that green bottle in the shack? I thought it was chicory."

Gridger dropped the hacksaw and took a sudden lurch towards her. Isabel didn't move, but Gridger was only feigning. Cackling with merriment he said, "It's dern pizen. Tangle-foot that Charlie brews up special, fer Injuns!"

"Where's the coffee?"

"It'll cost you," Gridger said with a lewd wink, pointing up into the hayloft. "Feel like going up for a tumble?"

"All right," Isabel said, egging him on. "I'm ready."

Gridger couldn't believe his luck. He gazed at her stupidly and said, "One-Ear'd kill me if he found us doin' it. Kill me stone dead."

"Of course he would, you miserable oaf!" Isabel retorted. "Good riddance."

Gridger grasped an imaginary hangman's noose, dropped it around his neck, with the knot against his left ear, and jerked his head to the right side. With his tongue lolling from the corner of his mouth, he staggered around for a minute. Grinning like a maniac, he went back to work.

Isabel went over to the potato patch. Missy ignored her. There wasn't the faintest light in her face, not the least sign of life, or interest.

Isabel's glance passed over a wall of loosely piled rocks to where a green lizard, perfectly motionless, was blinking its leathery eyes in the

April sunshine. With a flick of its pointed tail, the tiny creature vanished into a crack. Isabel crouched down beside Missy and tried to help with the planting, but the girl shoved her away roughly. "Go away," she said angrily. "Go away go away!"

Over at the barn, Gridger hitched a mule to a small wagon loaded with last year's potatoes, and drove it down a trail into the jackpines. Missy, going past Isabel to enter the shack, muttered something in a low threatening voice. The wagon went out of sight.

A curving arm of forested land concealed One-Ear's sloop and the shack from Bute Inlet. Turkey buzzards were riding loose-winged on warm updrafts rising from the beach — gaining altitude so that they could glide across the inlet without effort. Isabel removed her boots, rolled up her pant cuffs and waded into the sea, knee deep, until the icy water numbed her feet and legs. When she returned to the shack, Missy had fired up the stove and was frying potatoes and small chunks of fatty meat. The smoke inside was almost intolerable because the stovepipe leaked, but this at least helped to keep chiggers and other insects to a minimum. Bruised and aching, Isabel sagged on her sack of straw, while Missy took a dirty plate off the table, carried it to the door, and scraped bits of food residue to the ground with her fingers. She filled her plate with food from the iron skillet, grunted at Isabel, pointed at an empty plate, and sat on the floor to eat with her fingers.

The idea of greasy, half-cooked food set Isabel's stomach churning. She hurried outside, drank more water, washed her face, and dried it on her sleeves. Exhausted, she lay in a patch of sunlight on the beach, and closed her eyes. Scene after scene flashed into her mind, experiences that she would never be able to explain to Missy. She thought of London's parks, and of a boardinghouse for men where she had worked as a skivvy. She thought of Sunday afternoons and smartly dressed women, walking their dogs. Suddenly, she was transported to the cabin of the bootleggers' sloop. Now she saw ropes coiled loosely in a basket, and a fan of playing cards scattered on a filthy floor. With the remembered taste of raw liquor in her mouth, she saw the one-eared man reaching for her, felt the moist heat of his breath fanning her cheek as he unfastened the buttons of her cape. Isabel moaned as a shadow passed across the sky. She opened her eyes and saw green branches flailing against puffy white clouds and also Missy, standing above her, blocking out the sun.

"Why you run away, Trotter?" Missy said in a flat voice.

"I didn't run away," Isabel said. "One-Ear tricked me."

Missy put her head to one side and said, "What you doing along One-Ear?"

"Are you blind?" Isabel answered, her eyes flashing. "What do you think we've been doing?"

"No good along One-Ear," Missy said with more emphasis, pointing east. "Go away, Waddy Flats. Go away, quick."

Isabel leapt to her feet and stared irresolutely along the beach. She had to do something, but what? With Missy at her heels she left the beach and ran along the forest trail. The thin strand that connected her to Trotter and One-Ear was getting thinner and thinner; if she ran fast enough the strand would break and she would be shut of them.

One-Ear was working inside a shed, shovelling potatoes off the wagon and into a wooden trough. Gridger was screwing a newly trimmed piece of metal to a copper vat. Flames rose through the coils of a boiler in the shed and the air was redolent of sour mash.

A bear came out of the woods on two legs, followed by a raven-headed man and a sea otter. Frightened, Isabel ran deeper into the jackpines and burrowed in among the roots of a fallen cedar tree. When she raised her head, the bear had seized One-Ear and they were rolling together along the ground. Missy leapt upon the bear's back, giving One-Ear the chance to free a pistol from his belt and shoot the bear's eye out. The bear's wooden mask came off. Missy, stupefied with shock, picked the mask up and stared at it. When she looked up, One-Ear had vanished and the raven was rushing at her with an axe. Missy threw the mask at him and ran.

Gridger, slow to react, dropped his tools. Trying to follow Missy, he felt an enormous blow. His right leg was swept from beneath him and he collapsed inches away from the roaring still, gazing stupidly at his leg and seeing blood. There was no pain, only fear. He got to his hands and knees but when he tried to stand his leg buckled and he tipped over on his face. Scrabbling in the dirt, he was blindly clawing his way through clouds of smoke and steam when the sea otter impaled him to the ground with a battle-lance. More warriors came out of the forest. Two of them found One-Ear crouching in the shadows behind the still and backed him into the rear of the shed. Trapped, he emptied his pistol at his attackers and when they fell he flew at the back wall and hurled his shoulder against it. Flimsy timbers burst. He fell headlong, scrambled to his feet, and ran.

The warriors had dispersed in pursuit of One-Ear and Missy when Isabel came up from hiding beneath the cedar roots and crawled blindly away from the distillery. Coming to the forest margin above the barn, she lay on her stomach and saw that Missy had been over-taken. Isabel buried herself beneath another deadfall where she lay, shivering, as One-Ear's distillery was destroyed.

CHAPTER SEVEN

A HUMMINGBIRD FEEDING on pinesap buzzed the air with shimmering wings ten feet from where Isabel was lying. The damp cold earth, smelling of mould, was chilling her legs and belly and arms but she lay still, shrouded by branches, afraid to move, as weathered brown men moved all about. When they went away she continued to lie in that untrodden private place.

Isabel had lost her childhood overnight and found solitude. As a child, she had never been left alone for a moment. Before she discovered that there were worse things than benign neglect she used to think that the world's sorriest place was the Westminster Orphanage — an ugly, crowded barracks in London, with brick walls and spindly chimneys and drafty corridors. The only grown-up who didn't treat the inmates with cold indifference was Mister Jacks, the cleaner who, until he hanged himself with his own suspenders, followed girls around making obscene gestures with his forearms and fingers. He was notorious for lurking in the toilets, pretending to mop floors; instead of swishing he ogled children, trying to see their private parts in the only spaces in the building that had no doors.

When Isabel thought of the miserable years she'd spent locked up, with nothing to better to do than stare through barred windows, gazing at the smoke rising from a million chimneys above the reeking city, instead of being taught how to read and do numbers, it made her seethe. But she absorbed one lesson thoroughly: when the Westminster Beadle finally released her from this prison, he was never, ever, going to see her again. A lot of uneducated girl orphans became drunken streetwalkers, with unwanted children, and ended their days in the poor ward. Isabel promised herself it wouldn't happen to her. No, she was beautiful. Wealthy men would vie for her favours; in due course she would marry (a butcher perhaps, or a house-painter) and move in the highest circles.

On her thirteenth birthday, without her knowing the least thing about herself, or the world, or her place in it, the Beadle turned Isabel Jordan — and another girl called Molly Moggs — away from his orphanage, with a shilling each, and gave them both addresses where they might apply for work as scullery maids. Locked out, instead of in, they were quickly lost in a noisy maze of blind alleys and twisting lanes. Brick-arched entryways guarded mean little courts where the sun never penetrated. Collapsing apartments rained loose slates and bricks on to the homeless people who lived on the pavements. Parks and cemeteries, rampant with weeds and nettles, were hedged in with spiked iron railings and barred gates. Vacant building sites were undermined by the burrows of vagabond creatures, two-legged and four, which emerged by night, to prowl. The girls had scarcely ever set foot outside the orphanage in their lives, except on supervised visits to fenced playgrounds, when they had to march there and back in little squads, like soldiers. Now they went arm-in-arm along streets jammed with hackney-cabs, dodging heavy wagons that were contesting the right-of-way with broughams and carts and reckless horsemen and unwary pedestrians.

"So 'ow's about this skivvying lark?" said Molly. "'Ow's you feel about workin' in a big 'ouse as a skivvy-maid?"

"I don't know what to expect."

"Ain't you heard? Skivvies is worked to death," Molly Moggs said. "They're sweepin' grates and polishin' brass and deliverin' cups of tea to their betters from mornin' till night. And what thanks does they get? A lousy few quid a year! Well, I ain't havin' no part of it, no I ain't."

Asking directions from time to time, unaware that their hand-me-down clothes showed their poverty to every crossing-sweeper, the girls went past a gasometer and beside a railway line where black-faced firemen hurled shovels of coal into the fiery bellies of roaring steam engines, until Molly Moggs, perspiring in her rag bonnet and second-hand overcoat and high-laced boots, brought Isabel to a stop outside a public house. Neither was able to read the inn sign swinging above its front door, but a girl told them it was The Bellowing Mule. From appearances, the patrons of that ancient tavern, mostly sailors, had but recently returned from the Orient with pet monkeys and parrots, which they were plying with strong drink to the great amusement of several befuddled young women. Infant ragamuffins beguiled their time on the tavern steps, drinking watered gin, while their doting parents drank it neat inside.

"This is a likely place, Jordan," Molly said. "'Ow's about you and me stoppin' to 'ave a little nip of gin and hot water, to strengthen our 'earts?"

"Oh Molly! Wouldn't that be very foolish to start drinking gin and end up drunk, before we've even found a place to work, and sleep?"

"Place ter work! Yer don't *really* mean to work as a skivvy, do yer?"

"I will if they'll hire me. I'm to apply in Craven Gardens, if I ever find it."

"I'm supposed to go to an 'ouse in Brigham Terrace, but I ain't goin'. I ain't working as no underpaid skivvy, I'm going ter enjoy meself, is what I'm going to do."

"We won't be skivvies forever, and we're bound to start at the bottom until we learn our way about. Better things will turn up."

"Things don't get no better than this, not fer the likes of us, Jordan."

"We're as good as anybody else. Just think, Molly. Your shilling will be gone in an hour, and then what will you do?"

"I'll 'ang around on street corners, and wink at men, and enjoy meself."

"Say that you don't mean it, Molly! After all the things we've heard about girls, and gin..."

"Don't be so soft. They lied to us about everythin' in that orphanage," Molly scoffed, and pointed at the bibulous children scattered all around. "Look at them 'appy little nippers. Do they look 'appy, or not? That's what gin does, it makes yer 'appy, so I'm off inside."

Isabel ran to fetch a policeman, and asked him to intervene. He refused, on the grounds that no laws prevented young girls from entering licenced drinking houses.

Worried about her friend, worried because she had no job guarantees and if the Craven Gardens job didn't pan out she might have to spend her first night alone on the streets, Isabel went across a green park where bandsmen in red uniforms were playing marches for people in deckchairs. The seedy tripe-shops and pawnbrokers and rag-and-bone dealers of the orphanage district were left behind. After asking directions several times more, Isabel progressed by degrees into a residential area where a chimney sweeper's apprentice, resembling a sack of soot as he sat on a handcart loaded with long-handled brushes, stopped whistling to roll his eyes and shout, "Hey! And she's a proper corker, so give us a kiss, then!"

Resisting this, and other sooty blandishments, Isabel fetched up at Craven Gardens: a dismal, narrow cul-de-sac.

Number eleven was a weather-stained, four-storey brick edifice with "Commercial Travellers Boardinghouse. B. Bullen, Prop." inscribed on a sign tacked to its front door. The windows were all dark and shaded behind heavy velvet curtains. Isabel gave the door-knocker a timid rap. A front room curtain was drawn aside and she was surveyed from within by a shaggy young head with two unwinking little eyes. The head withdrew. Door bolts creaked, and the front door opened to the width of that same shaggy head.

"House for gents. No ladies. Go around to number fifty-four and tell Max that Cecil is returning the favour."

"Excuse me, please. Is this eleven Craven Gardens?"

"Who wants to know?"

"If it please you, sir, I'm Isabel Jordan. I was told that you might be in need of a scullery maid."

Cecil, for that was his name, opened the door fractionally wider. More of his face and part of a scarf-covered neck emerged, and Isabel was examined from head to toe by a sixteen-year-old boy.

"Hah! Hmph! I don't suppose you got no experience, neither."

"No, sir, I haven't."

"Are you another orphan?"

"Yes sir."

"Go around to the back, tradesmen's entrance, and don't you never go knocking on this front door again," the lad said, shutting the door.

The dark and airless alley behind Craven Gardens was narrow enough for people to lean out of back windows and shake hands with neighbours across the way. Isabel groped along the cobblestones, squeezing past overflowing dustbins, old bedsteads, and a dog kennel, aiming for a subterranean light gleaming dully in the near distance. She was unlucky enough to plunge her right leg down a drain and bark her shins because some wag had playfully removed its iron grating. Bending forward to rub her leg she banged her head against the bottom rung of a fire ladder. With an aching head and an aching heart, miserable with dire forebodings, Isabel arrived at stone steps leading down to number eleven's cellar, where Cecil was holding up a candle-lantern outside a barred and studded oak door.

CHAPTER EIGHT

DECKER AND BUSHRAT left Waddy Flats and rode south for three miles along the shore to MacCormack's ranch, an unsightly mess covered with unburned and unlimbed trees lying where they had been felled, months earlier. Apart from a two-roomed shack, and a vegetable garden fenced with cedar posts hung with white rattle-shells meant to discourage deer, MacCormack had little to show for a year's desultory labour, but for once, there were signs of meaningful activity on the place.

Seagulls and turkey buzzards had been making a racket on MacCormack's beach all night. When he went to see what all the fuss was about, he found a dead whale washed up. Frank Strongitharm helped him to slice the whale lengthwise with long-bladed knives, and pull strips of blubber off with blocks and tackle. They borrowed a whaler's kettle from Shanks, the blacksmith, and were boiling the fat for lamp oil when Decker and Bushrat showed up.

"Here's a bargain for you, Decker," MacCormack said. "All the oil you want, and only fifty cents a gallon."

"I'll take two barrels but you know my terms. You'll get credit in my store, no cash."

"I know that game. You buy with four-bit dollars and sell with eight-bit dollars."

"I thought we were friends."

"Friends or not. Give me fifteen dollars cash and we'll call it square."

"We can trade it out that way if you're really pushed."

"You know I'm pushed. Everybody in this godforsaken place is pushed. If there's a hundred dollars cash in the whole of Waddy Flats it's in your mattress," MacCormack said bitterly. "Fifteen dollars off you, plus the ten I have in a sock, will buy me a one-way ticket back to Victoria."

Bushrat clumped over and said, "I just been telling Strongitharm how to do it, but he don't listen. The trick with boiling whales is, you put water in the kettle along with the blubber. Water floats the dirt out, and don't hurt the oil, as long as you lets it separate before bottling."

"There," Decker said. "Bushrat knows all about blubber. A fellow told me that Bushy was born blubbering. He'll give Frank a hand while you and I go to your cabin and get away from this stink."

"I'm busy."

"Quit for ten minutes. We need to talk."

"Talk to me here."

"Listen. Are you going to come up to the house under your own steam, or do I have to drag you?"

MacCormack swallowed, blinked his eyes, and said lamely, "Oh, all right. Lead on, McDuff."

They walked up to MacCormack's house, where he drew water from his well and carried a bucketful up to the porch. Decker drank from a dipper and said appreciatively, "Tastes good."

"Drink hearty," said MacCormack. "I'm done with it."

"Done? Man, you put more sweat into digging that well than you've taken out of it!"

"Digging that well and trying to build a ranch was a waste of time. The question is whether I leave Waddy Flats now, or leave later, with a gun to my head. Mrs. Wilbur and Esau Knox spelled it out: this town is finished. When Trotter burned that kid, it was the last straw. There'll be no holding the Indians, now."

"It hasn't been proved that anybody's been burned. It's all a rumour, nothing more."

"Rumour be blowed."

"Mack," Decker said patiently, "don't take on so."

"You can cut out the soft soap, Decker, because it won't change my mind."

"We need settlers to tame this country, and grow with it. Waddy Flats will survive if ten of us stick it out. Ten determined men."

"Waddy Flats is a dead end. I've been breaking my back, and for what? This will be an isolated little backwater forever. Trotter's never going to finish that road."

"He could, if he made a reasonable settlement with the Chilcotin nation."

"Nation? They're a rabble and you know it. Stop trying to dignify them with fancy words. I don't like Trotter any more than the next man, but I'm damned if I want him accommodating a pack of wild Indians."

"You don't see that this is Indian country," Decker said sharply. "That they're the owners. What good does it do to belittle people? If you're going to live with them, you might as well make an effort to get to know them and understand them."

"We'll never see eye to eye. Indians hate us all, Trotter especially. They won't give him a minute's peace. His men are quitting because Indians have been slashing their tents at night."

"Tents that were put up on Chilcotin land without permission."

"Devil take it! What will it take to convince you that there's no such thing as Chilcotin land!" MacCormack shouted. "I say that a fellow who homesteads land, and works it, that fellow owns his land, by right, and can keep it!"

"Homesteading is one thing, Waddington's land grant is another. The government's done too good a job, giving away things that belong to other people."

"Which people?"

"The Chilcotins."

Incensed, MacCormack slammed a hand down on his knee and said, "They're right, you're an Indian lover. Nobody can say a word against them."

Decker fixed his attention on Bushrat, slaving away down at the beach, until he had a grip on his anger. "Dammit," Decker said, "the Chilcotins have a point. They don't mind settlers like you and me, with our few paltry little acreages. What they object to is Waddington, getting a road allowance across their whole country."

"By God, Decker, Indian lover or not, I admire you in a way. You've bankrolled this place from the beginning. There wouldn't be a dollar of cash money here, but for you."

"The road gang has cash."

"Maybe, but they don't spend. They're here to earn money and save it, they take it out when they go."

What MacCormack wanted now was to live in a place with theatres and cigar shops. A quiet city with decent clubs, where a fellow could drink brandy of an evening with a few civilised pals. He said, "Sorry, Decker. I've been losing my temper a lot, lately. That thing I said just now, about you buying with four-bit dollars..."

"Forget it."

"I wish I had your pluck, but I haven't and that's that. I'm giving my cattle to Strongitharm because I haven't the money to ship them anywhere. Quirk's taking my mule. Nobody wants to bother with my stump puller so if you can make use of it, help yourself."

"Put it behind my store. If it sells, I'll send the money on to Victoria."

MacCormack saw Decker looking inside his door. It was an untidy shambles, with dirty dishes on the table and blankets lying across the side of his bunk where they had been pushed aside when he got up. MacCormack said, "The place is a mess. That sometimes happens, when a fellow has no wife."

"That brings me to the reason I'm here. What were you saying about Trotter's wife yesterday?"

"I was hot when I said those things in the store," MacCormack answered, turning away to stare at the distant mountains. "I'm sorry now."

Decker took two cigars from his breast pocket, gave one to MacCormack, and lit them both with a match that he struck on a thumbnail.

"Sure. It's jealousy made me speak. I'm as jealous as any lovestruck kid, and that's a fact," MacCormack said, dragging the words out slowly. "Isabel's a bride-ship girl of course. Beautiful. But a fellow is seeding the devil's crop when he buys his wife the same way he buys his horses."

"Get this straight," Decker said sharply. "I won't have her maligned."

"I hardly give a damn, but I've a need to get something off my chest," MacCormack said, but his voice had changed. It sounded as if somebody else's voice was speaking through him. Decker guessed that MacCormack was ready to uncork some strong ideas that had been fermenting inside him for a long time.

"I've known Isabel since she immigrated to this country," MacCormack said. "I was on the dock in Victoria when the bride ship came in...."

Decker smiled inwardly. He'd been on the dock himself, together with James Douglas and Matthew Begbie, but so had every other able-bodied man in Victoria. Begbie and James Douglas were pressuring Decker to enlist as a special constable and enforce British law at the time, but they had halted their discussions to watch what was going on in the harbour.

Decker only had to close his eyes and he could see the bride ship as if it were yesterday. The ship was the *Tynemouth*. Ninety-nine days out of London with fifty female waifs destined for the colonial and matrimonial market. Instead of mooring at a wharf, the captain anchored his vessel offshore and mounted a deck watch to stop men in rowboats from climbing aboard and carrying girls off the ship by force. Decker had never seen an unrulier bunch, and the reason for all the excitement was a sharp-witted opportunist named Bert Graham.

Nobody seemed to know how Graham managed the stunt, but when he heard that helpless English girls were coming to Victoria he organized a club, The Female Immigration Society. If you wanted a maid, or a governess, or a wife, you had to go through the society and pay Graham ten pounds for the privilege. He put advertisements in the newspaper to let folks know that marriageable girls would be available. Tailors on Government Street were advertising new suits, for men wanting to make a good impression. When the *Tynemouth* did arrive, the town's bachelors had been talking of little else for months. Decker was remembering how Graham, and a reporter from the *British Colonist*, were the only ones allowed on board to see the girls. Describing them, Graham had Victoria's bachelors agog. According to his description, the immigrant girls were a mixed bag of handsome and homely between about twelve years old and some indeterminate age and according to Graham, the undoubted prize was a beautiful girl called Isabel Jordan.

So there they were, Decker, Judge Begbie and Governor Douglas, together on the wharf, watching, when the girls were ferried off the *Tynemouth* and a marine guard brought them ashore on HMS *Forward*, a navy gunboat. There was plenty of lusty cheering when the *Forward* landed and the watching men caught their first glimpse of the girls. They were herded into a fenced paddock on the wharf and met by an official greeting party consisting of four Hudson's Bay wives and two clergymen.

Decker had to admit that for all his defects, Graham had been right about Isabel Jordan. Decker had never seen a lovelier woman. Compared to the others she was like a full-rigged ship surrounded by rowboats.

One of the Hudson's Bay ladies gave a nice little speech to remind the girls that, until the money for their assisted passages had been repaid in full, they would be placed in selected homes where they could express their gratitude to God, and the colony, by performing their duties diligently, obediently, and without pay, for a period to be determined. The senior clergyman got up on the podium and pointed out that the country was filling up with Asians, Virginians, and other riff-raff. As English girls they had a duty to marry Englishmen, preferably English clergymen, and to populate the colony with decent people. A man from Virginia offered to punch the clergyman's nose and the dignitaries went home to the sound of boos as, disgusted by the whole performance, so did James Douglas and Matthew Begbie. Decker was too curious to leave. He stayed behind and watched as the girls — a mite bedraggled after ninety-nine days of close confinement at sea — were given soap, buckets, and fresh water. The hooting onlookers had a diverting hour, watching the embarrassed girls washing their small clothes and draping them on ropes to dry in the sun. Seeing those dainty garments, one delicate fellow fainted, because he had never seen a woman's small clothes in his life. He didn't even know that such things existed. Decker heard several men remark, more or less enthusiastically, that some of the girls did not seem to have any small clothes.

After finishing their laundry, the immigrants were paraded about the town under another marine guard, to be seen and judged. To their probable horror and fear, the girls were next corralled in the marine barracks, until Graham decided how they were to be distributed.

Going back to his lodgings, Decker hadn't been able to stop thinking about Isabel Jordan. With skin like gold, she seemed the blooming and unattainable essence of ripe maidenhood. Decker couldn't look at her smooth flowing limbs and the outline of soft breasts beneath her clothes without thinking of pillows, beds, and lewd pagan revels with cloven-hoofed satyrs and naughty shepherdesses.

Decker shook his head to banish that disturbing memory from his mind. MacCormack was still talking.

"Then Clarence Trotter showed up in Graham's office," MacCormack said, laughing. "By God, Trotter was livid. It was better than a circus. There was Graham, trying to auction Isabel to the highest bidder. But she wasn't a homeless waif, like some of the other girls. She'd been a servant in London. Clarence Trotter had arranged her passage out and paid the fare. He said she was his second cousin, or some such. Everything had been arranged by mail, but you know how slow and awkward that business is. Anyway. Graham and Trotter and me, we went to bail her out of the barracks."

"Why you, particularly?"

"I was thick with Graham in those days," MacCormack replied, waving his cigar as he relived the story in his mind. "Isabel was with the others in a large room, undressing for bed, when we went in..."

"Three uninvited men, walking into a bedroom full of girls! Are you serious?"

"They weren't girls to Graham. They were commodities," MacCormack said defensively. "Isabel was tired, a bit shabby. She had a faraway look. But damn, Decker, I should have offered Trotter my whole fortune and taken her for myself! By the Lord, it would have been better for me if I'd spent my money on a wife, instead of staking everything on this Godforsaken place. Well, Trotter proposed to Isabel on the spot, right there in that barracks. She bowed her head. For a moment, Trotter must have been worried, but Isabel nodded."

"She didn't actually say she'd marry him?" Decker interjected. "She didn't meet the fellow, and a minute later fall into his arms?"

"Isabel didn't fall into his arms, but she nodded, and that was good enough for Trotter. Graham and me, we took leave of the happy couple," MacCormack said, with a lengthening face. "Presume the usual and predictable aftermath..."

"But dammit, Trotter couldn't marry Isabel immediately! There's a formality of churches and priests. There's a procedure of banns and suchlike, to be got through first."

"I did not say there was a marriage," MacCormack returned. "I said there was the usual and predictable aftermath. I know it took place in a sleazy hotel room, beside a dark cluttered alley, with cats fighting in a yard, and lanterns swinging past the bedroom windows..."

"How come you know all this?"

"Graham told me."

"How could Graham possibly know?"

"Why so many damn questions? I'm doing my best to tell you the story, so just listen," MacCormack said. "The next public event took place a couple of hours later, in the Rat House Cafe. I was eating lamb chops at that small circular table alongside the kitchen when Trotter and Isabel arrived for their post ... when they arrived. Trotter was edgy. Isabel looked no different than she had earlier. The cafe was jammed and there was a muddle over tables. That sour-looking head waiter with a face like a hangman tried to sort things out. After an argument Trotter tried to bribe him with half a crown but it was no good. In the end they shared my table. Trotter ordered champagne, got drunk, and treated us to the secret longings of his heart." The thought made MacCormack shake his head. "As a speech it was awful, embarrassing. I've never seen an unhappier fool in my life. Trotter told Isabel — the whole room heard him — about his rise from penniless immigrant to lofty .... It was as if Trotter couldn't get his dreams and hopes untangled in his mind. Isabel must have thought he owned the Bute Inlet Wagon Road instead of being a paid employee. And his wild talk! It was a half-baked rant about Indians, and land grants, and thundering waterfalls and toll gates, and rolling wagon wheels."

"You think Trotter's mad?"

"If he isn't, he's the next thing to it. I tell you honestly, Decker, what I felt for that woman was more than lust. I've been half in love with her ever since I first laid eyes on her, and as soon as I found out she'd moved up here with Trotter, I couldn't wait to see her again.

She's one of the reasons I came to Waddy Flats, and settled. I went up to the Slough at the first chance, and we did manage to have one conversation, Isabel and me. I can tell you this much, Trotter's not her cousin. It was just his nonsense, they're not related in any way. Trotter met her in a London boarding house when she was a drudge, fresh out of an orphanage," MacCormack frowned. "I called at the Slough twice, after that, and we were able to talk for a while. She didn't whine but I knew she was unhappy. When Trotter came along he threw me out."

"Literally?"

"He waved a rifle at me and I cleared off. The next time I tried to go and see her, one of Trotter's lackeys turned me away at the gate," MacCormack got up off the porch with a quick impatient movement. "The hell with Trotter! A worthier cuckold never built a road."

"Hold your tongue, man! Remember the girl's honour, for God's sake."

"Aye, sorry. It slipped out."

"Slipped out bedamned. Your whole attitude is insulting. When a girl's honour is lost, it's lost forever, you bloody fool."

"I said I was sorry."

"It's too late to be sorry," Decker said. He moderated his tone and added. "Anyway, it looks as if Trotter's lost her."

"That's if she is lost," MacCormack said, and something dark came into his eyes. "By God, it's not pleasant, but I have to tell somebody before I burst. There's more. Isabel's been here. It was a month ago and I don't think I understood what ... Isabel! I made a fool of myself. I was working on a fence. When I turned around, she was there. I don't know how, but she came up behind without me knowing. She was wearing a white shirt with the top buttons undone, and knee britches. I threw myself at her. It wasn't a matter of thinking, or even choice. I kissed her on the lips and ... . By God, it was like kissing a statue, a marble. There was no flesh, d'ye see? Nothing human there, her lips were stiff and dry and cold. And her eyes! She stared at me with her cold damned eyes, Decker, as I demeaned myself!"

"You made love to her?"

"Love? To her! A kiss was enough," MacCormack said passionately. "By God man, she's the cure for love."

"Listen, Mack. You're a grown man, but you've still got some learning to do ..."

"That's as may be, but you're not my teacher," MacCormack snapped, and tried to stand up.

Decker grabbed MacCormack's wrist and squeezed, hard. MacCormack swallowed, and sat still.

"Isabel Trotter is married. Get that into your head," Decker said. "She and Trotter were married according to the custom of the country."

"What's that supposed to mean?"

"I'm talking to you about a country where there's more guns than preachers. Men and women make their vows to each other, and the next time a preacher comes around to their district, it might be in a month, or a year, they repeat their vows in front of him and it's all logged in the family bible. That's the way James Douglas was married. That's the way a lot of good people were married. If I hear you say one more malicious word against Isabel Trotter I'll take a horsewhip to you."

MacCormack went into his house and kicked the door shut.

As for Decker, he managed to stop thinking about MacCormack. He thought about Isabel instead, and not innocently; to him, her whole being suggested bursting fruit and forbidden delights, half-hidden in the long grasses of golden Dionysian afternoons. With a sudden lurch, he got up from MacCormack's porch and strode down to where Bushrat was still slaving away with whale-oil kettles. "Belay that, Bushy," he said. "I'm sick of this place."

***

Decker was leaning against his back fence with one foot resting on the bottom rail, watching freshly branded calves settle into enclosed pasture. The little Highlander, tamer now, took his face out of the grass long enough to size Decker up and find him uninteresting. With a snort the Highlander grazed away. "Eat hearty, old fellow," Decker said idly. He was hardly aware of speaking. He was not even thinking about the bull. He was thinking how quick men were to pin labels on people. Now he was an Indian lover. The hell he was. Decker tugged a shaft of sweetgrass from its stalk and chewed abstractedly as he wandered into the back of the store.

Bushrat was pouring hot water into a metal teapot. He stirred the pot with a wooden spoon, placed a knobby hand on his hip and straightened his back, saying, "My rheumatics is bad today. I need to get me a new copper bracelet 'cos I wore all the goodness outta my last one."

"Make yourself another. There's copper wire in that box under the work bench."

"Hit don't do no good to make your own bracelets," Bushrat replied as he filled two enamel mugs with tea and shoved one to

Decker. "Rheumatics bracelets needs to be made special, and then have hands laid on 'em by somebody with the gift. The Irish has the gift mostly, and gypsies."

Sudden gusts buffeted the building and made the chimney smoke. Decker looked through the window. Swells were lifting driftlogs onto the shores of Bute Inlet. Beyond the rolling waves, mountains gnawed the underbellies of clouds with sharp white teeth.

"The Highlander's shedding his winter coat quickly," Decker said. "It'll be a hot summer, I reckon. Thank heaven, because it's been a rough winter. Especially on the Chilcotins."

"They ran short of grub, right enough, but you know, hungry or not, Chilcotins prefer winter to summer. They can't wait for the long dark to come around, so they can dig themselves into their pit-houses. Regular Turkish baths, them pit-houses. They chant their winter songs and run their secret societies and have their dances," Bushrat said. "There'll be big trouble here before winter rolls around."

"Why?"

"Injuns is sayin' that white men is spreading the pox on purpose."

"That's not as far-fetched as some people might think. When you finish that tea, let's saddle up and see if we can find Klatsassan. There's no sense waiting here until somebody else brings me goods I don't need and can't sell."

"I got me an idea where Klatsassan might be holed up."

"Where?"

"In that spirit house that Cusshen The Scarface built."

"What's Klatsassan doing in a place like that?"

"Mourning. Praying."

***

The unnamed creek disgorged into a sandy cove behind a tree-covered island. As Decker and Bushrat dismounted and tethered their horses to trees beside the trail, a flock of oystercatchers feeding at the tideline took to the air and flew in skittering circles. Harbour seals, dozing on offshore rocks, raised their sleek mottled heads, blinked incurious eyes, and went back to sleep.

The lawmen scrambled up a rocky trail beside the thundering creek. Blackberry tangles, rose thickets and trout lilies fought for space between ancient firs and colossal cedars. Clouds of misty spray sparkled in the air above little waterfalls like the white skirts of a dancer. Away from the shore, the ground gradually levelled to a gentle incline. They plodded across a beaver meadow to reach a shed with a moss-covered roof about eight feet square. Its walls consisted of cedar planks, stacked between vertical parallel posts. Roof planks, weighted down with heavy rocks, could be pried apart from the inside to let daylight in, or let smoke out.

Bushrat hailed the house in Chilcotin, but there was no reply. Going down on all fours, Decker entered the shed by pushing aside a mat of woven grass that was draped across a low doorway. Crawling in on the earthen floor, his head brushed against something in the darkness and there was a sound like pebbles, shaking inside a wooden box. A few rays of grey light seeped into the shed through holes and chinks. More light came from the red embers of a fire, glowing within a circle of stones. A string of deer hooves dangled across the entrance. Crawling in, Bushrat set them rattling again.

Carved wooden animal masks were laid in a row on the floor, facing a naked female, dead of smallpox, who had been placed on a sleeping platform. The woman's shorn hair had been rolled into a ball and placed between her knees.

Bushrat said huskily, "Hit's Klatsassan's daughter."

"And those deer hooves?"

"Ghost catchers, to protect her and the house."

"Where's Klatsassan?"

"Watching the place from up in the trees, I guess."

"You're sure that's his daughter?"

"Certain sure," said Bushrat. "Sure as hell."

To which burning diabolical place, Decker was convinced, Klatsassan in his grief would now readily consign every white man in the territory.

CHAPTER NINE

DECKER AND BUSHRAT had been prepared for the worst but all the same it was a shock. Two flayed, headless corpses were suspended by their wrists from an arbutus tree, fifty feet up a sidehill off Trotter's wagon road. Under blankets of buzzing insects they looked more like tattered red flags than corpses.

"Great Jehovah!" Decker cried. "What kind of lunatics did this?"

"Don't look at me," the roadbuilder said. "How do you think I felt? I lost my breakfast, I did, when I stumbled across 'em."

Decker smiled thinly. The roadbuilder was a decent sort.

"Help! Murder!" he'd cried, bursting into Decker's store two hours earlier, covered in sweat, his eyes popping. "You're a lawman ain't you?"

"Right."

"You've got to come quick."

"What's happening?"

When the roadbuilder told them, the lawmen saddled up and went to have a look. It was a grim spectacle and the roadbuilder was anxious to be gone.

"Wait a minute," Decker said. "Who's going to clean this mess up?"

"Bury 'em, or leave 'em hanging for crowbait, it's all the same to me," the roadbuilder replied woodenly. A moment later, his horse was picking its way down the slope towards the wagon road.

"Perfeck," Bushrat said. "Now we been elected gravediggers."

Decker thought, This is the end of Waddy Flats. Contemplating the cadavers from a distance, he said, "Bushy. Have you ever heard of Indians flaying people like that?"

"Yessir. You should have seen what the Salteaux did to the Blackfoots after the Red Deer war. White Elk Horn was the Blackfoot chief, so he got special attention. Them Salteaux flayed White Elk

Horn alive and then they dismembered him one limb at a time. When he still wouldn't die they cut his heart and briskets out and nailed 'em to a tree."

Noisy crows led Decker and Bushrat to the missing heads. They were impaled on sticks a hundred yards away, on a bluff overlooking the wagon road.

"Hell fire!" Decker said. "It's Gridger and Missy."

Flies and crows had been working on the corpses. Cutting them down and dropping them into their graves was a sweaty, smelly business.

Bushrat said, "That other keg angel, One-Ear Brown. He ought to be around here somewhere."

"Have I ever told you how One-Ear lost his ear?"

Bushrat shook his head.

"You may find this hard to swallow. It happened a few years back. In those days, I was a sergeant of police in Victoria. We called him Charlie Brown, then. He'd been pinched for selling liquor to Indians and it was his fifth or sixth offence. His recipe was a small touch of alcohol, added to gunpowder, tobacco juice, blue vitriol, pepper, molasses, lamp oil, vinegar, and a secret ingredient. A pint of One-Ear's tangle-leg could drive an ordinary man into raging lunacy for about twelve hours and either kill him, or give him a headache that lasted a week. The best thing was, only about five percent of Charlie's customers went blind. Judge Begbie got tired of his nonsense so he sentenced him to wear heavy government jewellery for six months. Charlie didn't cotton to the idea. He picked up his ball and chain and made a run for it out of the court room. A constable and I chased him outside, shouting for him to stop, and when he wouldn't quit we both fired, and one of us clipped his ear. We changed his name with one bullet."

"That was pretty fancy shooting."

"It would have been better all round if we'd aimed four inches towards the centre," Decker said. "One-Ear did his six months quietly after that. As soon as we cut his chains off and turned him loose, he moved out of Victoria. He never learned a thing, though, never changed his endearing ways."

"Some folks ain't smart enough to learn. One-Ear's brain's about as big as a bar of soap after a hard day's washing."

"I'm not so sure. One-Ear's mean and vicious, but he's as smart as a cookhouse rat."

"There's no argument about Gridger, I guess. He didn't know tulips from turpentine, throwin' in with a no-good like One-Ear,"

Bushrat said, as he ranged in circles until he found the killers' tracks. He kept going, his head down and his nostrils twitching like a dog on scent, seeing bent twigs and broken branches and reading things in dislodged stones and leaves that Decker, following in the rear, missed completely. Bushrat took them between the trees and around a sunny marsh where ducks and geese rose up out of the water and beat away over the reeds, their wings stirring the air and bringing up the smell of mud and the faint scent of last year's orchids. The trail became well-trodden and easy to follow and soon they could have found the wreckage of One-Ear's moonshine factory with their noses. In the silence a patient mule, still hitched to a wagon loaded with potatoes, was cropping grass.

"This is where they done it. Bare footprints and blood everywhere," Bushrat said. "But I got a hunch One-Ear might have escaped. I bet he's still running so fast you could play a game of poker on his shirt tail."

Trees were throwing their last, long shadows and squadrons of crows were winging to their night roosts when Decker unyoked the mule and they followed it from the distillery to One-Ear's shack. The bootlegger's sloop was high and dry on the beach, with its sides stove in.

Bushrat took a looping stroll and said, "One-Ear kept two woman here."

"How do you know?"

Bushrat didn't know how he knew. He said, "All kinds of reasons."

"That's helpful."

"At least one of 'em was white. We seen the other woman hanging up alongside Gridger."

"Was it Isabel?"

"I reckon. She'd been collecting moss from off them trees out by the privy. And look at them sacks of straw she's slept on."

"No thanks."

"Hit's a good thing God don't tell young-un's what they're gonna run up against in this life, or I doubt they'd have the courage to get out of bed in the mornin'. They'd be too scairt to go nowhere and do nothin'."

"We all would," Decker said, walking down to the beach to look at the sloop and thinking about that strange, lost girl.

CHAPTER TEN

THE ROADWORKER DIDN'T waste a minute before spreading the news of his gruesome discovery. Rumour fed on rumour. Before long, there were people willing to swear that dozens of headless men had been found; more were dying of smallpox; Indians were massing for war, and so on. By general consent, Waddy Flats was doomed and blighted and cursed. Hysteria built. People left their farms; roadworkers deserted. Old Tsulas, fearing reprisals from the white men, crawled out from beneath Decker's porch and vanished like a ghost into the trees.

The exodus was in full swing when a mule-drawn cart with a busted tail-gate, its broken wheel-spokes braced with wired-on slabs of hand-sawn timber, rumbled down Waddington Street. Esau Knox, up on the unsprung seat with his wife, stared straight ahead as he went past the store where Decker, trying to write a letter on his porch, was shaking his head in disbelief as the lifeblood leached out of his town. Tim Knox, twelve years old, hiking alongside the cart in a pair of his father's cut-down overalls, gazed wide-eyed at the abandoned wagons clogging the road to the wharf.

All was abustle as roadworkers and prospectors and settlers jostled aboard the *Nonpareil*. Pigtailed sailors manned the gangplanks, selling tickets and checking passengers for signs of smallpox. Tim Knox helped his mother to dismount and she held his arm, speechless and defeated in a frowsy black frock and a black straw bonnet, while Esau Knox untethered the mule and turned it loose. Unattended, it ambled off towards the unstaked wilderness. Across the street, Shanks locked his smithy and hurried to the ship with the coals still glowing in his forge. Settler Quirk collected his family, and went; MacCormack and Strongitharm went. Everybody was leaving.

As passenger space diminished aboard the *Nonpareil*, panic deepened. A general lunacy possessed the townsfolk. To make way for living freight, sailors jettisoned everything except hand luggage. Headboards and eiderdowns and mahogany-framed mirrors and heirloom bureaus were thrown overboard, or deposited among the rank nettles. Schnurr's acquisitive instincts asserted themselves; the fat scrounger went around rubbing his hands and grinning like an imbecile, collecting wandering livestock and dragging disowned treasure into the lot behind his empty lodging house.

Decker handed a letter to Strongitharm and said, "See that Governor Douglas gets this, will you?"

Strongitharm, beside himself with worry, smiled absently and jammed the letter into a back pocket.

When the schooner departed, with a dangerously low freeboard, canoes and flatboats driven by bedsheet sails, drifted in its wake, carrying the last evacuees. The very dogs were thrown from the boats like so much rubbish. Decker and Bushrat watched in silent outrage as a faithful castaway dog dragged itself exhausted from the inlet, and ran along the barnacled shore, barking after its departed master.

"Great Gawd," Decker said.

"Hard to tell from his looks how far a frog will jump when you prod it, but I thought we'd a few starchier fellows livin' in this burg," Bushrat said. "I heard Waddy Flats called a garden of Eden more'n once, yet folks think there's a curse here. Manseed and womanseed don't take root."

"Nonsense. Folks will come to their senses when they've had time to think quietly. You watch, they'll all come back and we'll get the town going again."

"You're sayin' that because it's what you want to believe, boss, but you and me know better and there's no sense sayin' no different. We'll see no more of 'em. There was no child born in Eden, and none were born here. Even the Hudson's Bay gave up on this place."

"When?"

"Long ago. Their scouts come up here and got lost in icefields and ravines and snowfogs, ran out of grub, survived by eating their leather packs, and stumbled out of the mountains lookin' like a bunch of skeletons."

"They sound more like greenhorns than scouts. The Hudson's Bay used to train their people with more care." Decker looked Bushrat in the eye and said, "Do you want to clear out? Say the word and I'll pay you off. I won't try to stop you."

Bushrat let that one float by.

"There's not a soul left, except us and Schnurr. It's as if the Homathko has flooded its banks."

"That's good. Most of the rubbish has been flushed out. What we needs here, is a hardier bunch," Bushrat said. "Now, boss. How's about some coffee?"

"Sure. Coffee would be fine."

Strongitharm was leaning over the schooner's rail, looking up the inlet at the ruin of his dreams. Tim Knox, brushing past him along the crowded deck, dislodged Decker's letter to Douglas from Strongitharm's back pocket. It fell over the side, unnoticed save by hovering seagulls, as the ship surged onwards.

***

One-Ear had watched from the trees as rampaging Indians destroyed his distillery. When the destruction was complete, they took their axes to his sloop, and celebrated the rout by dancing and waving spears and chanting victory songs. The sun was falling below the horizon when the jubilant warriors abandoned the area.

One-Ear shivered with rage. To be beaten by Injuns! It was intolerable! By God, he'd get his own back. How? His thoughts led him straight to Isabel. Isabel, killed! His rage knew no bounds. What was it about her? Her beauty? The way she stood up straight, like a princess? No, there was something else behind that beauty. Tears dripped down his cheeks. Goddam those Injuns.

One-Ear was on the beach, opening mussels with a knife and eating them raw, when, looking up, he saw Isabel standing on a bluff. He wiped his eyes. "There you are," he said, recovering his usual cocky assurance. "I been wonderin' if them heathens wasted yer charms. They've all gone, you don't need to be scared. Come down here along of me, have a feed. A few mussels'll do you good."

Isabel saw the moist glitter in his yellow eyes. Without speaking she removed her boots, tied their laces together and draped them around her neck, and slid down the cliff on the seat of her baggy overalls.

He grinned at her. "Hey, listen," he said, "I missed you, so I did. I thought you was done for."

Isabel nodded and hurried away towards Waddy Flats.

One-Ear's warm feelings and pleasurable anticipation vanished. "Hey! Stop right there!" he shouted. "That ain't the way we's going."

She had quite a lead when he set off, puzzled and angry, pursuing her along hard, tide-combed sand. Isabel's lead increased as she weaved in and out of sight behind rock outcroppings in the failing light. Clouds descended and a chilling rain began. Water streamed off every leaf and branch. Oozy mud streaked out of the bush and ran in little brown trickles across the sand. A lonely black cormorant, standing on a rock with spreadeagled wings, was the only other living creature in sight when Isabel clambered through a mist of white surf around a broken promontory and disappeared into a stand of trees.

Breakers pounded the shore as One-Ear tried to follow her vanishing footprints before he became trapped by the rising tide. An errant wave carried him into the undertow and swept him out to deep water. His baggy cap floated away. Another enormous breaker heaved him onto a bed of mussels. Scrambling mightily, bleeding, One-Ear clawed up to a ledge as the tide flooded the beach. Shivering, he shuffled backwards and forwards along the ledge in his soggy clothes, swinging his arms to keep warm until, overcome by exhaustion, he crouched against the rockface, clasping his knees and shivering.

A half moon came up, and with it, the smell of woodsmoke. One-Ear waited for the tide to drop and sidled across the promontory in the dark, his arms and legs outstretched like a clinging starfish. The smell of burning wood was stronger now. Above the cliffs, black trees were dense except where their jagged edges made a moving fringe against moonsilver. He broke through a gulch matted with thorns and burrs. Invisible points snagged his buckskins, hidden stumps and rocks barked his shins. He limped to a grassy sward where a fire burned. Isabel was lying on a bed of cedar boughs in the shelter of a cantilevered bank. He heard her soft exhalation above the crackle of flames, saw her eyes, alternately veiled and gleaming, as embers fell.

***

The wagon road was little more than twin tracks through the forest, where wheels had compacted the soil. Wild rhododendrons and crowberries and alders were already starting to obliterate it. It was evening when Decker and Bushrat appeared on horseback and stopped outside Trotter's mansion.

The San Francisco-style house was five thousand square feet of elegant living space enclosed by three-storey turrets, gables, captain's walks, porches, beveled glass, stained glass, and gingerbread mouldings. Waddington had built it to impress visiting investors but its extravagances were absurd in that wild setting — it was like seeing a monkey in a suit. Now, with drawn curtains, the house looked cold and unwelcoming as well. Decker said facetiously, "All that's missing is a moat."

Curtains moved behind a window. In a moment, the front door opened. "Nobody's home," a white-haired man was informing them, when he took a closer look and said, "Is that you, Bushrat?"

"Blow me, it's Hayes. I figured everybody was long gone from here. How come you didn't light out to Victoria on the schooner with the rest of 'em?"

"I could ask you the same thing," Hayes said, as he came out of the house cradling a shotgun.

"Well, I never was one fer making sudden moves," Bushrat said. "I'm kind of slow and smooth, like cold tar."

"Trotter made it worth my while to stick around for a bit," Hayes smirked, "and my duties ain't exactly wearyin'. Since I fell and busted my knee a while back I've been on odd jobs here instead of on the road, sweepin' the barn and suchlike. I helped Miz Trotter with her chores as well, until she took off."

"We heard she left," said Bushrat. "What happened? Why'd she go?"

"Maybe she got tired of all the golderned noise," Hayes said. "Generally they was a bunch of Injuns camped here. Drummin' and yellin', day and night, they was, right outside the front door. I dern near went deaf. But they all took a powder a few days ago. Got some peace, now." Hayes spat and added, "I ain't sorry to be closer to town."

"Got tired of the boondocks?"

"No more'n usual," Hayes said, leaning his weight on the shotgun as if it were a crutch. "Things is different on the road gang since your day, Bush. Derned if you didn't pick the right time to quit."

"That's polite, but you knows I never quit. Trotter give me my walking papers."

"Don't matter. All I'm saying, the guys still workin' is countin' the days till they can collect their wages and clear out."

"Is Trotter pushing 'em hard?"

"Sure, he's pushing 'em, but the boys ain't scared of work. They're scared that Waddington's run out of cash and they won't get paid." Hayes looked at Decker and said slyly, "You found them head-hunters yet?"

"Am I supposed to be looking?"

Hayes grinned. "Well, you're a lawman, ain't you?"

Decker said amiably, "When was the last time you saw Mrs. Trotter?"

"A few days ago. I never actually seen her leave." With a widening smirk, Hayes added, "But I could tell you things about her, if I wanted to. Like..."

Decker said abruptly, "Where's Trotter?"

Hayes' smirk faded. "How should I know?"

"You're making noises like a man who knows things. Why don't you tell us how Trotter set fire to Klatsassan's son?"

Hayes moved his weight from one foot to the other and adjusted his gaze to a point near Decker's stomach. "That's a rotten lie. Nobody burned nobody. I know that for a fact."

"I've got other ideas," Decker said sharply. "What were were you doing that night? Scratching your ass, or dipping sugar cubes into Trotter's whisky bottle?"

"I was asleep, in bed," Hayes sputtered, terminating the interview by backing inside the house and slamming the door.

"Brother. You better not expect no favours from him," Bushrat said. "Were you needlin' him deliberate?"

"Sure. You take Hayes now. He and MacCormack were the fellows spreading rumours about Isabel. We know Hayes is a blabbermouth, but is he a hard case, or what?"

"Not a natural hard case. Just the opposite, because the thing about Hayes is, he ain't got no strong idears of his own. You know the kind? Hears what everybody else has to say, then goes along with it."

"The sort of fellow who would spread dirt on a woman's name? The sort of fellow who could help torture a lad, depending on who was pushing him?"

"Well, I'll tow that fish alongside fer a while, before I reel it in," Bushrat said, as he turned his horse and followed Decker back down the hill to Waddy Flats.

They left the wagon road behind and went across ground cobbled with loose rocks. Decker, one hand on the reins and the other gripping his saddlehorn, looked up from time to time at the melting snow-caps rising all around. Waddy Flats seemed cold and forbidding because all the familiar house lights that had once twinkled on the hillsides were dark.

"This country still suits you, does it, boss?" said Bushrat.

Decker rode without speaking for another five minutes. Dismounting, he led his horse into a creekbed where it lowered its head to drink. His cattle, bunched together chewing cud, swung their heads to watch. He thought of Isabel, who had often paused in this same place, for the same purpose. He imagined her patting the mare's smooth neck, imagined her talking to it in a soft, reassuring voice.

"Waddy Flats suited me better before," Decker said, slackening the chestnut's girth straps to let it blow.

CHAPTER ELEVEN

CLARENCE TROTTER AND Byron McEachren heard the gorge's thunder fifteen minutes before it came into view. Riding up a crest in cloudless sunshine they saw a dazzling rainbow hanging in the permanent mists above waterfalls a mile distant. Straddling the Homathko River and dwarfed by the mountains behind it, the rainbow's arc neatly encompassed Trotter's rope ferry and other changes that his men had wrought on the land.

On the east bank, trees had been cleared for a ferry landing and two small huts. On the west bank, the land rose from another landing to a crossing-keeper's house, where jackpine forest resumed, except for a narrow road leading to the gorge's western battlements. Beyond, where the Homathko had carved through solid rock and was expending its might on a series of cascades, a chain of swaying boardwalks could be seen, suspended from iron cables in the mists above the torrents.

Trotter drew rein below the waterfalls and sagged in the saddle that he was gradually moulding to his own shape. The rainbow's mighty arc had brought no gladness to his heart; it rested on his shoulders like a dome of iron. He felt his throat knotting with self-pity because he knew beyond contradiction that the cables and pulleys of the rope ferry were doomed. Soon, the ill-conceived road would revert to its former state of untamed desolation, untrodden save by cougars and grizzlies and Indians. History would remember this disaster of misdirected hubris as Trotter's Folly. The shame of it, and knowing besides that he was held in general contempt, was insupportable. Trotter's heart pounded when he reflected that Isabel had also fled. He lowered his head and tried to clear his mind, but it was no use. His humiliation was complete. His eyes were swimming and he was forced to blink and turn his face away from McEachren.

At the Homathko gorge, every drop of rain that fell on a million square miles of country had to squeeze through a chasm less than fifty yards wide before it reached the sea. And Clarence Trotter had squandered Waddington's fortune there, defying the forces of nature. Trotter knew himself for a failure; he had been sliding to this ruin since he left England for Victoria to meet his future employer. Apprenticed to Isambard Kingdom Brunel in London, Trotter had been taught the trade of a bridge and marine engineer and was recruited to finish Waddington's road on Brunel's personal recommendation. When Trotter shook hands with Waddington for the first time, at a hotel in Victoria, Waddington said, "I'm an entrepreneur, I dream large. Unlike other men, my dreams become reality."

Waddington did not seem vainglorious in those days; he was boyish, eager, excited. He entertained Trotter to a private dinner and with the soft light of candles falling on his face he looked about forty years old. When Trotter saw Waddington in daylight he realized that the businessman was at least sixty-five.

"I'm building a toll road from the head of Bute Inlet to the interior," Waddington declared, pointing to a line of red ink on a wall map. "A road for wagons, built entirely along the Homathko River. When finished, it will cut weeks off the journey to the interior goldfields and recover its entire costs in a single year. It's a daring scheme, I grant you, but the thing will earn millions. Millions! People say the road can't be built. James Douglas had the audacity to tell me that the terrain is too difficult, that I'm a fool to think otherwise. I intend to show Douglas and everybody else what grit and determination can achieve." Waddington drank a little more wine and reaching across the table gave Trotter a poke in the chest. "Mr. Trotter. I need a resourceful engineer to push the work while I attend to business affairs here in Victoria. Are you that man?"

"I hope so."

"Hope! Hope did you say? I didn't bring you all the way from London to listen to the likes of that."

"If the thing's doable, I'll do it, sir."

"Will you now? Will you indeed?"

"Yes sir, I'll do it."

"That's better, Trotter. A lot better, and let me tell you something else. I always speak my mind and I can see at a glance that you were nothing and nobody in England. But when a man travels to these colonies, he travels to a jurisdiction of wider possibilities," Waddington said as he refilled both their glasses. "In England, I was in trade and you were an apprentice. Here, our only limits are vision and enterprise. Vision and enterprise, my boy, and don't let anybody tell you different."

Trotter arrived at Waddy Flats full of enthusiasm, but saw at once the flaws in Waddington's armchair design — it was practically impossible to build a road entirely along the Homathko gorge. After making his own careful surveys, Trotter returned to Victoria and suggested changes which bypassed the gorge, added thirty miles to the length of the road, and increased costs by ten thousand pounds.

Trotter's reception this time was decidedly chilly. "Another thirty miles!" he said. "Another ten thousand! You must be mad. My God! What did Brunel tell people who told him that the Clifton suspension bridge couldn't be built?"

"Well ..."

"Come on! You're supposed to be the man who helped Brunel to build giant ships and tunnels and railroads and bridges. What did Mr. Brunel tell naysayers who said those feats were impossible?"

Trotter paused. He had no sense of mission; apart from an idle personal vanity which manifested itself in furtive sexual obsessions there were no passions in his life. He was quite content to bathe in the lustre of sturdier men if he were allowed to lord it over a few underlings. He thought, This is just a job. If Waddington wants to pay me a large salary while I waste his money, the more fool him.

Trotter told Waddington what Waddington wanted to hear. "Brunel persevered," he said. "Brunel succeeded."

"Exactly. It's dogged that does it," Waddington said, reassured. "Now, Trotter, listen to me. Just between the two of us, this road's costing me a mint of money, far more than I anticipated. I've been forced to borrow heavily, and bring in a group of partners. I've got to keep them happy, so I don't want anybody hearing what you've just told me. If they withdraw their support, I'm done for."

"Heaven forbid! Do you mean I might not get paid?"

"No no no, Trotter, you have my personal guarantee, but listen," Waddington said, sanguine as ever. "If you can't push the road through all the way along the east side, can you make me a crossing at the gorge? What's wrong with building a ferry across the river there, and continuing the road along the west side?"

"An ordinary ferry won't work, the rapids and cross-currents are too wild and dangerous. I might build a rope ferry, but why? The terrain on the west side of the gorge is almost as bad."

"What's a rope ferry?"

"You attach a flat-bottomed boat to an endless rope. The boat goes back and forth, like laundry on a clothes line."

"Tell me honestly," Waddington said, with impatience rising afresh in his voice. "Are my ideas possible, or not?"

"In theory, they are. But..."

"Never mind. But me no buts. Shoulder to the wheel, eh?" Waddington said, putting his arm around Trotter. "Build me that rope ferry and remember, the completed road will mean big money to both of us. I'm a generous man."

Trotter returned to Waddy Flats with a new wife on his arm, and new ideas simmering in his fertile mind.

The difficulties facing Engineer Trotter at the gorge were formidable. After reckless expenditures, all he had to show were modest improvements to an Indian trail. In many places the so-called road squeezed between rocky defiles and across dangerous rockfalls along a route hardly wide enough for a wheelbarrow. Lengthy sections of Trotter's improvements consisted of swaying boardwalks suspended from cables. There were seventy-nine switchbacks too narrow for mounted riders. Pack horses, spooked by the Homathko's swirling torrents, had to be led along blindfolded.

"That ferry's done you proud."

Trotter raised his face. "What's that?"

"Yon ferry," McEachren said. "It's done you proud, rides the water like a duck."

"Don't you worry yourself about the ferry," Trotter said, noticing the absence of a respectful title. "I can see for myself how well it's doing."

"Sure, I was only remarking," McEachren said, perceiving without unease that Trotter had lapsed into one of his surlier moods. But McEachren's eyes too had narrowed and he looked at his boss with stealthy contempt.

McEachren was older than Trotter, with dark hair and hooded eyes and a broken nose that had been badly set. Given that, and the wide set of his shoulders, he had an air of physical menace useful to a foreman of roughnecked men. However, McEachren was not without perception and he sensed in Trotter a corruption he had noted in men who were dying. Trotter's decline began when Isabel arrived in Waddy Flats.

When McEachren first laid eyes on Trotter's bride-ship prize, he saw a distant, beautiful girl with nothing to say. That was all right (Trotter had too much to say). He, and the rest of Waddy Flats, were happy to see Isabel, apparently demure and certainly uncommunicative in silks, with one slender hand holding her skirts above the mud to display an agreeable length of ankle.

In that country where white women were as rare as unicorns, she was lusted after mightily and the subject of endless gossip. McEachren could name the day when the ruin of her reputation began. A waspish-tongued fellow named Lemman, widely disliked on the road gang, told his mates that Isabel had winked at him. McEachren called Lemman a liar to his face, but it did no good. Other malicious tongues were soon wagging. MacCormack whispered that Isabel had been seen carrying her raised skirts into Schnurr's dark lodging house, from which she emerged the worse for drink. Hayes reported that she was frequently absent from the Slough, ostensibly riding, only to return dishevelled and intoxicated, on an unwinded horse.

In his pre-Isabel stage, McEachren recalled, Trotter had fumed at Waddington's refusal to face facts. As Isabel's reputation worsened and Trotter's relationship with her deteriorated, he hurled Waddington's diminishing store of money into make-work projects which never came to fruition, greeted news of fresh delays with equanimity, and smiled when unforeseen misfortunes added mightily to costs. And once, when Waddington's payroll was late, Trotter told McEachren that he was taking company shares in lieu of wages — Trotter now owned a fair chunk of the wagon road company.

Trotter turned away from the violence of the river. He stared at his foreman and said, "Like it or not, we're into this business up to our necks. It's all or nothing. If you'll stick by me we'll carry it off yet."

"I might stick harder if I knew where you want to go," McEachren said.

"I want none of your damned riddles, mister. What I want to know is whether I can rely on you?"

"You're playing a deep game, but I don't rightly know what it is," McEachren answered stubbornly. "Whatever it is, is it worth keeping on, and risking a war?"

Trotter's face darkened. "I'll tell you what my game is. It's a game for high stakes," he said, longing to kick the fellow off his horse and show him who was master. "Waddington's pockets are nearly empty. If there's an Indian war, the cost and delays will bankrupt him. That will be my ... our ... chance to take over the works. We'll finish the road ourselves, as partners, and line our pockets."

"It's a mighty gamble. We must have a perfect understanding."

"Say your piece."

"You've incited Indians deliberately."

"Who gives a damn?"

"I don't see the need for it. We burned Piell, and I've heard you blame Klatsassan for kidnapping your wife."

"And so he did. Who says he didn't?"

"I do. Klatsassan had nothing to do with it. Mrs. Trotter left on her own, her reasons don't matter to me," McEachren turned his head and spat. "I don't care if you lie to save face, but if you won't deal true with me I'll quit, now, while I still can. I'm a man with other fish to fry."

Trotter was livid and his collar had shrunk so tight that he could hardly breathe. He jammed a finger inside his collar to ease the pressure and give himself time to think. "Now listen to me," Trotter gasped, waving his hand. "If there's a war, it won't matter. With Waddington ruined and out of the way, I'll buy the road for practically nothing and finish it with a detour around this gorge."

"Where will you find the men to build it?"

"If there's a war, the Indians will be wiped out. With them out of the way we'll have no trouble hiring men."

"Let's say you're right. Who'll put up the money to finish the road?"

Trotter had no idea where the money would come from. Confused and upset by McEachren's pointed questions and insolence he couldn't think straight. By God, why wouldn't the fellow be civil? "I have backers in San Francisco," Trotter lied. "It's all arranged, every penny."

"Fine, but what's in it for me?"

Trotter closed his eyes. "One thousand pounds," he said, inventing wildly. "A thousand English pounds."

McEachren stared at him. He knew that Trotter was a knave, like Lemman and Hayes, but a thousand English pounds was more money than McEachren would see in a lifetime. It was worth a few risks. Later, he'd get Trotter's promissory note. In the meantime, he'd keep his eyes and ears open for treachery.

"Very good, I'm your man," he said. "You can count on me."

Trotter swivelled in his saddle. Fifty yards away the ferry was grounding into its landing after arriving from the crossing-keeper's side. Four workmen in overalls disembarked and trudged up a gentle slope towards the huts with picks and shovels across their shoulders. Two hundred yards away, a band of Chilcotins was snaking out of the jackpines.

First to come was an old chief, dressed in a waist-length eagle feather head dress, buckskin leggings, and a buckskin shirt decorated with rows of white sea shells. He was followed by four lesser chiefs. Young men and boys with bows and spears and muskets walked behind. Slaves came next, dragging lodgepoles and carrying bundles. Women straggled in last, hunched over with tumplines across their foreheads, carrying babies and baskets and other heavy loads. Except for the slaves, who owned nothing and were in various states of nudity, the Indians wore breech clouts, skin britches and shirts.

The chief signified his intention to make camp by driving his war lance into the ground, whereupon the men and boys sat in a circle near the huts. Women and girls dropped their burdens. Without pausing to rest they helped the slaves to erect tepees for the night.

A roadworker came out of a hut, locked the door, and hurried towards the ferry. The four workmen who had just arrived from the crossing-keeper's side changed their minds about where they were going and walked over to consult with Trotter. A roadworker took off his cap and said, "Excuse me, Mr. Trotter. We ain't comfortable with them fellers camping so close."

"Me neither," Trotter shouted, shaking his fist at the sky. "If they think they can camp on my road they're mistaken. Look at them! Dirty savages. Women doing all the work. The mistake I made when I came to this country was trying to hire those men as packers. I should have hired their wives, it would have saved me money and aggravation."

"Lower your voice," McEachren growled. "They might hear you."

"It's time they did hear me! I'm going to set them straight, tell them a few things. Come with me, McEachren. The rest of you stay put while I give 'em a talking to."

McEachren was starting to believe that Trotter's intense hatred of Indians had unsettled his reason. Snatching a horsewhip from its scabbard behind his saddle, he rolled the thong about its handle, and strode fearlessly towards the old chief without waiting to see if McEachren would follow.

McEachren swung his leg over his horse and dropped to the ground, saying, "Who's that bird in the long head dress?"

"Chief Tellot," said one of the workmen.

"Does he speak English?"

"Some. But Tellot is a wise old fellow. He doesn't need many words."

"Put Trotter's horse and mine on the ferry, and get set for a quick getaway. I don't like the looks of this."

By the time McEachren joined him, Trotter had marched into the circle of men and was facing Chief Tellot, who was sitting on the ground.

Standing with his legs apart and his arms folded, Trotter said, "Chief, a gang of you people spent a month picketing my house, before I got rid of 'em. Now you're setting up on my road. Well, I won't stand for it. This is private land. What's the meaning, camping here?"

Tellot, squatting cross-legged, closed his eyes until Trotter stopped speaking, then he opened his eyes and moved his head from side to side, staring as if to discover where Trotter's words had come from. He shrugged, apparently baffled — Trotter was invisible.

"Don't try your fancy stuff on me, Chief, I won't tolerate it," Trotter snarled, tapping his leg with the whip and ignoring some low threatening rumbles coming from the throats of younger chiefs.

McEachren, standing outside the circle, went down on his haunches. After a moment Tellot nodded. McEachren advanced to stand beside Trotter and whispered, "Are you crazy? Put that whip away."

"I'll put it away when I get the chief's attention."

"A chief with his people won't look up to any man."

"That's what he thinks."

McEachren bent his knees and sat on the ground facing Tellot from a distance of six feet. Trotter, his face working with annoyance, expelled a long breath of pent-up air. Another moment passed before he sat beside his foreman.

Tellot's skin was like smoked leather. Unmoved and unhurried, he watched the river bite into the gravel shore before his gaze flickered towards McEachren. He closed his eyes and said modestly, "You are a King George man?"

"No, Chief. I'm a Boston man."

"King George is a skookum chief. I talk to James Douglas, long time ago, and he tell me about King George. Now, King George men everywhere, should be nowhere on these lands," Tellot said in a deep, slow voice, raising his arm and sweeping it before him in an arc. "James Douglas give my people a cultus potlatch of molasses and biscuits, be friend of Indian. Now, white men think my people sleeping. They sell tangle-leg, bring pox to my people. They steal our women." He glanced at Trotter and added, "King George is a great humbug."

McEachren produced a plug of tobacco and gave it to Tellot. Tellot reached inside his shirt, brought out a small package wrapped in many layers of flannel, and gave it to McEachren. While Tellot bit a chew off the plug and passed it to his neighbour, McEachren unwrapped the chief's package and found a piece of the *Illustrated London News* of 1847 with a picture of Sir John Franklin's two Arctic expedition ships on the front cover. Written in the margin were the words:

Tellot, Chilcoaten chief, a good guide, faithful
and trustworthy. Capt. Thomas Price, R.E.

Trotter stretched out a hand. "Give me that," he said.

His tone of imperial condescension set McEachren's nerves jangling, but he handed it over. Trotter read it, sneering, and dropped it on the ground, forcing McEachren to pick it up and return it to the brooding chief. Tellot put his treasured keepsake away but the undercurrent of dislike that existed between the two white men had been noticed.

"King George wants the Chilcotin chiefs to put marks on a treaty so that I can finish this road without interference. In exchange, the chiefs will receive many gifts," Trotter said in a loud voice. "What about it?"

Tellot spat tobacco juice on the ground, closed his eyes, and said, "I mark nothing."

Acting like a man surrounded by inferiors, Trotter shook his head and blurted, "I'll pay a big reward to the man who returns my wife unharmed."

"We wait. We see," Tellot said, his eyes as innocent as black flints before he modestly closed them again. "By and by, Tellot will sit down and smoke another pipe with James Douglas."

"This is a big country, there's room for everybody. But the land you're sitting on is taken. King George gave it to Waddington. Now I want to know how long you intend to be camping here because my men will be doing work on it presently."

Tellot's hooded eyes flicked open for a moment, and he gave Trotter a look which made the hairs rise on McEachren's neck. "It take a long time put tepees up and take down," Tellot replied softly. "I will stay here a while. I will sleep on it."

Tellot's shy modesty misled Trotter. "Not good enough," he snapped. "I need to know, will you be here a night, two nights, a week?"

Tellot sighed, and closed his eyes.

Trotter brought a notepad and pencil from his pockets and said, "Chief, I know your name. I see Tappet here as well. I see Piem and Chassis and others whose names I know. I'm going to write these names in my book and send the book to Victoria. King George and King Pox will know who to punish, when the time comes."

Tellot's eyes opened. McEachren stopped breathing.

A hundred yards away, Trotter's workmen heard a sudden commotion and saw Chief Tellot and the sub-chiefs rising to their feet.

McEachren had overpowered Trotter and was dragging him through a circle of angry Chilcotins and over to the ferry. A warrior chief uttered a piercing cry. Before Tellot could prevent it, Chilcotins were rushing at the white men. They leapt aboard the ferry and it pulled away from the shore.

CHAPTER TWELVE

ISABEL DREAMT THAT she was aboard the *Tynemouth* again, locked in an airless hold with the other girls to protect them from the lascivious attentions of the crew. When one of the girls died mysteriously, the captain ordered she be buried at sea. Terrified because a similar fate might await them all, the girls demanded to be put ashore on the Falkland Islands, but were cast adrift in a small boat with their dead companion. A storm came up and the boat began to sink.

Isabel woke up from her dream shivering in the dark, to find her fire almost out. One-Ear, delirious, was lying nearby in a puddle of water. She dragged him deeper under the overhanging bank and stoked the fire with bits of dry brush that she found in the darkness, then held him for warmth as the temperature dropped and wolves howled. One-Ear groaned unceasingly. She thought, So this is life, a man and a woman, lying together as they died by inches. She slept, and woke feeling weak and feverish; worse, her face and body itched maddeningly, as if she was being bitten by thousands of insects. When she tried to stand, her knees and ankle joints ached and she pitched dizzily forward. She was making a second effort to get up when One-Ear rolled across the dead fire and said, "I'm dying," in a quavering voice.

Scratching herself until her fingers were sticky with blood, Isabel passed through the trees and around a tidepool full of darting crabs and bullheads to the shoreline. It was low tide and there was a seaweedy smell in the cold wind. Isabel tasted salt on her lips. Disoriented and confused, half out of her wits from the accursed itch of her skin, she retraced her route unwittingly across that harsh wilderness of beach and surf and rain, back towards One-Ear's cove. Spring was ripening in the country. Dune-grass was greening and flowers spotted the forest marge with purples and yellows, and reds that matched her bloodied overalls. A deer stepped out of the forest.

She was pale brown and the size of a greyhound with legs as slender as willow branches. Isabel went on along a shore floored with clamshells and moonshells and bits of driftwood and the egg-casings of sea rays and dogfish. At a rockfall she climbed across an enormous cedar with an upward-curving trunk that had slid down a cliff with tons of loose earth and was now trying to re-root itself with barnacles and mussels anchored to its living bark. Falling several times, contemplating the desolation about her, and the desolation within, Isabel got to her knees and crawled. She saw One-Ear coming towards her with his arms outstretched and remembered her dream of the dead girl, but she knew it wasn't entirely a dream; half of it was memory. A girl *had* died at sea. They had buried her in a graveyard on the Falkland Islands, but the terrible thing now was that Isabel could not remember the poor dead girl's name, or what she looked like. She was trying to remember when One-Ear seized her limp arm, and dragged her along the sand to his shack. Much later, she saw that he had started a fire in the stove.

One-Ear woke up in the shack feeling sicker than ever, with the itches driving him crazy, trying to think out his situation. Meat that Missy had stored in the food safe was going rotten, but there was plenty of weevilly meal in a tin and some old potatoes. One-Ear put the rank-smelling meat into a pan with unpeeled potatoes and a handful of meal and set it all boiling. He took all his clothes off and rubbed his body against the rough planks of the floor as a way of curing the itch but that did nothing except make him bleed. By the time he wearied of scratching himself and had vomited a few times the pan had boiled almost dry on the stove. The food was a disgusting half-burned gruel that wasn't even fit for hogs. It didn't matter. One-Ear ate a few mouthfuls with a spoon that he found on the floor and didn't even notice that he was scalding the inside of his mouth.

Isabel was rolling around on the floor in wet overalls, crying and carrying on like a dog with fleas and being a doggone nuisance in general. One-Ear shoved gruel down her throat to shut her up. But something funny was happening because it turned out that a lot of the noises he heard were coming out of his own mouth. Jesus, he felt sick. To his horror, he saw that he had turned red. Damn. Now where in hell is Gridger? Why isn't he here to light the lamp? Do I have to do everything myself, as usual? Isabel ought to be doing something, instead of acting crazy.

By God, he thought, It's funny. My mouth is burning. My skin is itchy and cold and hot at the same time. How is that possible? And why is that white-haired old Injun man sitting on my stove, crooking a finger at me? Let him stay there and burn his ass. He'll move out of the way if I put more wood in the stove. There. Sticks of firewood, shoved them into the stove, right underneath him. Christ! This itch is making me mad!

One-Ear went outside. Now the old Indian man was standing beside the water butt. One-Ear shoved him out of the way, and put his head deep into the water. My, he thought, This cold water feels nice.

CHAPTER THIRTEEN

WITH CHIEF TELLOT'S warriors throwing spears and lofting arrows into the air all around, Clarence Trotter and his roadworkers raced ashore off the ferry and up to the crossing-keeper's house where they were beyond the range of the bowmen on the opposite side of the river. But Trotter's problems weren't over.

A muleskinner named Prior poked Trotter in the chest and cried, "Ain't you got a lick of sense? Are you trying to get us all killed?"

A look of incredulity came across Trotter's face. "Mr. McEachren!"

"Yes sir."

"You'll stop that man's wages immediately! That'll teach him to remember his place and who he's talking to in future."

Morley Clarke, a stocky, fifty-year-old man, pushed himself forward and said, "Prior was talking to an idiot! You think you're above us, Trotter, but your balls hang in a bag, same as ours."

"I saw the whole thing. The fat pile of shit insulted a chief and put his name in a book!" another declared. "Don't you know that writing's a mystery to Injuns? Putting an Injun's name in a book is a mortal insult, it's like locking up his soul. What's the matter with you, are you feeble minded?"

"He thinks we're mongrels to be kicked," Prior said, leaning forward. He seized Trotter's shirt and was set to deliver a punch when McEachren stepped in and shoved him away, but Prior's jaw was obstinately set and he yelled, "If I had a pistol I'd shoot the fat swine in the guts and laugh at him!"

"Be damned to the lot of you," Trotter blustered. "If you don't like it here, get the hell off my job. See if I care."

"By God, that's the limit! I quit right now," Clarke roared, as more roadworkers appeared from along the boardwalks. "I've had my fill of your damned job. It's not enough that you put our lives at risk, you don't even pay us what we've earned by sweating our guts out!"

Somebody pointed. Chilcotins were attempting to swim the river, but the current was too strong. The swimmers were being swept downstream and back ashore on the other side. The diversion was short lived and once again there were cries of "Slit the bastard's throat!" "Heave him into the goddam river!" and the like.

"Steady on, fellows," McEachren said. "This mischief has gone far enough."

"The hell with you too," shouted another grizzled labourer. "I'm fed up with your blasted job and I'm fed up with this blasted country, as well."

"What Trotter done is the dumbest thing I seen in my life!" cried another. "That's the finish for me. I'm packing my bags, and leaving as soon as the coast is clear! But I'm not leaving without my wages!"

Sweat was pouring down Trotter's face as he began to see how bitterly his men hated him.

McEachren's loyalty had wavered but now he said sternly, "Back off, lads. What's done's done. Mr. Trotter will pay every man's wages this minute. Isn't that so?"

It was a bitter moment for Trotter. Baited by the least of his underlings he back-tracked to his horse and unbuckled a leather bag from behind his saddle. "Every man here gets his reckoning in full," he said, his dripping face distorted with hate. "Nobody loses a penny..."

Chief Tellot's bivouac was breaking up across the river and as the Indians departed tensions eased, until Trotter tried to pay the men off with cheques instead of cash. There were more jeers and threats when, flanked by McEachren, Trotter withdrew to a small storage shed away from the crossing-keeper's house, and barred the door.

"You'd better pray there's no booze among 'em, otherwise you'll be a dead duck by morning."

"Fiddlesticks! Those cretins know which side their bread's buttered on," said Trotter, flying into another passion. "There isn't a man among 'em with any guts."

"Come to your senses, damn you! I'm the only thing standing between you and eternity!" McEachren snapped. "If I walk away the men will bust the door down and drag you out in a minute. See how much good fancy talk does you then."

"I'll have my vengeance," Trotter muttered, as he sat down clutching his leather bag to his chest in a corner of the shed.

"Stow your guff, mister," McEachren growled, controlling his temper with an effort. "And don't go thinking that I've stuck with you because we made a deal for a thousand pounds. I'm here because we've a dozen men working at the upper camp who don't know what the hell is going on. If Tellot and the Chilcotins don't calm down those workers will be in more danger than you are."

"If that's the case, there's nothing I can do about it."

"There's plenty you can do. First thing tomorrow, we saddle up and ride north to raise the alarm."

"But if it's dangerous and..."

"Hellfire and damnation! Would you leave our men up there helpless, and do nothing?"

"But how will we get back across the river and home ourselves if we don't leave with this gang tomorrow?"

McEachren hadn't thought of that. He jammed his hands into his pockets. Thinking out loud he said, "Smith, the crossing-keeper. When he takes the men across the river he'll have to bring the ferry back for us and wait here for a day or two. It'd be risky, though. You'd have to promise him something."

"How much?"

"A few pounds might do it. I'll sound him out."

"What if Smith says no?"

"We'll be out of luck, because come hell or high water, you and me are heading for the upper camp in the morning."

McEachren put his eye to a crack in the door. The roadworkers had lit a campfire outside the crossing-keeper's house but its embers were sputtering and hissing in a cold rain and the men were going inside. The foreman shivered and said, "It'll be snowing, higher up."

"I'm hungry," Trotter said.

"What do you want me to do about it?" McEachren snapped. "Take grub out of your saddlebags and feed it to you, a mouthful at a time?"

"Try to be civil," Trotter said. "There's a good fellow."

Shaking his head in the darkness, McEachren said, "By God. You take the bloody biscuit, you do."

Early the next day, with Trotter slinking out of sight, the crossing-keeper ferried ten roadworkers and two pack mules across the river, and they began the thirty-mile tramp back to Waddy Flats.

McEachren watched anxiously until Smith brought the ferry back, and told them that he'd wait for three days more.

With a thin sleet driving into their faces, Trotter and his foreman mounted their horses, and headed north for the upper camp.

***

Davy Lemman had walked away from the ferry twelve hours earlier, with the rest of Trotter's men. He was glad to be going home. As a new hand on the road gang, Lemman had gone around introducing himself, so that everybody would know who he was, and what he stood for. Pretty soon, within a week, Lemman knew that his mates put no stock in his words. They didn't like him, figured him for a showoff. Well, that was rough because it wasn't his fault. It didn't matter how hard he tried, men always disliked him — he got along better with women. That was understandable, because he was better looking than the average fellow. Handsome, get right down to it, and that wasn't just his own opinion, neither. There was that girl, for instance, the one in the Rialto Bar. She had remarked on it, said he was the handsomest date she'd had in a year. Why would she say that if she didn't mean it? She liked his mustache, and the beard that made his chin look bigger. He'd sure been glad when he grew up and could grow a beard. People stopped calling him the chinless wonder then. By God, he'd like to meet the fellow who'd call him a chinless wonder today. Well, when he got back to Victoria he'd go around to the Rialto with money in his pockets. He'd look her up and see if she remembered him, because she was a feisty little whore.

And that was another thing. Trotter's cheque had better be good for the back wages he was owed. By God, he was tired of excuses. It was all to do with high finance. Financiers in San Francisco and London, they were in back of all this mischief. One of these days, Lemman told himself, he'd take a look into this financier business, and see if there was anything in it, for a wide-awake fellow.

Lemman was walking up front with the pack mules when he tripped on a loose stone and his boot heel broke off. A few more hours and he would have been safe in Waddy Flats. Cursing, Lemman found the heel, removed his boot, and sat by the side of the road, trying to pound the heel back on with a rock while his mates kept on going. Nobody offered to stay with him, not one dern soul. Dern selfish bunch of swine, they weren't even fit to lace his shoe strings. But yet they hated him. Why? It wasn't fair. Folks figured he was lazy. Everybody said he left the heavy lifting to the other fellow. He could blame McEachren. One day he overheard McEachren say, "Well, Lemman, I guess he won't be having no heart attacks from overwork."

"Only if it's from overworking his mouth," a fellow called Thwaites had said.

It was because he'd made a harmless little remark about Isabel Trotter winking at him. Couldn't they take a joke, for God's sake?

Thwaites and McEachren, thought Lemman, a couple of nobodies. "Well, the hell with 'em," Lemman said aloud. But he couldn't get the heel to stick. The cheap dern cobbler that had made these cheap dern boots in the first place had used cheap dern nails. Now they were all bent and twisted. And those fellers as were supposed to be his mates were a mile ahead, already.

A cloud of little grey birds sliced the air with scimitar wings as they ducked and weaved through a stand of cedars. Lemman followed them with his eyes and saw Morley Clarke straggling along the road, last, as usual, and limping on that dud leg of his. Old Morley. Had to be fifty, fifty-five years old if he was a day. The only good thing was, he had a shotgun with him. A fifty-five-year-old rearguard with a gammy leg and his best days long gone, still swamping for a bunch of no-good labourers. By God, it wasn't going to happen to Davy Lemman. At fifty he'd be retired, sitting pretty. Maybe a financier. Maybe a gambler on one of them river boats.

Indistinct voices rang in the woods and several arrows whistled overhead.

Lemman took off running with one boot on and one boot off, misstepped, and rolled down an embankment. Clarke was staring at his companion in that slow stupefaction with which all men contemplate their own inevitable destinies when six Indians burst into view wielding war lances and axes. Clarke took aim with his shotgun and fired both barrels and the red men swerved out of sight into the forest. Cursing furiously, he reloaded and careened down the embankment to find Lemman burrowing into the undergrowth. Apart from a slightly sprained ankle, Lemman was uninjured.

"By Christ!" Clarke roared. "Seein' them red-faced terrors scared the tar outta me but I tell you what, buster, the sight of their naked asses heading into them trees is somethin' I'll never forget."

With Lemman whining that he couldn't walk because of his sore ankle, Clarke hooked his arm across his shoulder and they were three-legging it when they heard noises beside the trail. In a moment, an old Indian man appeared with three little children. Black with bear grease, the Indians saw one trembling King George man in tears and another pointing a shotgun at them, and fled.

Lemman cried, "Shoot 'em, Clarkey, afore they gets us!"

Sighing, Clarke lowered his gun.

A ten-foot yew-wood war lance with a fire-hardened point entered Clarke's neck and severed his spinal cord.

Lemman made his run. He travelled fifty yards and there were four arrows in his back when he fell, face down, and lay without moving, as men with axes approached.

***

Decker had killed a young porker, and Bushrat was carrying an arm-load of split maple across to the smokehouse, intending to convert that porker into bacon, when a bloodied mule loaded with bloodstained pannier bags wandered into view. Bushrat dropped the firewood and led the mule over to the house, shouting for Decker.

"There's a sorry looking moke," Decker said, coming outside. "How did it get cut up like that?"

"Hah! If only that moke could speak. See, it ain't cut up."

Decker came off the porch and looked the mule over carefully, "There's probably a sorry-looking muleskinner back along the trail somewhere, if that blood is human."

"If that blood is human, the man who spilled it ain't got a whole lot left."

The lawmen saddled up their horses. Hushed, they followed the mule's trail back. Halfway up to the Slough, a dark shape lay on the road and when they reached it they saw a roadworker who had bled to death.

Bushrat looked at the body, and looked away.

"Tonight we'll stay put in Waddy Flats with the doors locked," Decker said. "Tomorrow we'll pack blankets and grub. See what else we can find up there."

***

Wind-ruffled scarves of white mist draped the snowy mountains below the Franklin icefields and heavier black snow clouds were darkening the Homathko Glacier when Decker and Bushrat lit out of Waddy Flats on horseback the next day, leading a pack mule. Before long, cold rain was lashing the hills, causing mudslides where the roadbuilders had removed trees. The sullen sky lowered until the visible terrain was reduced to grey monotones, except where white foam leapt in the wild river. After riding a few miles without seeing a living animal the lawmen came across a ravine, where crows were tearing at bits of scattered clothing. Nearby, a black bear was rooting at something half-hidden beneath a cedar tree.

Decker dismounted and walked to the edge of the ravine to take a closer look. Cold and boredom had combined to dull his wits, but the sight of a dead man being dismembered by a bear set his nerves tingling.

Bushrat lifted his rifle out of its scabbard on the horse and levered a round into the chamber.

"Hold it," Decker said, "don't shoot."

"Hell fire, boss. We can't let bears eat him, and do nothin'."

"Just a minute," Decker growled. "Keep quiet, and listen."

Above the rushing river, they heard the muffled chant of Indians.

"We'll go up there," Decker barked, pointing to a ridge. "Lively, now!"

They had scarcely got themselves and their horses out of sight in the trees before ten warriors, led by a tall man with a single eagle feather in his black braids, appeared from out of the trees and stopped below the road. These natives were soon joined by ten others and there was a short parley before they all headed north.

"Who's the big fellow?"

"Klatsassan," Bushrat hissed, as the warriors passed along the road. "He might have Carrier blood to thank for that height, and that nose."

"His men are well armed."

Bushrat took his felt hat off, wrung water out of it, and plopped it back on. He said, "I'd like to know where they got them muskets from."

"They probably got them from Trotter. He's been bartering stores and muskets since he ran out of cash."

"More fool him."

Long peals of thunder were rolling out of the sky when Bushrat and Decker went back down to the road and looked into the ravine. The bear had gone, dragging its trophy with it. Without a word, they headed north. At a gravel bar on the river there was a sudden terrified scream from Bushrat's skittish horse, and the lawmen found seven dead and mutilated Europeans scattered across the green hillside like red flowers on a mat. Bushrat groaned. Every man had had his throat slashed, and chest cavities gaped where some had had their hearts cut out. The lawmen recognised a few faces. Three dead Chilcotins lay among the rocks where a creek joined the main river.

"There were sharp-shooters among the roadworkers. They got all three Indians with bullets through their brains," Decker said. "There's something funny, though. It isn't normal for Indians to leave their comrades lying for the birds and the bears."

"Since the pox got started in among 'em, they've given up on regular buryings. They either dumps corpses in the river, or they drags them out of sight, in the trees." Bushrat frowned and said, "I'm not up to doing any buryings myself, right now. Not with them fellers around here."

Decker nodded and got up on his horse.

Sombre but vigilant, their boots full of cold water, Decker and Bushrat resumed their journey. Bushrat dismounted frequently to check the trail and said at last, "They's ten minutes ahead."

The lawmen tethered their horses and the pack mule five hundred yards off the road, and investigated on foot — flitting from tree to tree and stepping around moss-covered deadfalls with their rifles cocked until they had a good view of the crossing-keeper's house. The natives had smoked Smith out. His body was tied to the wall in plain sight with his arms and legs extended.

"Clever fellows," Bushrat said. "Got him without damaging the building. I hope that keeper was savvy enough to shoot hisself, first."

"Christ, yes."

"Them warriors'll be cosy inside till morning, while we's freezin' in the rain."

"Could be a lot worse," Decker said.

"How?"

"Ask that crossing-keeper."

They spent a miserable night under the dripping trees. There was scant feed for their animals and those unhappy creatures stamped and neighed while Decker and Bushrat, cold, soaked, patient in the dark, built a brushwood shelter, covered it with their oilskin slickers, and coaxed a fire into existence. Hot coffee and beans made the effort worthwhile.

Bushrat said, "Do you think Trotter's still alive?"

"I wouldn't hazard a guess."

"If he is, the only hope he's got is he might know that Klatsassan's coming, and digs in, because there's no way he can hide from them trackers."

"Trotter's showed no marked signs of high intuition so far. He may not even realize he's in danger."

"He prob'ly thinks he's still two steps ahead of everybody else," said Bushrat. "Trouble is, now he's falling, others are being dragged down too."

Shivering in the chill, moist air, Decker reconnoitred in time to see a column of Indians striding north from the crossing-keeper's house the next morning. He returned to his own camp and stood near the fire while Bushrat dumped beans out of a billycan onto a thick slice of bread and offered it to Decker.

"Let's get cracking," Decker said. "I don't like the look of this weather."

"Where we going?"

"To the upper canyons. It'll be pure hell. The road isn't fit for horses, or horse-riders."

Bushrat, on his knees by the fire, straightened up slowly. Putting both hands on his hips he rocked his body gently backwards and forwards to ease his spine. "What kept you tossin' and turnin' all night? Thinkin' about weather?"

"As a matter of fact, I was thinking about Trotter, and Isabel."

"She's worth thinkin' about too."

"Bushy, I thought you were above such nonsense."

"You mean too old? I don't know when a fellow gets too old. It was a girl show that set me goin' down the wrong trail in life."

"Are you brave enough to talk about it?"

"Yes sir, I am," Bushrat said. "Way back, me an' Woodruff Key got paid off from a mustang herdin' outfit and we was told about this dirty girl show they had over in 'Frisco. Barbary Coast gals they was. Rode dern near five hundert miles, me an' Woodruff done, and all because a feller told us there was a six-bit show with girls showin' their bare asses. Well sir, we had ten days of hard ridin' an' when we found that show it weren't nothin' but a fraud. There was a woman with a beard, and a feller tattooed all over, and a three-legged monkey in a bottle of gin, and two dancin' girls in long white knickers kickin' their heels inside of a tent. Woodruff said to that shyster that was runnin' the show, 'Where's them dirty girls at?' and he got told that to see them gals up close it'd be an extry five dollars over an' above the six bits we already just paid. Well sir, me an' Woodruff figured that what with one thing or another, we might as well fork over the five dollars apiece, so that's what we done, and we sat on a bench seat in another tent there, just waitin' our turn along with a whole bunch of other young fellers what had the same idears what we had. Now this is where the tragedy kicks in. The shyster pulled back a curtain, and what we seen was girls in clothes holding up pictures of dirty girls with bare asses. Next thing me an' Woodruff know, that tent was in ruins and we'd got busted over the head by constables with nightsticks. Me an' Woodruff an' the rest of them fun seekers wound up arrested into the San Francisco jail fer creatin' a disturbance. Only consolation we had, that shyster was in there with us."

"You ought to write that story down, Bush, and act it on a stage."

"Hit weren't over yet. That magistrate there, when he heard our case, he fines us all a hundert dollars, or six months on the rock pile, but you know he was a crooked magistrate because there was a feller showed up immediate who'd pay our fine if we'd agree to shovel gravel on the Mucho Oro gold claim. On the American River that gold claim was. Me an' Woodrow shovelled dirt for six months and our share was five dollars a day. We blew the whole wad on whores and booze in a week."

"That must have been some week," Decker said. "A week to remember."

"It weren't nothin' special. More fool us. We thought you got your excitement spendin'. Now, I know different. Best fun I had was hopin'. Havin' ain't like hopin'. Hopin' beats all," Bushrat said ruefully. "After that, I chased every gold strike. I thought nothin' of goin' on a thousand-mile jaunt with nothin' in my pocket except a dry biscuit. I always chose the risky kinds of ventures, because I never thought I'd grow old. I never did figure to settle down comfortable in no regular job."

"What happened to Woodruff?"

"Died of the cholera. When I buried him he didn't weigh no more'n ninety pounds."

Decker watched Bushrat pour himself another cup of coffee and scratch his whiskers and he waited until Bushrat said, "When do you reckon the governor will send the army to Waddy Flats?"

"It doesn't look too promising. I sent him a letter, and the settlers that quit have been pressuring him to do something, no doubt, but Waddy Flats might not be important enough to concern the governor. If the army's coming, it should be here soon. Depends whether the navy lends the governor a transport steamer."

Bushrat turned to stare at the glacier. "Hit's snowin' over there," he said. "It'll be snowing here too, before long."

"Snow! At this time of year? It'll be May soon!"

"It snows up here anytime," Bushrat said. "I've seen big dumps of snow in July, August."

"Snow or not, let's see if we can get across that river."

***

Chraychanuru and Lowwa and Tahpitt and Cheddecki and Squinteye and Hachis smoked one pipe of tobacco together.

Chraychanuru said, "When Klatsassan's second daughter by his first wife died of the pox, he put her in a tree grave. Then The Creator spoke to Klatsassan. In thanks to The Creator, Klatsassan burned a canoe and six blankets. After this burning, to gain extra favour from The Creator, Klatsassan threw two muskets into the sea and killed a slave. Klatsassan then took his number two wife Toowaewoot, and his two daughters by another wife, and his son Piell Who Was Burned In A Chimney, and Cusshen The Scarface, and together they travelled to The Crossing, going to the lake country. Smith The Ferryman refused to show his face. Klatsassan shed many tears because Toowaewoot was big with child and she could not cross the Homathko. Klatsassan asked Cusshen The Scarface what to do. Cusshen The Scarface told Klatsassan to kill Smith The Ferryman because he was a King George man who had seen Klatsassan's tears, and because Klatsassan's second daughter by his first wife had been killed by King George's pox."

Lowwa said that his daughter had run away to lie with a white man. This white man had promised her a fine gown to wear, instead of a blanket. But after the white man lay with her, what became of her? Why, she was laughed at. Other men had their way with her against her wishes. After making her lie with them all, the white men sent her away.

Now, Lowwa's daughter cried all the time, and she was useless.

This is what Squinteye told his wife:

Chief Tellot was angry when Trotter put his soul into a black box of papers and made a lie about stealing Trotter's wife. Tellot never stole Trotter's wife. Trotter put fire to Piell Who Was Burned In A Chimney. Tellot had never heard of such a thing in his life.

And Squinteye told his wife that he was frightened of King George.

Chraychanuru and Lowwa and Tahpitt and Cheddecki and Squinteye and Hachis took up their lodges and went to join Klatsassan's lodge. That was when Klatsassan became a grand war chief against King George, and other men joined his war lodge with his wife Toowaewoot and his two daughters by another wife and his son Piell Who Was Burned In A Chimney and Cusshen The Scarface.

CHAPTER FOURTEEN

JAMES DOUGLAS WAS in his garden, when Governor Arthur Kennedy came strolling along the street, twirling an umbrella.

"Have you heard the latest, Jim?" Kennedy said. "A bunch of settlers have just reached Victoria from Waddy Flats. There's been a terrible Indian massacre, they say. Dead bodies all over the place."

Douglas scowled. He didn't like being called Jim, and he wasn't over-fond of Kennedy, either. Kennedy couldn't seem to get it into his head that he was the governor of Vancouver Island now, not Douglas — Douglas had retired.

"I wouldnae describe the deaths of two backwoodsmen and a bootlegger's concubine as a massacre," Douglas growled.

"So you've heard all about it, Jim?"

"Aye, to my regret. People seem to think I've nothing better to do than listen to idle rumours. As you'll soon find out, Mr. Kennedy, things are a bit different here in the west than they are in your old homeland."

"They certainly are," Kennedy laughed. "There are no snakes in Ireland, for a start."

"If there was anything to this particular yarn, my constable, Decker, would have sent us a note. Now, if you'll excuse me, Mr. Kennedy, I ..."

"Decker did you say? Who's he?"

"Waddy Flats' policeman. I sent him up there myself."

"So what I'm hearing, Jim, is that in your opinion I shouldn't waste my time worrying about it, eh?"

"Do as you please, Mr. Kennedy. I'm sick to death of Waddy Flats. My major regret in life is that I didn't hang Alfred Waddington, years ago, when he first proposed his damn fool road. It would have saved me a great deal of aggravation."

With that, James Douglas went inside his house and slammed the door.

Bad-tempered old bugger, Kennedy thought.

With nothing else for it, Kennedy looked into the massacre story personally, and interviewed one alleged eye witness; a fellow called Quirk who said he had seen a headless body, lying on a beach. When Kennedy pressed him for details, Quirk would not swear unequivocally that the body was European; it had been badly decomposed. Pressed further, Quirk conceded that the object had not necessarily been human. It might have been a rotting seal. As for other supposed victims, nobody had seen them. Somebody (perhaps) had found two bodies above a wagon road, and had buried them. Kennedy concluded that any and all of Waddy Flats' deaths had probably resulted from smallpox. He washed his hands of the matter and got on with something really important — he was asking Whitehall to increase his stipend by a thousand pounds a year. That is where matters remained, until Alfred Waddington returned to Victoria from San Francisco.

Waddington, already at the boiling point because he had failed to get the financial guarantees he desperately needed and was close to bankruptcy, heard about the alleged massacre and went straight to the new governor's office.

Kennedy received Waddington at short notice and invited his visitor to sit.

Alfred Waddington was a rash, self-deluding individual. Closeted with Kennedy, he did not waste any time on pleasantries. "What's the meaning of this!" he shouted. "Are you the governor, or not?"

"I am sir, since this time last month. Just getting my feet wet, I am, feeling my way, don't you know, so I'm delighted to make your acquaintance at last."

"I'll have you know that work on my road is at a standstill and people are being killed. And you sit here, doing nothing."

"Bless your ould boots," Kennedy said with a laugh. "The entire resources of Vancouver's Island are at your disposal sir. Why, it isn't ten days ago that I was talking to James Douglas about your problems, so I was."

"Douglas? You were talking to Douglas about me?"

"I was indeed," Kennedy said, leaning forward to tap Waddington playfully on the shoulder. "Thinks the world of you, Jim does."

"Jim?"

"James Douglas. A regular booster he is, of the Bute Inlet road."

Waddington, taken aback by the Irishman's cordiality, sat down in a chair. Kennedy, doing likewise, shot his cuffs, took a hunter out of his waistcoat pocket, stared at it, and said, "Now, it's three o'clock. How about a drink, sir? A drop of whisky?"

"I didn't come here to drink whisky, sir, I came here ... I came here to demand something."

"So you did, Mr. Waddington, and what was it now, just exactly, that you'd like me to do?"

"Ships. Guns. Marines. We need the Royal Navy up at Waddy Flats right now."

"Ah, now there, I'm afraid, I can't help you at all, much as I'd like to. My warrant doesn't extend to the Royal Navy. But I tell you what. Why don't you pop over to the mainland, talk to Governor Seymour."

"Governor Seymour? How many governors are there in this damned country, for God's sake?"

"Just me and Seymour. When Douglas retired they split his job in two. Seymour's running things on the mainland, and I'm doing my bit here on Vancouver Island."

"Waddy Flats is on the mainland," Waddington mused. "I suppose it is Seymour's business, really."

"Certainly it is, it's what I've been telling you, Mr. Waddington. I wish to God it wasn't, though, because I can see that you're a damn fine chap and there's nothing I'd have enjoyed more than joining forces with you. Together, arm in arm, we'd blast those Waddy Flats rascals into the sea..."

Encouraged by Kennedy's fulsome reception, Waddington left Victoria in buoyant mood, but his spirits had flagged by the time he'd taken an uncomfortable boat trip across the Strait of Georgia to New Westminster, on the Fraser River, to seek out Governor Seymour. To his disgust, Seymour had not yet arrived from England. During his absence, none of British Columbia's official representatives would have anything to do with Waddington. In the end, he was received by Arthur Birch, the future governor's private secretary.

Birch, an amiable, twenty-five year old lesser son of the British upper classes, demonstrated cool, unruffled calm when Waddington took the same hard line with him that he'd taken with Kennedy. Waddington, thought Birch, was not a gentleman, dammit. But Birch tried to be fair. Waddington had, after all, risked his capital to improve the country. Birch drew his lips back over his teeth in a cold smile and said, "What would you like me to do?"

"You, sir? A young whippersnapper of a damned secretary?" Waddington yelled, screwing up his indignation. "I expect nothing from you, but I expect Governor Seymour to do his duty, sir! I expect him to send a gunboat up to Waddy Flats, and teach those murdering rascals a lesson."

"Which murdering rascals are those?"

Flabbergasted, Waddington leapt to his feet and roared, "Indians, of course. Chilcotins!"

Birch, disappointed by Waddington's churlish manner, forbore to point out that Waddington's problems in Waddy Flats, of whatever nature, were his own fault. The obstinate fellow had been told on all sides that trying to build a road up the Homathko River was a fool's notion. His face smooth, Birch said, "My dear sir, restrain yourself. Please sit down."

"I'm damned if I will," Waddington blustered.

"If we cannot conduct ourselves like gentlemen, we will make little progress."

"This is no time for diplomacy, sir, it's time for marines. It's time for guns and bayonets," Waddington bellowed. "I want action, not government shilly-shallying."

Birch rested his elbows on the arms of his chair, made a steeple with his fingers, and gazed through the arch. Waddington thought that Birch was thinking about Waddy Flats, but he was mistaken. Arthur Birch was thinking about a certain summer afternoon in Devon, where, long ago, he had spent pleasant hours chasing butterflies with a net. This mental strategem, which Birch resorted to whenever the pressures of office grew unbearable, had the desired effect. His passions cooled. Birch brought himself back to reality with a sigh. Beyond the high windows of his room, uniformed sentries were marching across a parade ground towards a large, wooden, two-storey building where an extremely tall, black-bearded man, wearing a black hat and a black suit, was standing on the steps. It was Judge Matthew Begbie. Begbie saw Birch watching, and raised his hat politely.

Waddington said, "These colonies are going to rack and ruin because nobody will lift a finger to protect private property. My property sir, my valuable property."

"Sir, you must have the goodness to attend to me."

"I warn you, Birch, my fortune's at stake. I don't want doubletalk!"

"Very well, I will speak plainly, since that is what you demand," Birch said. "First, let me point out, there has been no verifiable uprising..."

"That's nonsense..."

"There has been no verifiable uprising in Waddy Flats," Birch persisted. "What's more, esteemed sir, if I may be blunt, such an uprising would be the probable result of your neglect to pay wages and discharge other shortfalls."

"That's a vile slander," Waddington cried. "I'll sue you for this."

"Do as you please," Birch said coldly. "But, since I wish to protect you from immediate unpleasantness, please leave my office at once."

"I'll go straight to the newspapers. I'll tell 'em what's what, and they'll light a fire underneath you sir, that'll scorch your trousers!"

"My dear man. Visit newspapers. Tell them that your hare-brained scheme to build a road through impossible country has backfired."

His tolerance at an end, Birch grasped Waddington's elbow. There was, he perceived, nothing to be gained by further discourse, and besides, one does not argue with a cad. Easing his visitor out through the door, Birch said, "Tell the newspapers whatever you please."

"I'll sue! Mark my words!"

"Present my compliments to your solicitors," Birch replied. "In the interim, take ship to Waddy Flats, and judge matters for yourself. While there, pay your workers what is owed to them, and see if that improves matters. And now, sir, good day to you."

Fuming, his head down, hands in his pockets, Waddington marched the streets, thinking furiously. In the darkness of his vision he heard people saying that he was a failure, that the toll road was beyond him. He was just a deluded shopkeeper who had got in over his head. Waddington came to his senses outside a newspaper office.

A man was crouched over a desk behind a large plate glass window, writing furiously. It was John Robson, editor of the *British Columbian*. Occasionally, Robson crossed pieces out with violent slashes of his steel-nibbed pen; from time to time he crunched papers into a ball and hurled them into an overflowing wastebasket. In an inner room, an elderly typesetter and a dirty little boy, both wearing green eyeshades and grubby white shirts with black sleeve protectors, were ready to set type on a sloping table. Waddington put his hand on the office door, hesitated, changed his mind, and proceeded to the city wharf.

Captain Johnson, master of the *Belle*, a screw-schooner with a compound steam engine, was exceedingly cool when Waddington approached him about a charter.

"Charter my eye. I know you, Waddington, and I'm sick of your promises and bafflegab," Captain Johnson said waspishly. "You owe every captain in the port. I'm still owed fifty pound for that last job I did you."

"My dear captain, the money is forthcoming immediately. My accountant is already working on the..."

"Yes, and pickled eggs grow on trees!" the captain yelled, as he turned his back on Waddington and made to go below. "If you must get to Waddy Flats, take a canoe, you devious old rascal, and paddle it there yourself. See how you like that!"

Waddington received a similar reception from two more sea captains. Stymied, he trudged back into town.

Editor Robson was still behind his window, still writing furiously, and still hurling crumpled scraps of paper into a wastebasket. Waddington braced himself, and entered.

"Out, Waddington! Out out out!" Robson cried. "My next edition's due by morning and I'm still working on my lead story."

"I've got a lead story that will knock your eye out," Waddington said. "A lead story that will increase your circulation and save this colony from the forces of anarchy at the same time."

"Is that so?" the editor roared. "Well, let me tell you something, Waddington..."

"No listen, this is serious. Fellows are being murdered at Waddy Flats."

"Nonsense! There's nothing to that Waddy Flats business," Robson said, with slightly improved civility. "The trouble is, you don't pay your reckonings, and it makes people angry."

"There's a slight irregularity in my fiscal affairs, but it's temporary. Next week, at the latest, I receive a fresh infusion of cash from a syndicate in San Francisco. In the meantime, I am being ruined. Our spineless leaders refuse to act. Why can't we send one of our precious navy ships and a few of their idle marines to protect British citizens and British property?"

"Hmmmm!" Robson said thoughtfully. "I must say, true or not it's a good yarn. What these colonies need are born leaders."

"Quite. Fellows like Chartres Brew. Or that gold commissioner, what's his name?"

"Cox."

"Right. Commissioner Cox. Send either of them to Waddy Flats. They'd sort things out in a hurry."

"Hah, hmmmmm. Cox and Brew, eh? Ecod, Cox is a slippery dog, and Brew is a thrusting sort of ferret, but they are both good fellows in their way. We could do worse than send both of 'em," Robson mused aloud, as he seized a blank sheet of paper and dipped his steel-nibbed pen into an inkwell. "Get out of here, Waddington. Leave me in peace. But be sure to buy tomorrow's paper."

When Waddington left, Robson rubbed his hands together, thinking, What an ass! Chuckling, he dipped pen into ink. "Alfred Waddington's gross deceptions and indiscretions now endanger the whole of this colony," he wrote. "There can be no doubt as to the diseased state of the old gentleman's mind, but nevertheless, Police Inspector Chartres Brew might be despatched to Waddy Flats, to investigate poor Waddy's charges..."

Across the Strait of Georgia, in Victoria, Amor De Cosmos, editor of the *British Colonist*, was also struggling with his lead story.

"Nothing short of lead or hemp will bring the lawless tribes to their senses," De Cosmos wrote. "This was fully demonstrated by the lamented Captain Robinson when he sent several broadsides from his gunboat into the camp of Haidas at Cape Mudge, and brought them to their knees a few minutes after the first gun was fired. The lesson then taught the savages lasted for some time. These efforts are now nearly forgotten, and another lesson is required to teach them how to behave in civilized society..."

CHAPTER FIFTEEN

WHEN KLATSASSAN AND his band of warriors reached The Crossing, his slave Chessus was the only man who understood the ferry's mysterious workings. Klatsassan ate his pride while Chessus proudly shoved the magic lever which moved a vane beneath the hull and drove the boat. Klatsassan resolved to keep an eye on Chessus, in case he forgot his lowly caste and tried to move up from his station beside the door of Klatsassan's lodge.

Because big trouble was already brewing in Klatsassan's lodge. Squinteye, whose mother was a noblewoman of the Raven Clan, had been acting strangely. The sons of noble mothers were permitted a certain amount of strangeness. They could kill slaves at feasts or to gain favour with The Creator. They could starve slaves, beat them or use them carnally, but the sons of noble mothers were expected to be courageous. Squinteye was a coward. In the recent battle with Trotter's men, (that glorious victory would be sung in Chilcotin lodges for a thousand years), Squinteye's war lance never left his hand. It was a conspicuous disgrace. Instead of risking an honourable wound, or death, Squinteye had stood behind a slave while other valiant warriors fought bravely. Three slaves had covered themselves in immortal glory; even now their slave souls were waiting to be reborn to noble mothers. In the next life, surely, Squinteye would return as a snake.

After ending the crossing-keeper's life, Klatsassan read signs on the earth and saw that Trotter and McEachren had recently departed on horseback. It was too late to follow them and so Klatsassan would sleep in the crossing-keeper's lodge. Tomorrow, if The Creator willed it, Klatsassan would meet Tellot, and between them, they would rescue stolen souls from Trotter's magic box of papers. People would have reason to say that Klatsassan and Tellot were mighty chiefs. That would be very fine.

And thus it followed that the next day, Klatsassan led his people north along the swinging baskets that Trotter had built along the chasm for men to walk on. These baskets were wonderful. Klatsassan had never seen such iron ropes. They would take the weight of many horses. Yes, these swinging baskets of wood and iron were very fine, but they were a puzzle. Why would men put swinging baskets above a river when they could walk around a river? This was King George magic, and Klatsassan would not even try to understand it.

***

At this elevation, in this country, it could snow at any time and April snow was falling when Trotter and McEachren rode out of The Crossing. Taking horses along the boardwalks under wintry conditions was a test of nerves and endurance, as well as skill. They wrapped their horses' feet in sacks to prevent them from slipping on the frozen boards, and moved gingerly along, tugging their reluctant mounts with mittened hands. Chunks of ice fell off the cliffs, smashing against the wooden slats and making the suspension cables twang like violin strings. The walk was too narrow to turn a horse in so, once committed, there was nothing for it but to keep going. Sweating and cursing in spite of icy winds, it took them an hour to travel half a mile.

"This boardwalk won't last," Trotter gasped. "It was built for show, to impress Waddington's investors."

"You've told me that before," McEachren answered. "What you haven't explained is where Waddington finds such people."

"The world is full of greedy fools," Trotter said arrogantly.

It was the wrong thing to say. Did Trotter think him stupid? McEachren remembered the countless little slights and ironies and sarcasms he had endured from Trotter, and was filled with anger and self disgust. He thought of Piell, being burned in a chimney and was soon burning with self-loathing himself. By the time they got through the chasm and remounted their horses, he had made up his mind to quit; there wasn't enough money in the world to keep him at Trotter's beck and call. They were ascending a steep slope when suddenly, McEachren's horse reared up on its hind legs. Caught unawares, McEachren fell out of his saddle sideways, with his left foot still jammed in its stirrup. Trotter watched the bolting horse drag its rider for about a hundred yards, before McEachren's ankle snapped and the foot came loose. The riderless horse was racing out of sight when twenty warriors came out of the trees. In a moment, a war lance had pierced McEachren's heart.

Trotter's horse bounded forward of its own volition and the unexpected momentum sent Trotter reeling backwards. With his mind
frozen in a slow paralysis he held onto the reins by instinct and
remained in the saddle as his panicked horse galloped blindly past the
ambush. It charged on for a few more seconds before it skidded
across a patch of ice and Trotter was catapulted into a stand of snow-
laden juniper bushes. Dazed, bleeding from cuts to his face, Trotter
got to his feet and when his eyes focussed he saw Indians rushing at
him. His brain began to work and with a frightened moan he yanked
a pistol out of his belt and fired two wild shots which made them
duck for cover.

Running away clumsily, Trotter stubbed his toe on a hidden stump
and went flying down a bank in a cascade of bushes and stones,
slamming into a thicket of pines just short of a ravine. Warriors with
axes and spears moved down the slope towards him. Trotter was
thinking about headless bodies when he put the muzzle of his pistol
between his teeth and pulled the trigger. The bullet passed through
his jawbone and exited his cheek without causing a fatal wound.
Trotter was making a second attempt to end his life when the hammer
clicked uselessly — the magazine was empty.

But the warriors did not kill Trotter. They did not even touch him.
They hemmed him in with their spears and axes, as if he were a
dangerous bear, and herded him back up to the road where, smiling,
his eyes closed, a great and modest chief humbly asked Trotter to
release the stolen souls from his box of papers.

***

Three miles north and a thousand feet up the mountains, it was
snowing hard. Elijah Oppenshaw and John Nieumann, skidding
jackpine logs off the roadway with four yokes of oxen, stopped work
and stared in surprise at the snorting, riderless horse cantering
towards them. Waving their hats and hollering, they diverted it to a
side trail and shooed it down a narrow canyon. Oppenshaw caught the
runaway's reins. Whispering, praising it, he put an arm around its
steaming neck while the pumping heart slowed and the hot breath
brought unreadable news.

Unimpressed by this sentimental display, Nieumann snatched the
reins and tried to mount the still-terrified horse. Its back arched and
every one of its four legs left the earth; its back hooves were still
kicking air when Nieumann hit the ground on his knees. Oppenshaw
hid his thoughts. What he admired in animals he admired in men:
courage and humility. Calling it a brave horse and a good horse,

Oppenshaw led it quietly into camp while Nieumann, cursing all dumb and ignorant beasts, hobbled along behind.

Trotter's northern camp — a break in the wilderness at the mouth of a thickly forested box canyon — consisted of four eight-by-twelve tents and a big grub tent with plumes of blue smoke rising from its chimney. Accumulated snow had split Nieumann's tent along its seams. When Nieumann saw his ruined canvas and soaking blankets, he yelled with rage and hammered the camp's iron dinner triangle. The camp cook, McBeth, dozing inside, woke up and came running out of the grub tent in a panic to be met by Nieumann's tremendous punch to the side of his head.

"Son of a whore!" Nieumann yelled. "Why you not sweep offa my tent?"

Half stunned, McBeth rushed back inside, and was reaching for a carving knife when Nieumann's next blow knocked him unconscious and broke every knuckle in the Dutchman's right hand.

The dinner gong brought Joseph Fielding — the straw boss — hurrying back to camp together with James Campbell and Basil Henderson. Nieumann was hobbling about in a swoon of pain, nursing his broken hand.

Fielding, a fifty-year-old Cornish giant, calm as a monument and as expressionless, listened quietly while Oppenshaw explained what was going on. Fielding checked the captured horse and saw Byron McEachren's initials stamped on its saddleflaps.

"What's it mean?" Henderson asked.

"What the hell do you think it means?" Fielding growled. "That horse was hauling McEachren's ass up here, and it got spooked."

Nieumann said angrily, "I clearing off to Waddy Flats. Nobody don't make a fool of me no more. Tomorrow, I pulling up stakes, I quitting this damn camp and go looking for Trotter, you bet!"

McBeth crawled into view, spitting blood and holding a meat cleaver.

Fielding waved an admonitory finger at McBeth. Staring Nieumann in the eye he said, "There's long weary miles between here and Waddy Flats. Think you'll make it on those knees?"

"By Gott, I do it, if it kills me, you bet!" Nieumann snarled. "I sick of working for promises."

McBeth, groggy and confused, heard the last part of Nieumann's commentary. "He won't be on his own, mister. I'm sick of cookin' fer promises, too. You guys wants your dinners, cook yer own," McBeth said, and went back into the grub tent where he collapsed over a table and sat with his head cradled in his arms.

James Campbell, a young English surveyor, said diffidently, "Well, chaps, I think Nieumann has made a jolly good point. This isn't exactly a holiday camp and chaps can't be expected to work here for nothing."

Nieumann misunderstood Campbell's remarks. Balling his swollen fist he waved it under Campbell's nose and shouted, "By cracky, English! You better not say no more, or I bust you too!"

Campbell — half Nieumann's size — stepped backwards, crying, "Think so, do you? Well, take your chances, but be warned!" and with both arms extended defiantly in a fair imitation of a professional pugilist, he danced on tiptoes around the huge Dutchman.

Nieumann was getting ready to deliver another enormous blow when Fielding stepped between them and said, "Jimmy, you'd better go shovel snow off your tent before you get killed. As for you Nieumann, shut the hell up!"

"Say what you like, boss, but this sure as hell ain't no big rock candy mountain and I for one am just about ready for a showdown," a man called Pollack said. "I ain't pointin' no finger at you, Mr. Fielding, but that feller what's supposed to be running the show is doing us wrong."

Fielding set his feet apart, shoved his hat back on his head, and folded his arms. "What's that, Pollack?"

Pollack swallowed, and said nothing.

Fielding said, "Fine, Pollack, that's what I thought you said. Now, I better take a look up the canyon, see if there's any sign of McEachren. He might be lying in a gully with a busted head."

"I'll come with you," Campbell said.

"One man'll be enough, I daresay," Fielding said. "You stay here, Jimmy, but don't go stirring Nieumann up or I won't be responsible."

Fielding left the camp at a studied saunter. His face bore no expression because he had been raised to listen, instead of talk, and to take the rough with the smooth, but he was beset by problems. The men were cranky and suspicious, and there was constant bickering because they had started gambling and IOUs were beginning to mount up. Charlie McBeth was in over his head and by all accounts Elijah Oppenshaw was the big winner.

Fielding heard footsteps coming up behind. He stopped walking until Oppenshaw caught up and said, "With all the excitement I clear forgot about my oxen. I'd better bring them in before it's too dark."

"There's something on my mind and I've been meaning to have a private word with you. It's this gambling business. You know I don't like it."

"I know you don't, but it's a way of passing the time."

"Mebbe so, but I'm putting a stop to it."

"It's a bit late. I'm through the minute Trotter gets here with my wages."

"You've been paid."

"Sure, in scrip. What I want is cash, in my hand."

"Why, so you can collect on your gambling debts?"

"I haven't claimed any debts," Oppenshaw said unemotionally, as a cold wind whistled and shivering trees dumped their burdens in the white silence. "Am I the sort of man who goes around dunning his mates?"

Fielding remained silent for a moment. Ashamed of himself, he stretched out his right hand. "Sorry, Elijah. Forget what I said, eh?"

Oppenshaw shook hands readily and said, "I hate to be lumped in with that beggar Nieumann, but I've had enough too."

"Steady on, now," Fielding was saying, when an animal bellowed and a horned ox, still collared to its half of a double wooden yoke, charged out of the trees. Its eyes rolling in terror, the beast went crashing into the Homathko with its neck twisted over by the uneven burden and churned through fifty yards of broken shallows. The ox was trying to swim across a narrow channel of deep water when the powerful current swept it out of sight.

"That's Hannibal!" Oppenshaw said, hurrying forward. "How the devil did he get loose..." and stopped dead in his tracks. Fifty yards away, in the lee of a bluff where the oxen had been sheltering, four warriors were kneeling in the snow, butchering and quartering one of Oppenshaw's beloved animals.

"Why you murdering devils!" Oppenshaw hollered. "Get your-selves away from that!" and ran towards them waving his arms. In a moment, the Indians had flitted into the trees carrying some of the meat.

The sight of the felled beast's head and entrails, steaming in the reddened snow, was too much for Oppenshaw. "May I be struck blind, if I ever saw gallanter oxes," he said, turning his face away from the gory remains. "What the hell's to be done about it, boss?"

Fielding put a finger to his lips.

Five hundred yards down the road, Oppenshaw's surviving yokes had bolted into another canyon where a Chilcotin chief, indistinct in swirls of snow, was directing his people. Women and slaves were erecting tepees.

"That's the limit! By God, I never saw the likes," Oppenshaw cried. "I believe they're going to slaughter my whole team."

"Pipe down," Fielding said in a low voice.

"What the..."

"I said pipe down! Shut up. Let's get back to camp. There's nothing that two can do against fifty."

"You don't mean..."

"What's the matter with your head, man?" Fielding said. "An hour ago we were wondering about a runaway horse. Now, Indians are butchering our oxen!"

"D'ye mean there's maybe deliberate harm come to McEachren?"

"Your guess is as good as mine."

Back at the roadworkers' camp, lamps had been lit and tents glowed warmly in the twilight. McBeth had suspended his mutiny and was drawing food stores from a bear-proof wooden box behind the grub tent. Henderson and Mayhew were talking outside. Nieumann, still fuming and cursing, was crouched on his haunches, cooling his swollen hand in a snowbank. Everybody else was inside the grub tent.

The fifteen-by-twenty-foot tent had a plank floor and wooden half-walls, four feet high. An iron cookstove, its tin chimney constructed of square coal oil cans, stood in the centre heating a huge, black, iron tea kettle. From time to time the kettle was topped up with water; every few hours, depending on its specific gravity, McBeth added more tea leaves to the brew.

The back half of the interior space was roped off — it was McBeth's exclusive domain, sacrosanct and inviolable. Within that sacred ground (trespassers risked being cleft asunder) there was a chopping block, a serving table, sacks of dried food, and makeshift shelving for dishes, utensils and sundries. McBeth's warm, comfortable bed, a very treasure and the envy of all, was a real three-by-six feather mattress set on a raised wooden frame and concealed from the rude public gaze by dangling bedsheets.

Three long tables with benches occupied the public half of the tent, where the road-gangers congregated as long as they did not interfere with the cook, or (a heinous crime) beg for treats. There was a wooden sink outside for rinsing dishes. When Fielding and Oppenshaw entered the grub tent, its greasy water was developing a sheen of ice.

Oppenshaw couldn't contain himself. "There's mischief brewing," he said. "Indians have killed my oxen, and now they're camped down the road."

"Is that right? Well, they better stay there!" McBeth shouted, coming inside the tent with a sack of potatoes. "Them cadgers better keep clear of me. I had my fill of their dern whining and begging last year. It's all I can do to keep you boys fed, without fattening them fellers as well."

"If Indians show up here, everybody's going to be real nice and polite," Fielding said firmly, as the tent flap opened and Nieumann came in, breathing murder. "And them's my orders."

Everybody started talking at once. "I taking no orders no more," Nieumann shouted, making himself heard above the din. "I taking nothing from nobody."

"You'll take my orders and like it," Fielding returned. "Any more guff from you mister, I'll haul you out by the short hairs and leave you shivering till you're properly cooled."

Nieumann, his broad muscular shoulders hunched and his arms bent, growled something, and Fielding slammed the flat of his hand down on a table. This rare show of emotion made Nieumann blink. Fielding had said enough. Nieumann poured himself a mug of tea and sat on a bench, glowering.

There were more subdued complaints about Trotter and their wages but the workers by and large had the usual stoicism of men who engage in lonely occupations and gradually their tempers calmed. Elijah Oppenshaw took off his jacket, rolled up his sleeves, and helped McBeth to peel potatoes.

Fielding went back to his own tent. Sitting on a homemade chair at a folding table, the straw boss was immersed in thought. He and his road workers might be trapped and he was worried about McEachren, but he did not see what could be done about anything until daylight. Dammit, he thought, Basil Henderson was the likely cause of this bother. The oversexed bloody fool had messed around with an Indian girl that he saw hanging about the camp. Before Fielding found out and put a stop to it, a few of the other men had had a go at her as well. Curse the bloody lot of them, Fielding thought, I hope they wind up with the clap. Putting those thoughts aside, he spent the time before supper writing in his log book.

It had stopped snowing when the metallic echoes of the dinner triangle rang across the little camp and Fielding put his books away. Clouds parted to reveal a half moon. The forest, dense and silent, cast long, black shadows. Crusted snow crackled underfoot. Halfway across the clearing to the grub tent, Fielding changed his mind and walked back up the canyon to see what was happening. The bluffs beside the road were thick with jackpines and scrub alder half invisible in the moonlight, and yellow campfires flickered up the road where the Indians were roasting oxen. Fielding was heading home when a warrior appeared out of the darkness carrying a carved wooden box.

Fielding's heart pounded until he saw that the warrior was unarmed. They faced each other in the snow and Fielding wondered how this man endured the freezing cold in thin moccasins and leggings and an unlaced buckskin shirt. Bowing gravely, the warrior placed his box on the road, gestured for Fielding to pick it up, and merged once more with the night shadows.

The foot-square object had been made from a single piece of thin, flat wood. Its corners and joints had been vee-notched with a knife, then bent to a box shape after the wood had been softened with hot water. Joints were pegged with wooden dowels and sealed with pine resin. A recessed lid was held in place with braided twine.

Fielding put the box under his arm — it was surprisingly heavy — and returned to the grub tent. The men were finishing supper when he laid it on a table. Campbell said cheerfully, "How nice, a bit of bentwood."

"A pretty piece of work," Fielding said, as he helped himself to a heaping plateful of boiled salt-cod and hot potatoes. "I found it on the road."

"Hey, Henderson," Openshaw said facetiously. "Maybe it's a gift from your Injun girlfriend."

Basil Henderson, grinning like a fool, shook his head.

"Clever things, those boxes," Campbell remarked, when people stopped laughing. "Completely watertight, and there isn't a single nail in 'em."

"What is it? A peace-offering, maybe?" Pollack ventured. "Kind of a token?"

"Don't be daft," McBeth said. "It's a trick, that's what it is."

But the men were intrigued. The box had a ripe smell, and Campbell thought it might contain smoked salmon or oysters.

"Come on, boss. Don't keep us in suspense," Pollack said. "Open it up."

"You open it," Fielding said. "I'm eating my dinner."

Pollack had short fingernails and couldn't undo the knots to get the lid off. He cut the twine with a knife, removed the lid, and lifted out an object the size of a football that was wrapped in layers of cloth. Conversation ceased as he unwrapped the first layer.

"Pollack," Openshaw said. "What's that red stuff on your hands?"

It was blood.

Pollack's eyes widened with horror and he dropped the package. It fell off the table and rolled along the ground, the wrapping unravelling as it went until it struck Nieumann's foot. When it came to rest, a ghastly object was revealed.

Pollack's legs turned to jelly and he collapsed onto a seat. Henderson rushed outside, vomiting. This triggered Mayhew's gorge and he was also losing his dinner when the tent canvas was split asunder in several places by screaming warriors wielding battleaxes and knives. Nieumann, McBeth, Pollack and Oppenshaw were killed immediately. Fielding survived for a minute by grabbing the steaming iron kettle and swinging it in an arc as he tried to reach the door, but his legs were hacked from under him and an axe split his head like a ripe melon. Campbell had the wit to duck beneath the bedsheets into McBeth's domain and dive under the feather bed.

Henderson, outside when the attack started, ran blindly into the forest through the tangled bush and up a snow covered hill. Gasping with fright he raced through moon-shadow to an unscaleable wall of sheer granite, where he threw himself flat and lay trembling. Two warriors passed within five yards and continued along the rock face, jabbing with spears as they tried to flush him out. Moving like a blind man in the black forest, Henderson came out above the road where a few hours earlier Oppenshaw and Nieumann had been skidding logs. Misstepping, he slid into a creek. He crawled out onto the snow, hatless, with his wool trousers, wool jacket and shirt stiffening with ice, and crouched in a patch of bush. After a few minutes the cold was unendurable. Henderson's brains were congealing along with his blood when he remembered something that a fisherman had once told him about winter survival. Undressing himself completely, Henderson wrung all the loose water out of his clothes by hand and put the damp wool back on. In those straits, he waited for morning.

Back at the camp, everybody except Campbell had perished. Trapped beneath McBeth's bed, Campbell watched through flaming tent canvas where the victorious Indians were celebrating. Choked, half blinded by smoke, with the wooden half-walls of the grub tent blazing all around, Campbell crawled to the door. The last thing that he beheld before he died was a great chief, holding a yew-wood war lance.

CHAPTER SIXTEEN

ISABEL ROUSED FROM her miserable stupor enough to see One-Ear go outside and dive into the water butt, head first. Now his legs were wriggling. Was he trying to get out? It didn't make any sense. He never should have gone into the water butt, especially not now, when she was frightened and longed to tell him things — to tell someone anyway — before she died and was forgotten, far from England, far from The Bellowing Mule. She would have liked to hear One-Ear's opinion: Did he think that it was very shameful to take little orphans from their beds and carry them along dark corridors at night, to be thrashed? Did One-Ear have an opinion about beadles with canes? And cleaners who liked to watch naked little girls?

One-Ear was a bad egg, but perhaps Molly Moggs would have thought him good company, on a level with jolly sailors in The Bellowing Mule (where, after all, Isabel had learned to enjoy herself and smile at talking parrots and tame monkeys). And gin! Saturday-night-in-London gin, with bottles shining behind the bar. And remember those gaslights! Remember those leather settees; remember those cut-glass partitions where a girl might be kissed discreetly. And as for kisses, what about the forwardness of a certain male lodger, Trotter by name, forever loitering on the back stairs of a boarding-house? And of being frightened in that cellar by the same boarder hiding in the dark? And trying to keep up with her work while Trotter followed her everywhere, with his restless hands and his whiney promises. All lies. Trotter's lies of roaming with Isabel, his queen, across wide dominions, if only, if only she would go to his room tonight and love him with her knickers off. Just once, before he ran to Canada and made his fortune. And she remembered one absolutely perfect day when Trotter's letter came, a Canadian miracle. Tears of joy in the downstairs kitchen with Cook, a candle on the table, while

Cecil read the letter to them, twice. Great delight all round, although it meant the end of The Bellowing Mule and England.

***

Waddington's Road compared with the worst that Decker had seen, and Decker had survived the Crimean winter roads of 1855. He had been on the heights above Balaklava, when Colonel Foster of the Royal Horse Artillery died in his arms. With cold and disease killing more British soldiers than the Russian foe, Decker's troop fought alongside the Turks as Russian infantry stormed up the hill from their redoubts until the Turks wavered and retreated. Decker and a few men braver than the rest continued the fight until most were killed and buglers sounded the retreat. One man who cut and ran with the Turks was caught afterwards and operated on by the regimental farriers. Fifty lashes they gave the poor devil, and Decker, the adjutant, had to count the strokes as the farriers laid on. Decker shook his head to banish those memories of valour and disgrace.

After fourteen hours of mixed walking and riding, Decker and Bushrat were once more on foot, leading their horses and the pack mule across a series of boulder-strewn ledges fit only for mountain goats. The horses moved along with their heads down and their ears drooping, snorting plumes of white vapour into the freezing air with every step. Here and there on the rocky crags and buttresses, tree stumps showed where Trotter's men had snaked jackpines off the trail and dumped them into the river. How this goat path could be developed into a road wide enough for wheeled wagons defied imagination and if it were ever finished it would be snow bound six months a year.

Since leaving The Crossing, Decker had seen no roadworkers and he was thinking that Trotter and his men were already dead. Cold and weary, he rekindled his vigilance by reflecting that his own greying scalp might soon adorn a warrior's collection.

"A Injun is like a bear with pepper up his ass, when he gets riled," Bushrat said unexpectedly. "They knows us pilgrims is following, and is sending this weather to make us miserable."

"Nobody controls the weather."

Bushrat — who looked like a fur-bearing animal in his frosted beard — touched the side of his nose to intimate inside knowledge. "Indians has powers us folks knows nothing about," he said sagely. "Take Euclataws. Some of them Euclataw women can lift fogs."

"How?"

"They calls up a wind. I seen it done."

Decker shook his head. Bushrat was full of these unlikely stories.

All the same, Decker had an edgy feeling. They were entering an eerie world. Here, unnamed glaciers and peaks swept across the limitless country like the waves of a vast ocean. Far away, where earth and sky linked, an immense plateau rose up. Uncountable acres of unexplored muskeg and forest, broken at long intervals by huge lakes and prairies, stretched endlessly to unscaled mountains and perpetual ice. Divided by rivers, this wild desolation was the Chilcotins' ancient hunting grounds but here, even Indians were usurpers. Sometimes these hardy souls perished in the long dark, when the oil froze, when the caribou and mountain goats and rabbits that men subsisted upon vanished.

A wind came up when nightfall was two hours off. Driven snow stiffened on Decker's slicker and froze his eyelashes. Waving tree branches cracked like whips and thin drifts of ice cobwebbed together in the Homathko's slow eddies. Decker's thoughts returned to Bushrat, and his queer yarns. Indians loved the long dark, but they also feared it. They sat huddled in their lodges for months, telling stories and smoking pipes, seldom venturing into the spirit-haunted night, where every tree and animal and bird might be a soul-snatching visitor from the other world. No Indian soul was safe unless it lay under the protection of a medicine man. Now, spirit medicine was failing against European magic and European diseases, and the Chilcotins were afraid of the new. Fear had its own contagion. Had madness spilled over into the white man's world? What else could account for Trotter's bizarre and dangerous posturing? And Isabel: what weird notions had impelled her to leave Trotter's mansion? Come to that, why was he, Decker, persisting with this dangerous, uncomfortable, and probably useless chase? How could two little men uphold the British law here? Besides, Trotter and the men in the upper camp were probably dead and only the laws of God could help them now. Tidewater was forty-five miles south and a few thousand feet of elevation warmer. He might be warm and cosy in Waddy Flats, sitting beside the stove with his feet up, instead of here, on this thankless errand.

Bushrat's voice, muffled by the wind, intruded into Decker's speculations. "Over there," Bushrat said, pointing, "just when we needs it most."

It was a warning — Decker should have seen that pit-house for himself. He would have seen it if he had been thinking of the road, and its dangers, instead of daydreaming. But there it stood — half-hidden by trees, and fifty feet off the trail — a conical earth hummock, five feet high and twenty feet across, rising up from the forest litter. A tilted log, notched for steps, jutted up through a manhole in the centre of the hummock.

Decker and Bushrat dropped their reins and crouched over the hole. A peculiar smell, of humanity and smoke and mouldy earth, rose out of it, along with the resonating echoes of Bushrat's voice as he hailed the house in Chilcotin.

There was no reply. "Watch out fer pox," Bushrat said, as Decker climbed down the notched log.

Entering this stone-age dwelling was like going into the belly of an earth-devouring dragon. Twisting entrails were the roots of trees and other vague grey organs distinguished themselves as his eyes grew accustomed to the darkness. He saw shelves dangling from ropes, dried-out fronds of sweet balsam, a pile of kindling wood. The pit-house's last nomadic occupants had departed months earlier, taking with them their mats and baskets and other portable possessions.

Bushrat unsaddled the horses and rubbed them down while Decker lit a fire in the pit-house and by its yellow blaze examined his surroundings. There was safety and comfort in this earth womb. With seven feet of headroom at its highest point, the circular house had a pole roof covered by a foot of clay. A raised earthen sleeping platform, three feet wide, circled the perimeter. As the interior space warmed, hibernating vermin and insects came to life, and their scuttering presences were accompanied by little avalanches of newly dried soil, falling through the overhead supports.

Bushrat brought the saddlebags in and started to make beef and potato stew. The place warmed quickly and Decker shivered when he went outside into crackling frost and wind to survey the road.

Under stars and a half-moon, the trail stretched forward for a couple of hundred yards before it disappeared into a black tunnel of jackpines. Trees continued along the escarpments as far as the eye could reach. Nothing moved out there. Relieved, Decker went back, past the staked and blanketed horses.

Half a mile away, Basil Henderson was facing death. All day he had persevered, dragging himself south along the frozen road, aiming for the pit-house. Rest was seductive; the funny thing was, even though he had been exposed to intolerable cold for nearly twenty-four hours, when he rested he felt quite comfortable. But his brain told him that death was approaching, that if he rested again, death would wrap him in its cold arms and squeeze the life out of him forever. And Henderson didn't want to die. He was afraid to die, because he was a miserable sinner. His mates were already dead. Henderson wondered whether any of them were roasting in hell yet? He couldn't remember: were sinners judged immediately, or did they have to wait for thousands of years, fretting and worrying, before God pronounced His verdict on people? So he hobbled on, thinking of death and sin, and of the Indian girl who had led him into temptation.

"Gee whittaker!" Bushrat said, as Decker brought an armload of firewood into the pit-house. "All we needs is a couple of goose-hair mattresses and this here is a regular hotel."

"How much grub is left?"

"Plenty."

"Good. Game's rather scarce in these parts, if you ask me. Deer will be down in the bottom country, and you could hunt for a week before you got within range of a mountain goat."

"That's right," Bushrat said, leaning forward to spit on the fire. "Now, I got somethin' to say, boss."

"Must be serious. I've never known you to ask permission before."

"Maybe, but I'm some misgive. This is a serious case."

"Keep talking."

"There ain't no place for us to go, except down. It's a dead immortal cinch that we's in a predicament with a bad outcome if we keeps headin' away from Waddy Flats. Injuns will beat us."

"What's your remedy?"

"Turn around."

"I mean to keep going until we get to the end of Trotter's road," Decker said. "How would you feel if it turns out we might have been able to save a few lives, and didn't?"

"Depends whose lives you're talkin' about, boss."

Decker climbed through the smoke and stood on the roof contemplating the wildness around him as a wolf clamouring on the slopes fell silent and listened to its own echoes. Clouds had hidden the moon and covered the sky to the south when the horses pricked their ears and started whinnying. He reached for his six-gun and moved behind the chestnut. A man, moving slowly and stiffly, was approaching the pit-house.

"Hold it! Who goes there?" Decker cried.

"By God, is that you, McEachren? It's me, Henderson. Basil Henderson."

"I'm Decker. Is McEachren with you?"

"Nossir, I've been looking for him along the trail."

"Are you alone?"

"I hope to God I am alone. Apart from you and me, the only white men left in these parts are ghosts," Henderson said, his voice cracking, and told Decker about seeing Trotter's head in a wooden box, and the midnight raiders.

"Was it Tellot's bunch?"

"I don't know who it was. But they killed every man in the upper camp, plus Trotter and, I guess, McEachren."

Henderson took a few more clumsy steps saying, "They finished the best part of me, as well."

"You'll do," Decker said, hooking Henderson's arm over his shoulder. "Let's move you out of this weather."

Decker and Bushrat helped Henderson to get down the ladder into the pit-house, took his frozen clothes off and wrapped him in blankets. His feet had bled earlier. Now, his flesh was like marble. Seeing it, Bushrat shook his head. In the flickering darkness of the dragon's belly, they gave the exhausted man hot water and fed him a few mouthfuls of stew, before he turned his head away and fell into a daze.

"He's frostbit all over, and won't get much rest. I frostbit a finger once, and that was bad enough," Bushrat whispered. "His marrow will be on fire soon. He'll think there's men breaking his bones with iron bars."

Decker stared at the falling embers.

As Henderson's body warmed and his veins throbbed, his face and fingers and toes became livid and swollen. The lightest touch caused agony. Decker and Bushrat watched Henderson's nose and ears swell to twice their normal size. In a few hours, his feet and hands were like inflated balloons.

Henderson floated in a sea of fire. Sometimes he saw faces in the flames, sometimes he heard drums, and voices. He saw the Indian girl, crying as he had his way with her, and he saw Charlie McBeth, sitting on a rock in that sea of fire, but when he tried to swim towards the rock, fiery water ran into his eyes and ears and mouth and everything vanished behind a glowing red veil. This is hell, he thought, I'm already in hell. Henderson stopped breathing for a moment, and when he opened his eyes he saw an old man, sitting across a fire of burning embers. Another man was trying to pour liquid fire down his throat.

"Drink this, Henderson," Decker said. "It's whisky."

Henderson tried to open his mouth as burning waters flooded over him.

Decker put the cork back into his whisky bottle.

"There ain't nothing you can do fer to help him, boss," Bushrat said. "Short of cutting his throat."

"I won't have to, if the Chilcotins catch us," Decker said. "We'll get out of here at first light."

"He's in no shape to sit a saddle."

"We'll tie him to the pack mule," Decker said. "Better get some sleep, we'll be making an early start."

Nobody got any sleep — Henderson's ravings kept everybody awake. As soon as it was light enough to see the trail, they put him on the mule and with Decker holding the reins they moved south, down the mountains. Snow turned to rain at the lower elevations. Rabbits, washed out of their burrows, were nibbling in a meadow before Bushrat shot one of them. He tied the rabbit's back legs together with a length of twine, looped it over his saddle horn, and rode on. They cooked and ate the rabbit in the crossing-keeper's house, and rested there for a few hours.

Decker said, "Henderson might lose his ears. Some toes."

"Is he gonna hang onto that little old pecker?"

"Let's hope so."

"It won't matter so much," Bushrat said. "No woman's gonna look at him now. He sure won't be no oil painting."

"That description," Decker said, without smiling, "applies to many of us."

Henderson was still in one piece when they lit out for Waddy Flats in a rainstorm.

Decker and his party were met by columns of rising steam and smoke when they reached Waddy Flats. The whole rainsoaked town had burned; bits of it were still smouldering. One of the Slough's three-storey turrets had survived and it stood, a blackened ruin, looming over a couple of loose cows. More cows, and a mule, were placidly grazing near the embers of Decker's vanished store and Schnurr's lodging house and the smithy. In the pouring rain, the wharf seemed intact, until they got closer and saw that it was a gutted shell. A breached fence near Decker's hissing hay barn showed where the Highlander and his harem had kicked through to freedom.

Bushrat rested a foot on the collapsed lintel of Decker's front door and said, "Sons a bitches. All this dern smoke and I'm out of tobacco."

Decker grinned. If Bushrat could put a good face on it, so could he.

"The stove and chimney look serviceable," Decker said, as a cock crowed, and Decker's chickens came out of the forest to cluck and complain around their former roosts. "And whoever did this was thoughtful enough not to burn our chickens so we'll have something for dinner at least," he continued cheerfully, to hide his strong feelings.

Decker and Bushrat lifted Henderson off the mule and did what they could to make him comfortable, under a tarpaulin that they found in what was left of Schnurr's yard. Using iron tools taken from Shanks's smithy, they tore useable timbers off various burned-out buildings and by nightfall they had rigged a waterproof lean-to shelter against the store's chimney. With firewood crackling in the stove they dined on a chicken and six moderately fresh eggs that Bushrat had found somewhere. Henderson was too ill and too crazy to do anything but thrash and moan.

Bushrat and Henderson spent the first part of that night by the stove while Decker, a rifle cradled in his arms, squatted cross-legged on guard under a dripping tree, where he had a good view of the lean-to they'd just built, and what remained of Waddy Flats.

There are codes of behaviour known intuitively, Decker thought. One such code, perhaps, argues against razing a whole town whatever the provocation. In the moonlight, he gazed at his favourite view: a curve of trees diminishing into the darkness above a shore where, until now, there had never been a permanent habitation. He broke off, sighing, his thoughts having come full circle. The error, it might be, lay in building a town here in the first place. Bushrat relieved Decker at midnight, but Decker got little sleep because he was wondering: What sense would it make to try and rebuild?

At daybreak, the smell of boiling coffee restored Decker's spirits, and sustained his optimism, even when his temporary roof began to creak. Above his head, accumulated rainwater was weighing down the roof tarpaulin between the rickety crossbeams.

Decker said, "Where'd you find that coffee?"

"There's a whole pile of cans lying around in the ruins that ain't burst. The only trick is to figure what's inside of 'em now they ain't got no labels. But I found us coffee, and bully, and peaches to be going on with."

Henderson slept through breakfast.

Decker and Bushrat salvaged more construction materials and rebuilt the barn above Sally's hole. Sally and her shoats arrived to watch the finishing touches. By the second night, the chickens were in new roosts, Sally and her piglets were snoring, and the horses were out of the rain. Until Bushrat figured out that the numbers stamped into can lids were an index to the contents, they had interesting meals for a while, getting peaches when they were expecting bully beef, and plum duff when hoping for sardines.

It wasn't all fun and games. Henderson's ears and his large toes and several fingers turned black, so Decker amputated them, without benefit of anaesthetic, to stop gangrene from killing him. Henderson cried, when he found out what they were doing, and it was difficult, holding him still. The tip of Henderson's nose and the flare of a nostril melted away by themselves. Decker had no ointments so he treated the wounds with dabs of melted tar, and hoped for the best.

After a few peaceful nights, Decker cancelled the night watches.

CHAPTER SEVENTEEN

WHIRLWINDS DARKENED THE sky over Waddy Flats and fear laid its black shadows over Henderson's mind. He sat weeping by Decker's stove, speaking to a disembodied head that he saw in a crumpled red blanket. He talked about killing himself.

Henderson woke Decker up one night. Falling across his bed he cried, "Forgive me, Father."

"The worst is over," Decker said. "Things'll improve, you'll see. And we'll stick with you."

"You don't understand. People are spreading wicked lies about me, Father," Henderson sobbed. "I've been bad, very bad."

"Nobody's talking about you, it's just imagination."

"They are. They say I had my way with an Indian girl, but if I did, I'm sorry now, and I'll never do it again. I only did it because the devil was in me."

"You had your way with a girl?"

"I did things, but it wasn't really me, it was something that was in me, a demon. I did it to her first..."

"What? What are you saying?"

"I wasn't the only one. She came to the upper camp, and showed me her body. What else could I do?" Henderson was saying, when he broke down in wracking sobs.

Tut-tutting, Decker put him back to bed. "Poor fellow," Decker said. "His delusions are getting worse."

Conscience reduced Henderson to gibbering idiocy, and he became the bane of Bushrat's existence. "I got enough to do," he'd say. "I ain't playin' nursemaid to no dern complainer." There was the house to work on, and a barn. The Highlander had returned with his harem. In addition, Decker and Bushrat were rebuilding the smokehouse. They came home one night after a hard day's work, longing for peace and quiet, and Henderson swept down on them, blubbering like a spoiled infant, seeking comfort they couldn't provide because his problems were in his head. Bushrat was fed up. In his uncomplicated opinion, Henderson's injuries were nothing. Bushrat got started on a story about two prospectors who just about froze to death on the Cariboo trails and survived even though the only functioning members they had left were their peckers. "Whores loved 'em 'cos they was 'armless," Bushrat guffawed. "Every time them boys give a girl an all-nighter, they got an extra lie-in, because they couldn't shake a leg in the morning." The sound of the Highlander, bellowing in the night, put a stop to his noise.

Decker blew the lamp out, reached for his rifle, and crawled across to the back window. Outside in the corral, dark shapes were moving between a screen of black trees and the barn. "There's three or four of 'em out back."

"Chilcotins?"

"God knows. Grab your rifle, Bushy, and go see what's happening out the front."

Bushrat crawled across the floor and said, "I don't see nothin'. It's the same like always."

"Stoke the fire but keep the lights doused," Decker said, as men flitted across the flats. "The sparks will let 'em know we're awake."

"Have you got 'em in your sights?"

"Yes."

"Give 'em have a round of buckshot," Bushrat said fiercely. "What's stopping you?"

"Just stoke the fire, Bushrat."

In a few minutes, the trespassers had gone. At daybreak there was blood on the ground, and Sally was missing.

Two days later Old Tsulas turned up, gaunt in his steeple hat and his dog-hair cape. He stood quietly in Decker's doorway, staring at his bare feet. Decker didn't know what to do with him. Indians who collaborated with whites would die first if Klatsassan came back; in the meantime, Old Tsulas was hungry. Bushrat cooked him a big dinner and fixed a bed for him in the barn.

Thereafter, at intervals, lone Indians arrived at Decker's place in daylight. Bushrat sent them away with little gifts of bacon, eggs, potatoes, jerky. Sally's remaining shoats — still resident in the pig-hole — thrived and fattened. No more stock was lost.

Spring coho showed up in Bute Inlet. Decker rooted out fish hooks and line, and built an eight-foot fishing rod out of willow wand and haywire. He was making lures and flashers out of bits of shiny tin when Old Tsulas came over and said, "Crazy woman living alone One-Ear's place. Need medicine."

"Indian woman?"

"One-Ear woman," Old Tsulas said. "What you making?"

"Casting gear."

"Nets easier."

"Not as much fun, though."

"Fun?"

"The challenge, and so on."

Old Tsulas shook his head and went back to the barn.

Decker strolled down to the beach to try his hand. Warm spring winds ruffled the maples. Blowhole spray glittered in the sun five hundred yards offshore, where a pod of killer whales was feeding. Miles beyond, mountains rose out of Georgia Strait and receded in diminishing shades of grey until the land and the sky came together.

It's Isabel, he thought. She's alive. Decker tried not to think about Isabel and considered Klatsassan instead, a man no more aware of the juggernaut he had set in motion than a child whose candle has just set fire to the curtains of a house. The mighty processes of British law would inevitably assemble in Victoria. One of these days, with or without legal niceties, Chilcotins would be hunted down and hanged.

Decker hooked a six-pounder and played it into six inches of water. Wading in, he stunned it with a wooden club and hooked a finger into its gills. Henderson hobbled over on his crutches and stood by while Decker removed the fish hook and dropped the coho in a basket as company for the two already in there.

"This is the life. And take a look at that whopping killer whale," Decker said. "Its dorsal fin must be seven feet high."

Henderson did not raise his eyes. "You look at it. I'm sick of whales and trees and wilderness," he replied joylessly. "Give me a city, any time."

Decker's next cast dropped his lure into the middle of a salmon ball that was churning twenty yards offshore. "We'll build a city here," he said. "You and me and Bushrat. There's empty land, waiting to be homesteaded."

"Waddy Flats has been cursed by the devil, it will never be settled."

"You might be wrong. Pre-empt Wilbur's place, or MacCormack's. Rebuild your life and start a farm, before somebody beats you to it."

"Farms need men," Henderson said grumpily, "not half-men."

"You're a man."

"For God's sake! Stop patronizing me. Things are bad enough without your condescending blather."

"That's the spirit," Decker said, grinning. "Give me hell, I deserve it."

Henderson's eyes filled with tears.

"I'm taking Bushrat away for a couple of days, so you'll have the place to yourself," Decker said, as another coho took the lure, felt the hook, and jumped in a flashing, four-foot arc.

"Here," Decker said, offering Henderson the fishing rod. "Bring this one in. Work up an appetite for your dinner."

"No thanks."

Decker said, "Old Tsulas just told me there's a woman, living in One-Ear's cove, and I want to check it out. You can come along if you want."

"Why?"

"Wouldn't it be better than staying here, feeling sorry for yourself?"

Decker's words caught Henderson like a blow. His jaw slackened and he moved back a step, white patches showing around his mouth and eyes.

"Cheer up, for God's sake. Are you going to be an invalid for the rest of your life? You could sit a horse, if you tried."

Henderson turned away. Carrying his weight on his heels, he muttered his way back to Decker's house.

Henderson was sitting by Decker's stove when he heard the voice again.

"Look at me," the voice implored him. Henderson had told the girl that she must never speak to him when Decker and Bushrat were around.

"Look at me," she repeated.

"I don't want to look at you," Henderson said, closing his eyelids tight. Was there to be no escape from the importunate hussy?

Goldeneyes, grebes, surf-scoters and widgeons had been flying in for weeks. Thousands of them were resting and feeding along Bute Inlet before they commenced the next leg north when Decker and Bushrat led a pack mule past MacCormack's old homestead the next day. Bitterns and teals and coots and pintails nosed about on the mudflats. Ravens, flapping low to cheat the gusts, added their own ill-tempered squawks to the general cacophony. Here and there, gumweeds poked yellow heads up between silvery driftlogs. Redberry elders and patches of wild rose waved their spring flowers on the forest margin.

Violent crosswinds rolled down the Homathko from the great upland icefields as the riders continued south with their heads down, along the shoreline trails and beaches. At mid-afternoon, Decker and Bushrat reached a headland, where steep cliffs rose straight out of the sea and ascended for a thousand feet to a densely treed plateau. Clouds were blanketing the west when they dismounted out of the wind, to rest their horses until the tide turned.

A series of monster heads had been chiselled into a sandstone cliff. Galleries of painted stick-men danced around the heads, together with birds and sea lions and wolves.

Bushrat pointed across the inlet to a snow-mantled mountain. "Look close," Bushrat said, "you'll see Raven. There's his beak, and his eyes, and his feet."

It was true — the mountain was a black raven. Its eyes were rings of snow, its beak was a jutting ridge.

"The Homathkos say that Raven made everything. Raven made insects, men, whales, trees. Did 'em with rock and paint, first, then breathed on 'em, and they was summoned to life."

The receding tide brought an offshore wind and more heavy rain. Decker and Bushrat left the petroglyphs behind and rode around the headland in waves deep enough to wet the mule's belly. They came out on a sheltered cove. One-Ear's wrecked sloop lay on the shore with seaweed dangling from its crippled spars. Footprints showed where somebody had tramped back and forth between the beach and a forest trail. Something moved in a potato patch, two hundred yards away.

Low black clouds arched over One-Ear's cove like sheets of rumpled black velvet. Isabel, trying to drag a partially filled sack of potatoes across a field from the barn, was shivering in her wet overalls. Her legs became water and she collapsed. Panting in the mud, picking absently at the scabs marring her cheeks, Isabel waited until her heart stopped thumping and then forced herself to get up. Clutching the sack with both hands she tried to move it. Dizzy, confused, with an aching head and aching bones, she watched dully as two horsemen rode into sight. Dropping the sack she crawled along muddy furrows to hide in the barn. Rain hammered the roof as she burrowed among the hay bales and made a nest for herself in the warmth, where summer heat still resided in the hay, and fell asleep, with the pleasant smell of horses lingering in her nostrils.

Bushrat said, "What do you think Isabel's playing at?"

"God only knows. Maybe she thinks we didn't see her."

"And maybe she's another Henderson, and ain't right in her head, neither."

Rain masked Decker's footsteps as he went inside the barn and rested a boot on the bottom rung of a ladder. Wet prints showed where Isabel had just gone up. He said, "Mrs. Trotter? This is Decker. I'm here with Bushrat Wright."

A faint whimper became audible above the noise of water against wood. Decker went up the ladder. Rays of pale light coming through cracks in the siding showed Isabel lying in the straw with her feet towards him, wearing ill-fitting faded brown overalls and a pair of muddy men's boots. She was very thin. In the darkness, the scabby blemishes that disfigured her beauty were almost unnoticeable.

Decker sat on his heels. Two robins were hopping in the shadows.

Bushrat came into the barn and said, "Where the hell's the sense in it?"

Decker shook his head and said he didn't know.

"Ain't you sorry you come down and found her like that?"

"I'm sorry about a lot of things."

"What do you aim to do with her?"

"Nurse her."

"You might get sick as well."

"I tell you what," Decker said. "I don't give a damn."

Decker wrapped soft cloth around Isabel's hands and strapped her arms to her sides, to stop her from scratching herself and causing needless scarring. It stopped raining and the sun came out as the lawmen carried her to the shack and laid her on a bed of fresh straw. That night, Decker lit a candle and looked down at Isabel's sleeping face, austere and angular in the flickering light. He watched her for a long time. The candle flame swayed when he moved past it to sit on One-Ear's stoop. Bushrat was stretched out on a horse blanket, using his saddle for a pillow as he watched the northern lights. He said, "How old is she?"

"Twenty. Eighteen. I don't know."

"Eighteen or eighty, smallpox is a bad piece of business," Bushrat said, as sheets of electric flame danced in the heavens. "You take them lights, there. Beautiful they are too, but they don't last. You no sooner start admirin' one of them particular lights, when it's gone, and there's another just as pretty takin' its place. Hit's the same with that little girl. We just got used to seein' how lovely she was, then it's taken away."

CHAPTER EIGHTEEN

A NORTH WIND was bending trees when Decker and Bushrat, splitting maple for the smokehouse, stopped work to eye Isabel who had just left her cabin and was carrying a bucket down to the beach at low tide.

Bushrat, who felt more like talking than working, watched her start raking for clams. He put his maul down and jammed his hands into his pockets. "She's some kid, ain't she?"

"She's a hell of a kid."

Waddy Flats had doubled in size lately. In addition to the little cabin that Decker and Bushrat had built for Isabel, there was Henderson's place — a canvas-and-wood shelter with a tin chimney where, except for occasional visits to Decker's house, the crazed road-worker had isolated himself, doing woodwork.

Most of Henderson's carpentry projects ended up with Isabel. He presented her with a table and two nice chairs. Then he made her a food safe. For this, he had received little thanks. "Please don't make me anything else," she would say, as he delivered yet another lovingly crafted artefact. "Stop fussing over me, please," and Henderson would slink off to sulk out of sight somewhere. Another of Henderson's useful contributions had been a trip to the Slough, from which he returned with some of Isabel's old gowns that had survived the fire, but she continued to wear overalls.

"Let's butcher a calf tomorrow," Decker said. "Old Tsulas can divvy some of it up among his brethren."

"Well, boss, I'll get supper started," Bushrat said, and went into the house.

Decker looked at Isabel, bending and gathering clams while seagulls circled and cried above her, beating their wings to hold their stations in the wind. She raised her head and smiled at him. Decker put down his tools and went across to talk with Old Tsulas in the barn. The old man was chatting with a stranger who leapt to his feet and ran away as soon as Decker entered.

Up at the house, Bushrat was rattling pots and pans and scratching his head. Henderson came in and sat on a kitchen chair warming his crippled hands at the stove. Bushrat made one or two attempts to engage him in conversation, but he stared at the floorboards. Bushrat hid a grin and facetiously suggested that Henderson build himself a canoe.

That caught his attention. He looked up and said, "Build a canoe? Why?"

"So's you can clear off to Victoria."

"I'll wait for a schooner. One's bound to arrive, sooner or later."

"Don't count on it. Waddy Flats is off the beaten track, outta bounds. The rest of the world has forgot all about us. If I was you, I'd make my own way south. You could paddle there in, oh, mebbe a month. That's if you don't drown, or get lost."

Henderson shrugged.

"Are you scared of drownin'?"

"I'd rather be drowned than hanged."

"There's always a chance them Cape Mudge pirates will kill you out of spite," Bushrat said helpfully. "Hate white fellers, them Cape Mudgers do. Always watchin' the coast to see if there's a likely victim driftin' by. Better give 'em a wide berth. If you decide to go, I'll make yer a map."

"If getting to Victoria is so simple, how come you and Decker don't go?"

"Cousin, we could go any time we wanted. Decker's got a standin' offer of a sergeant's job down there, and I could be his deppity, same as here. But Waddy Flats suits us just fine. We don't want no bright lights and noise and city ructions keepin' us awake nights. Nossir, we're country boys."

"I'm turning into a country boy myself."

"I seen that. I seen you start turning into a country boy the minute Isabel landed here. Only, you ain't no country boy at heart. At heart, you're a city feller."

"Isabel's being here has nothing to do with it."

"And clouds don't have nothin' to do with rain, neither."

"Well, let's suppose you're right. Let's suppose I did go to Victoria. What would I do for a living?"

"Fer a guy with them missin' fingers you ain't a bad carpenter. A bit more practice and you'll be a regular cabinet-maker. How about going into the coffin trade?"

"Eh?" Henderson said, smelling mischief.

"Build coffins, dig graves," Bushrat replied. "Hire yerself out as a professional mourner. Wear black suits and a black hat."

Henderson gave Bushrat a severe look. "Lay off," he said, when it dawned on him that he was being teased. "If you weren't such an old fool I'd knock you down."

"Oh, go boil yer head," Bushrat said endearingly. "The folks I'm used to, they don't talk about knocking people down, they goes ahead and starts throwin' punches."

Henderson rushed outside and almost collided with Decker.

"Hold it," Decker shouted, as Henderson ducked past. "I want a talk with you."

"Go to blazes," Henderson cried, and went into his shack.

Old Tsulas had just delivered disquieting news about Henderson. Decker thought about confronting him immediately, but decided to leave it until he'd thought matters over. He went into the house instead.

"Listen," Decker said. "Has Old Tsulas said anything to you about the goings-on at the upper camp, before the massacre?"

"No, why?"

"He's just told me that some of the roadworkers in the upper camp had been fooling with Lowwa's daughter."

Isabel walked up to the beach towards her cabin. Henderson came rushing over, waving his arms, "For heaven's sake, Isabel. Don't you think you're overdoing it?" he said. "Let me carry that bucket for you."

Isabel refused his help. If she let him, Henderson would overwhelm her in a minute. She closed the door and leant against it until she heard him going away. Taking her waterlogged boots off she put them to dry near the stove and stoked it with firewood. She cut up some potatoes and added them to the pot, and lay down on her bed.

The cabin was full of noises; they came seeping through the walls as in the old orphanage. The muffled clang of London's church bells had been the background music of her childhood; now, at night, she heard lashing winds, the faint wail of wolves, hooting owls. Isabel moved and the rustling straw in the mattress beneath her brought its own memories. Her eyes closed and she thought about One-Ear; saw lust in his yellow gimlet eyes. The memory was too painful. She couldn't bear it and opened her eyes to the bare rafters of the roof. God, how she hated this monotony. "Come to me, Decker," she said aloud. "Come here, come here, come here!"

With a pang of sharp despair she thought, Decker will never come. No decent man will look at me now. Not after smallpox, not after One-Ear.

She turned her head to look at the bubbling pot and got up to light a lamp. The damp overall cuffs chafed her ankles when she moved. She adjusted the pot off the heat and sat down again, clutching her breasts with her hands and staring at her ruined face in a looking glass.

I have come a long way, she thought; from being the toast of The Bellowing Mule to a bootlegger's woman. She remembered the back alley behind Craven Gardens. She remembered that first day, when Molly Moggs went into the public house and she followed Cecil's flickering candle through cellars and along a dark, low-ceilinged corridor to a large windowless kitchen lit by a pair of gas mantles. It was beef-stew night in the boarding-house and there it was, savoury and delicious, in a huge tureen on a coal-fired cooking range. A yellow canary was singing to the room's shiny copper pans. Loaves of bread were rising on a scrubbed wooden table.

A plump, middle-aged woman swept into the kitchen from upstairs: it was Cook, Mrs. Carlisle, wearing an enormous floppy white cloth cap and a matching white pinafore over a black dress.

"Here's the new scullery, Mrs. Carlisle," Cecil said. "But she don't have no references."

"Another bad hat, or an orphan without experience?" Mrs. Carlisle said fiercely, glaring at Isabel's institutional clothes and hand-me-down boots.

"She's all right," Cecil said. "We've enough bad hats in this boarding house already, without letting another one in."

Isabel's dream deepened. She dozed until Decker's voice rose above the shrill winds. He was calling her name. Somebody knocked on the cabin door. She came out of her memories. There was Decker, standing in her doorway holding a lantern. And when he came in she remembered how he had nursed her when she had been ill with smallpox; how he had talked to her and comforted her when he'd thought she'd been asleep, saying things that he probably wouldn't have said, if she'd opened her eyes. Now, he hardly seemed to give her a thought. Once, when she had been watching Decker's horses in the corral, she had turned around suddenly and found him staring at her; not undressing her with his eyes, as Henderson did, but speculatively, as if he were trying to understand something.

"There's a schooner, anchored down the inlet," Decker said. "It's the *Nonpareil*."

Isabel's overall hung like a sack from her thin shoulders; she looked defeated, tired. Now she shook her hair out, and smiled. By God, he thought, she was still beautiful, skinny and pockmarked and all. Decker hid his feelings. The *Nonpareil* would soon take her away from him; he'd never see her again. It would hurt like hell, but then he'd get over it.

She looked at him with great earnestness and went behind a screen at the back of the room. A moth circled the lamp. Behind the screen clothes rustled as Isabel spoke about a tiny mink she had seen among the rocks when raking clams. Decker, dissecting every word for the meanings he wanted to hear, remained silent until she came out wearing a blue dress, her long hair tied with a blue ribbon. In the darkness her face and her long neck were like white marble and when she reached him she held out her hand and he took it. This was the first time that he had touched her since her illness. He felt the frail bones beneath the skin of her small hand and in that subdued light her face was pale with an expression which might have been longing.

"I've been making my supper and you're welcome to have some. I hope you don't mind potatoes with their skins on," she said, turning away to put two plates on the table.

She sat down and stared at her hands. Shrill winds made the door rattle in its frame.

He thought, She's sadder, older. There she was, sitting in a lamp-lit cabin, with a ship out there ready to take her away from him before he ever got to know the least real thing about her, except for what she looked like at that moment, staring at her hands.

"The ship will come in at first light. I'll be giving the skipper letters, for the governor and Judge Begbie. To tell them what's been going on up here," Decker said. "There'll be room for passengers."

He sat at her table. A mile away out on the inlet riding-lights burned in the *Nonpareil's* rigging and reflected off the water. Decker leaned forward and took her hand and told Isabel about his life. About a man called Montgomery, now dead, who had been his best friend. He told her that he would be sorry when she left Waddy Flats.

"I'm not ready to leave here," she said. "Not unless you do."

Another gust of wind made the door rattle.

CHAPTER NINETEEN

THE *NONPAREIL* HAD been and gone before Henderson came out of hiding. The ship had faded out of sight down the inlet when Decker entered Henderson's shack without knocking and found him sitting at his work bench.

He knows, Henderson thought, as Decker slammed the door shut. Old Tsulas must have found out somehow, and told him.

Henderson put his carpentry tools down and sat hunched in front of his fire, elbows on his knees, cradling his face.

"What are you, insane?"

"Me and a fellow called Mayhew started it," Henderson said in a muffled voice.

"All this foolishness of yours, all this moping and whining and carrying on. Waking me up at night and crying. It wasn't just fantasy and bad dreams. It was bad conscience because it really happened."

"It happened. I was the worst."

"Who is Mayhew?"

"One of the fellows in the camp. We ... me and Mayhew promised her things. A gown, stuff like that."

"Did you rape her?"

"Rape? I don't like that word."

"You're too sensitive?"

"I'm not going to say that I raped her."

"What will you say?"

"She was pretty," Henderson whispered. "A pretty young Indian girl. Mayhew watched me do it, and got excited, by the watching. After that, some others had a go."

"So that's what started it?" Decker said. "A fellow called Henderson messed about with an Indian girl. And six or seven or a hundred other fellows did it after you, because they got excited?"

"Yes. That's the way it happened. I'm very sorry."

***

"Here," Corporal Braden said, marching into the New Westminster police station with a copy of the *British Columbian* under his arm. "Old square-toes got his promotion."

Constable Patterson was polishing his boots. "Eh, corp? What's that?" Patterson said, puzzled. "Who are you talking about?"

"Old square-toes, James Douglas. Queen Victoria's knighted him, it says so right here," Corporal Braden replied, opening the paper and laying it flat on the guard room table. "Listen to this," he said, reading aloud. "Word has just been received that Queen Victoria has honoured James Douglas with a knighthood and elevated him to the rank of Knight Commander to the Bath, prior to his retirement as governor."

"Douglas is retiring?"

"That's what it says in this here newspaper. Arthur Kennedy's the new Governor of Vancouver Island. A bloke called Frederick Seymour's been made Governor of British Columbia."

"Seymour? Never heard of him."

"He was Governor of British Honduras, before," said Braden. "But there's more," said Braden, continuing to read. "On March 14th, Sir James and Lady Douglas will be travelling to New Westminster, when Colonel Moody is to arrange a farewell banquet..."

Patterson put down his shoe brush, scratched his chin, shook his head and said, "Old square-toes? I've heard James Douglas called all kinds of things, but I never heard him called square-toes."

"Oh that feller whatsisname, De Cosmos. He called him that, when they was having one of their rows in the legislative council."

"All I know, corp, it'll be duty as usual, for you and me," Patterson returned gloomily. "While Colonel Moody and the bloomin' bigwigs is entertaining Douglas and his missus at a posh banquet, us bleedin' perishers'll be standin' by with rifles over our shoulders, same as like always."

***

On April 20th, HMS *Forward*, steaming up the Fraser River past Homer's sawmill, fired the first of a seventeen-gun salute. Cursing the noise, Frederick Seymour, who had been dozing in the captain's stateroom, went on deck in time to see a handful of New Westminsterites ambling towards the dock to witness his arrival. When the *Forward* drew close, the city brass band struck up with "Rule Britannia."

Corporal Braden and Constable Patterson comprised the honour guard. "Cor blimey. Is that him?" Patterson whispered, as the frail, bald, and anaemic-looking man appeared on deck. "That little bloke?"

"Must be," Braden whispered back.

Seymour turned to Arthur Birch who was standing beside him and said, "Good God. Is this it?"

"I'm afraid so."

"You can't seriously mean to say this is the capital city of British Columbia?" Seymour said, gazing with incredulity at all the empty hotels and houses with "To Let" signs nailed across their windows. Shaking his head at the sight of decaying stumps and fallen trees blocking the empty thoroughfares, Seymour added, "What the devil happened?"

"Since the Fraser River mines started to play out, things have taken a bad turn."

"Heaven forbid. And just think, I gave up palm trees and sunshine to come here."

After listening politely but inattentively to a few welcoming words from Colonel Moody, Seymour, accompanied by Secretary Birch, was escorted to his quarters which, he discovered, consisted of two rooms in a canvas-roofed building. The jail, next door, was a miserable wooden rookery inhabited by murderers, horse-thieves, debtors and felons.

"Damn!" said Seymour, taking off his hat and flinging it towards a rack of antlers nailed to a wall, which it missed, falling to the dusty floorboards. "Here's a jolly mess."

"Indeed," Birch murmured, as he picked up Seymour's hat, dusted it off, and hung it on the antlers.

Seymour, wincing at the noises issuing from the jail, sat behind a desk, clasped his hands and said, "This isn't the Caribbean."

"I'll take my oath on that, sir," Birch responded fervently.

"Well, Birch. Suggest something, for God's sake."

"I suggest we build a new government house, for a start."

"Jolly good idea."

"And some people want a hospital."

"What for?"

"To house smallpox victims and so on."

"It's not as if I wasn't warned."

"Sir?"

"Well, Reggie Blackstone told me all about this place. But you know Reggie, always exaggerating. 'BC's an uncouth backwater,' he said. 'Nothing but savages and misfits.' "

"Reggie's right. It's worse than New Zealand," said Birch. "Worse than Australia."

"That's what Reggie said. 'Remote and useless, a constant drain on the Privy Purse.' "

"Yes sir."

"I say, Birch. Did you say something about smallpox?"

"It's a regular scourge to the Indians. It'd be a smart thing if you did something about it."

"Smallpox?"

"That's it."

"Good heavens, Birch. What can I do about it?"

"The simplest remedy would be to ship all the savages back north, to where they came from. That would go down well with the public, and get rid of a nuisance at the same time."

"Damn the public," Seymour said. "Shipping the afflicted out of sight isn't a remedy. What those poor devils need is shelter, and medicine."

Birch frowned at a cockroach running about on the floor, and Seymour contemplated his fingernails.

"That's all, Birch. You may go," Seymour said, leaning his elbows on his desk and holding his head. "My brain's beginning to ache."

"I'll round up some fellows," Birch said. "Have this place cleaned up."

"What about our dinners, Birch? And a spot of whisky, eh? Wash down some of the dust of this confounded place."

"I'll see what I can do, sir."

Governor Seymour, Arthur Birch, Police Inspector Chartres Brew, and Sergeant Herrold took horses from the government stables and rode out to inspect more of New Westminster. On an earlier day, Seymour had visited the public school — a small building erected near a bog. Dejected, he continued on to inspect the mint, the assay office and the land registry office. Now, Seymour wanted to see an Indian settlement.

Circling there, Seymour's mind seethed with ideas. He ought, perhaps, to investigate this up-coast massacre yarn that Alfred Waddington had been pestering him about. But there were other matters requiring immediate attention. First, he would use his own money to design and build a spanking new government house. Something decent, with a ballroom, and private suites where fellows could play cards and smoke cigars and have a bit of fun. When it was finished he'd invite everybody to the opening ceremonies. Perhaps he'd talk to Judge Begbie and see about a general amnesty. Yes. He'd lay on a bang-up feast. Beef and venison. Bring in a few cases of champagne. Seymour made a mental note to order a hundred commemorative canes from England, with, say, silver-gilt tops engraved with a crown. Seymour was turning these ideas over as the party entered the enveloping darkness of a wood and he became aware of a death-like stillness. Birds had stopped singing. The only sound was the thud of hooves as they rode beneath trees. And what on earth was that appalling stink? Perhaps dead fish were rotting on the banks of the Fraser?

The morning sky was still thinly sprinkled with stars when Seymour's party rode up to the Indian camp and saw human bodies decaying on the short grass. Dozens of tepees stood in the silence with their tent flaps open, as if their owners had just left, intending to return momentarily. Campfires had burned down; there were no barking dogs to announce the white intruders. Boxes, guns, knives, beads, and carved wooden masks and whistles and drums were scattered across the grasslands. Of the two hundred Indians camping there a few days previously, none were found alive. Survivors had fled down river in canoes, taking their sick with them.

Overcome with pity, Seymour inspected a carved alder mask that was lying in the weeds. It was a smallpox mask, in the shape of a bird, with a moveable lower beak. The bird's forehead and cheeks were covered with raised wooden pegs, painted red.

Without a word, Seymour turned his horse and went back to his quarters. Pale, shaken by the smallpox tragedy, he dismissed Birch and sat down to write a personal account of it for Viscount Edward Cardwell, Duke of Newcastle, Secretary of State for the Colonies. Seymour lifted up his pen, laid it down again, and paced backwards and forwards. Still too agitated to compose his thoughts he threw himself into a chair and re-read John Robson's latest editorial in the *British Columbian*:

> We are quite aware that there are those among us who are disposed to ignore altogether the rights of the Indian and their claims upon us — who hold the American doctrine of 'manifest destiny' in its most fatal form, and say that the natives will die off and make way for the Anglo Saxon race, and the quicker the better; and under the shadow of that unChristian doctrine, the cry for 'extermination' is raised at every pretext.

Seymour took up his own pen and described his findings for the Colonial Secretary in London. He added:

> There are rumours of an Indian insurrection at Bute Inlet. I would most respectfully point out to Your Grace that should a real war

break out between the Indian population and the whites, the former numbering 60,000 and the latter 7,000, I may feel compelled to follow in the footsteps of the Governor of Colorado, and invite every white man to shoot every Indian he may meet. Such a proclamation would not be badly received here in case of emergency.

Seymour put the letter into a despatch box along with Robson's editorial, and Birch put it on the mail steamer for England.

One week later, Arthur Birch dropped the latest edition of the *British Columbian* on Seymour's desk.

HORRIBLE MASSACRE REMEMBERED: The schooner *Nonpareil* has arrived from Waddy Flats, en-route to Victoria, bringing further news. She is the ship that weeks ago brought as passengers, settlers and roadworkers who were the survivors of horrible murders by Chilcotin Indians. This newspaper asks: When will Governor Seymour act, and bring these murderers to justice?

"There's nothing for it now, Birch," Seymour groaned. "Fetch Inspector Brew, immediately."

Birch was turning away to comply when there came a terrific hammering on the door and Alfred Waddington cried, "Open up, Seymour! Let me in this minute, I say, or I won't be responsible!"

"Let him in," Seymour said resignedly. "I'll try to mollify the old nuisance while you find Mr. Brew. Bring the sergeant, as well."

***

HMS *Forward* was a hundred-foot gunboat armed with twin howitzers and a thirty-two-pound cannon. With black smoke and occasional sheets of flame emerging from its spindly funnel, the ship stirred every heart as it steamed out of New Westminster at its maximum speed of five knots. Past the crowds of flag-waving citizens it went, past the brass band, past the breakwaters, heading for Waddy Flats with an expeditionary force.

A gang of lusty men (unable, alas, to join the expedition themselves because of flat feet, doubtful bladders, weak knees, and the like) peopled the banks of the Fraser River, waving, and wishing to God that they didn't have flat feet, and so on, otherwise they'd be aboard the *Forward* too, bedamn! Their faint cries carried across the water and touched the captain's heart. "Rout those devils!" cried the would-be volunteers. "Teach them varmints a lesson!"

Strong winds and a chilling spray thrown up by the ship's paddles soon drove most people off the deck. The *Forward*'s commander, Lieutenant the Honourable Horace Douglas Lascelles, RN, stood behind the helmsman on the bridge with Chartres Brew, listening to the sounds of drunken riot issuing from the ship's main saloon.

Lascelles said stiffly, "I trust that your accommodations are satisfactory, Mr. Brew?"

"Perfectly," Brew said, thinking of the tiny, cockroach-infested cabin that he was having to share with Alfred Waddington, who had insisted on joining the expedition.

"Happy with that drunken rabble down there in my saloon, are you?"

"I'd be happier if I had command over proper British soldiers, or regular policemen. As it is, I have to make do with volunteers," Brew was saying, when the saloon door burst open and a crowd of buffalo hunters, settlers, trappers and gold miners appeared on deck.

"Americans, I understand?"

"Yes. They're tough enough, mind you, there are no shrinking violets among that lot. As soon as they've consumed all the liquor they managed to smuggle on board, I'll establish proper order and discipline."

"I'll establish discipline now, if you want," Lascelles said. "Give me the word. My marines will teach them how to behave."

"Let's overlook it for now, eh? It's just high jinks and the party will soon be over. They'll settle down soon enough."

"They'd better," Lascelles said. "This is a ship of the Royal Navy, not a public house."

The volunteers had shuffled aboard with their tracking-dogs and backpacks and whisky bottles, five parts drunk for the most part, and every man of them hated authority. Their common motto regarding Indians was simple: Hang Indians first, then call a jury and find guilty or not guilty.

When the *Forward* stopped in Nanaimo twelve hours later to fill her coal bunkers, Brew's volunteers overpowered the deck watch and swarmed down the gangplank en masse. Roaring into the town's pubs to carouse and refill their canteens with whisky, the buffalo hunters were soon engaged in drunken fights with a band of peaceable Indians camping along the shore. Led by Brew and Lascelles, the ship's marines sorted things out with a baton charge. Six Indians were already laid out and groaning with broken bones. Brew sent three volunteers back to New Westminster in leg irons and reminded the others that, as legally sworn constables, they were subject to military discipline. The *Forward* steamed out of Nanaimo with twenty-eight volunteers.

As the Coast Mountains drew closer, Brew bemoaned his inability to deputize a few marines, but this was expressly forbidden by Lord Gilford, commander of the North Pacific naval squadron.

Lascelles was occupied by his own thoughts. As an experienced officer, he knew better than to question higher authority. Nevertheless, he knew that deep political games were afoot. Governor Kennedy had shuffled responsibility for Waddy Flats onto Governor Seymour. Seymour, in turn, had done everything possible to get the Admiralty involved, but Lord Gilford viewed the massacre as a private dispute between Alfred Waddington and the Chilcotins. Under duress, Gilford had reluctantly provided this tiny old tub as a transport ship. Accommodating the ship's normal complement of forty officers and men was bad enough; now, besides the noisy volunteers, a dozen mules and six dogs were crammed on board, along with supplies and weapons. Not to mention that cantankerous old busybody, Alfred Waddington. Well, thought Lascelles, it wasn't his worry, thank God. In another year, with luck, the Admiralty would post him to the Mediterranean; after that, everybody on this godforsaken frontier wilderness could go hang. He didn't envy Brew though. Waddington and these smelly volunteers would keep him on his toes.

Lascelles looked to his own immediate business. There were no buoys or channel markers in these waters; he was using charts unimproved since Captain George Vancouver had made them, seventy years earlier. HMS *Forward* steamed past sheltered coves, where smoke rose from longhouses and barking dogs marked their passing. Sometimes, tiny figures appeared on beaches, to shout and wave at the giant Fire Canoe. Lascelles conned his slow ship across the mouth of Desolation Sound, and with lookouts posted on the bow and in the masts, set a course for the channel between Cortes Island and Redonda.

CHAPTER TWENTY

DECKER COLLECTED A dozen eggs from the chicken roosts and delivered six of them to Isabel's cabin. He had grown used to seeing her in overalls and he smiled to see her now, sitting quietly, profiled against the grey window with her hands folded neatly in her lap. He said, "My, you're looking fancy. What's the occasion?"

"You are. I'm happy to see you."

By God, she was astonishing. He put the eggs on the table, but what he wanted was to throw his arms around her again, hold her tight; he wished it was last night again.

She was glad he'd noticed her dress.

"One of these days, you'll have to tell me all about your voyage out here on the bride ship."

Isabel did not say anything. There were things she wasn't ready to tell Decker yet. About living in an orphanage, about the back cellars of a boarding house. Now, while it lasted, she had her own cabin. It was the first thing of value she had ever owned. It was funny, but she really had Trotter to thank for everything.

"Marry me," Trotter had said, bursting into her cellar room one night, when she was getting ready to go out. "Forget those fellows in The Bellowing Mule. Take me, instead."

"I can't," she said. "I don't love you."

"I'll kill myself if you don't," he said throwing her onto her bed and fumbling with his trouser buttons. "I'll be good to you, I'll treat you like a queen."

It was pathetic. Tears were running down Trotter's chubby face and he couldn't set his pole. She pushed him off and shook a finger at him.

"Do it with me, please," he wailed, waving his flabby little radish. "I'll pay you. Don't pretend you're a virgin."

"Put that thing away and be quiet," she said patiently. "Mrs. Carlisle will hear."

"I don't care! Don't you understand that I'm offering you the world?"

Isabel thought, But only if I give you my life.

She'd rather be dead and buried and forgotten than do it with a fellow who couldn't make her laugh.

Molly Moggs called her a fool. "Marry him," she said. "As Mrs. Trotter, you'll want for nothing."

"He's a joke, not a man."

"Who cares? Just think, dearie, he's got a job in Canada, you'll be a pioneer."

The evocation of distance and space did it: Isabel hated England. No, that wasn't right: she loved England, the idea and the beauty of England. She just didn't want to live there.

Trotter went off to Canada, still promising her the world. She thought, He's weak, but maybe he will send for me. Then his letter came, and with it a ticket to Fort Victoria.

She came out of her memories and heard Decker say, "I'm going."

"You don't have to go yet," Isabel said. "Stay a while."

He bent and kissed her.

"Will you come again tonight?"

Nodding, smiling, Decker went home in the pouring rain.

"You girls, git!" he said cheerfully, shooing chickens off the front porch and going into his house. "Go spread your lime on my spud patch, where it'll do some good. Shake a leg, Bush," he went on, rattling the stove with a poker.

Bushrat glared at him from under his blankets. "Sounds like a gulley washer outside."

"It is a gulley washer."

Scratching his crotch, Bushrat rolled out of bed in his longjohns and reached underneath for his carved leather riding boots.

Decker stood listening to the hiss of wind and water. "I'm hungry," he said. "What's for breakfast besides eggs?"

"You know I can't think with a full bladder," Bushrat said, opening the door and admitting a blast of damp air when he went outside. "You been lyin' about the weather, boss. Hit ain't no gulley washer," he said, coming back in with wet grey hairs plastered down his face. "Hit's a barn floater."

Decker felt that all was right with the world and smiled.

"Somebody took a lantern out of this house last night," Bushrat said darkly, "and forgot to bring it back."

"Thanks for reminding me," Decker said amiably. "I better stroll on out to Isabel's, later, pick it up from where I left it. That's if I have your permission."

It was dark in the house. Bushrat took a lamp down from the shelf and lifted off the glass chimney to wash it at the sink. When the chimney was clean he trimmed the lamp wick with a pair of scissors and lit it with sliver of cedar ignited at the woodstove.

"I could get used to this life," Decker said.

"We done good, didn't we?" Bushrat said, grinning and making a noise with his pans while he decided what to scorch for breakfast.

A moth came out of a corner and flew at the lamp's hot chimney again and again, until it dropped to the ground and ran in circles, flapping its useless wings. Bushrat stretched a foot out and mashed it beneath his heel. "You was out early."

"I was out all night."

"Just watch your ass, is all I say."

"Thanks."

"That girl can ruin your life, and I ain't telling you nothin' you don't know."

"A wise man told me that moths do their navigating by the moon," Decker said, looking at the moth. "Every bright lamp is a little moon, to them. They're so set on the idea of reaching it they lose sight of everything else." Decker grinned. "There's a heavy moral there, if only I was smart enough to figure it out."

Bushrat thought, Yeah, well, I can figure it out easy. I just hope that little gal don't burn you up too, boss, like one of them there moths.

CHAPTER TWENTY-ONE

HENDERSON WAS HAVING a nightmare, until he opened his eyes and saw the inside of his cabin. He lay in his blankets, feeling warm and gradually relaxing as his night terrors subsided. His left ear began to itch. Yawning, he reached up to scratch it, and discovered to his horror that his ear was gone. Howling, scratching a phantom itch that had been sent by God to punish him for his sins, Henderson came frantically awake. He had not been dreaming after all. He had been remembering. Remembering a terrible freezing journey to a pit-house, where he had found Bushrat Wright and Decker.

Decker! He hated Decker worse than this accursed itch. Decker had told the whole world what he had done to the Indian girl. Never mind that he had been driven to carnal excess by a devil. Never mind that he had truly repented for forcing himself on her against her will. Never mind that he went down on his knees every night to beg God's forgiveness for his sins. What more could he do? What was done was done. It could not be undone, except by God. Henderson knew that suffering could bring forgiveness. He would even be reborn as Christ's emissary — especially, if Isabel would befriend him. She was so lovely, so chaste, so perfect. But why, why did she keep out of his way? Maybe she knew about his secret sin! The thought filled him with terror. Isabel knew! Why else did she treat him like dirt? He fell to his knees with his hands together and the answer came from God. She treated him like dirt because Decker had told her everything. Now she hated him. Why? Because she was a woman! The devil was inside all women. Isabel was the devil!

Isabel, sewing by her window, saw Henderson come out of his shack barefoot and naked, and rush towards her. She cross-barred her door on the inside, just in time, as he hammered on it with his fists, demanding she return his table and chairs this minute. Calling her a painted harlot, he fled down the hill and vanished into the bush. Thorns tore at his flesh as he plunged through a ravine. He came up tight against a large cylindrical rock so perfectly shaped that it might have been carved by man. Should he go this way, or that? Uphill? Downhill? Henderson fell to his knees among the thorns, and God spoke to him in a very clear voice. Destiny was revealed. He was to go to Victoria. In Victoria, he would become an undertaker. He would wear black silk hats. In the evenings he would make beautiful coffins out of exotic woods.

When Isabel saw Henderson return to his cabin, she went over to Decker's house, but the lawmen were in the corral, saddling their horses for a trip along Decker's fences. Henderson re-emerged from his cabin and went scuttling across the flats and into the trees.

"Poor silly creature," Isabel said to herself, as the naked man's head emerged above some bushes behind the barn.

Decker also noticed. He shook his head. Henderson was up to his old tricks. First, he'd watch Old Tsulas through cracks in the wall of the barn. Then he'd flit across to Isabel's cabin and try to get a peek at her. "What next?" he said to Bushrat. "Henderson's ready to crack completely, in my opinion."

"He ain't dangerous, though. Too dern wishy-washy."

"I'm not so sure. I don't like leaving Isabel alone, with him acting this way."

Bushrat was preoccupied by something else. "I need to get my eyes checked," he said, and pointed. Old Tsulas had come out of the barn with a visitor, and seemed agitated.

"What's wrong with your eyes? You've got eyes like a hawk."

"I must be seeing things, then. If I didn't know better, I'd say that was Tahpitt over there."

Decker didn't know Tahpitt, but he knew what Tahpitt stood for. "Let's get back to the house," he said. "Something's wrong."

Isabel was standing on Decker's porch when they got there. She said, "We need to talk about Henderson. And who's that with Old Tsulas?"

"Hit's Tahpitt," Bushrat replied, puzzled. "Only, Tahpitt's supposed to be with Klatsassan."

Old Tsulas and Tahpitt were waving their arms and shouting at each other.

Decker and Bushrat were already carrying holstered revolvers. Decker grabbed a rifle from his gun cabinet and said, "Bush! Get your Winchester and come with me. Isabel, please stay here in my house."

When the lawmen were halfway to the barn, there was an explosion. The Highlander was staggering. Falling slowly, the bull sank to his knees. Puzzled, shaking his head, he toppled and buried one horn into the earth. With a final bellow of outrage and defiance, the Highlander died.

Henderson rushed out of the trees, wailing, and there was a second explosion. Henderson threw his arms wide, folded at the waist, and collapsed.

There were several more shots. Old Tsulas collapsed with blood pouring from his mouth.

Men with war-striped faces came running out of the woods. Screaming, waving muskets and battle axes, they advanced across the flats. Ten warriors closed in on the barn; an equal number were positioned for an attack on the house.

Decker and Bushrat fell to their knees behind the Highlander and emptied their Winchesters. A few Indians fell and all the others swerved back behind the barn. Bullets and arrows were flying all around as the lawmen retreated to the house. Bushrat missed his footing and sprawled headlong, striking his head against a rock with sickening force. Decker grabbed his arm and dragged him up across the porch and inside. Isabel had taken a shotgun out of the cabinet and was trying to load it when Decker barred the door. He took the gun off her and said calmly, "Dump a bucket of water over Bushy's head and try to bring him around."

Decker rested his shotgun on the windowsill. Taking careful aim, he fired both barrels and reloaded the Winchester while the warriors fell back to regroup. Decker was giving Isabel a crash course in weapons-loading when Bushrat opened his eyes.

"They'll come again," Decker said. "We've got to get the hell out of here, only Bushrat's not fit to travel."

"That's what you think," Bushrat grumbled.

"Are you ready to ride?"

"Where? How?" Bushrat said. "They got us pinned."

"They're shot up and now they've lost the advantage of surprise as well. They're carrying their injured back into the trees and they'll be licking their wounds for a bit," said Decker, thinking furiously. "Isabel!" he said, speaking over his shoulder as he manned the window, "Grab a side of bacon, cans of beans, coffee, anything edible. Stick it all in a bag. And round up some blankets."

"Box matches too," Bushrat added with a groan. "Wrap 'em in oilskins and we'll stick 'em in our pockets."

"Where can we go?" Isabel said. "They're everywhere."

"We'll try and make it along the beach trail, towards MacCormack's old place. Wherever there's the least of 'em," said Decker. "The horses are already saddled and we'll ride like hell."

The panicked horses were stamping in the corral as Isabel and the lawmen ran across, firing at anything that moved. Bushrat mounted the bay. Decker leapt on the chestnut and lifted Isabel up behind his saddle. They were whipping the horses for MacCormack's, until they saw Indians massed directly ahead. Swerving, they swung away and with nothing else for it galloped north along the wagon road, muskets blazing away behind them.

CHAPTER TWENTY-TWO

Hms *FORWARD* STEAMED into Waddy Flats in the rain with shaggy volunteers drooping over every railing. Sick from too much whisky, they were vomiting, pissing, cursing, and getting their buffalo coats wet when a look-out on the ship's foremast raised a hail. Lascelles put a telescope to his eye. Indians were running out of houses into a clearing. A few of their ragged, unexpected musket shots sent sailors and volunteers ducking for cover, before the Indians fled into the trees and were gone.

Lascelles brought his ship up to Waddy Flats' burned-out wharf, saw its useless condition, and reversed into the channel to anchor a hundred yards offshore. Waddy Flats now appeared to be deserted.

"What do you suppose all that shooting was about?" Lascelles said, up on the bridge with Chartres Brew and Alfred Waddington.

"God knows," Brew said.

"I've a good mind to rake the town with grapeshot. Blow those houses up. My gunners need the practice."

"Don't you go raking my town with your guns, not unless you have enough money to replace them," Waddington remarked sourly, as Sergeant Herrold, Brew's second-in-command, climbed out of the ship's forward hold and headed for the bridge.

Lascelles gazed stonily at Waddington, turned his back on him and, taking Brew's elbow, led him underneath a canvas awning. "The stories we heard about Indians burning the town are all true, obviously," Lascelles said. "There's not much to blow up, come to think of it."

Wind was driving the rain horizontally. Waddington followed them under the awning but was soon drenched below the waist. Herrold arrived on the bridge and said, "Bad news, I'm afraid sir. I can't find all our tents. We ordered four for the men, and a big 'un for the mess, but there's only two little ones aboard."

"Try looking for the rest in the after hold," Brew said.

"I've already done it, sir."

"Very good, Herrold. Carry on."

Herrold marched off.

"Damn! That's a bad start," Waddington said. "Where the devil am I to billet my volunteers, tonight?"

Brew, furious at Waddington's casual assumption of command, said stiffly. "I'll have you remember, Waddington, that I'm in charge of this expedition, not you."

Waddington marched off the bridge in a huff.

"All the same," Lascelles murmured, "somebody ought to have checked your supplies before you left home."

Lascelles tried to conceal his amusement. Brew's expedition had been organized too quickly and mixups were to be expected. As for Waddington and the volunteers, Lascelles thought they were an undisciplined rabble; unlike Brew and Herrold, they didn't appear to be the kind of valiants to follow the Queen's standard unflinchingly into the cannon's mouth. And he wouldn't allow them to spend one unnecessary hour aboard his ship. The marines were likely to rise in a body, and chuck them all overboard. Latent bad feeling between British sailors and American buffalo hunters had come to a head after the trouble in Nanaimo. Tempers flared. A dust-up broke out when a hunter insulted Queen Victoria, and in the ensuing riot, the hunters gave as good as they got.

"I tell you frankly, Lascelles, I'm not sure this scheme can work," Brew said. "Waddington's an impossible nuisance and I don't like the look of things. It might be best to have a quick reconnaissance, then return to New Westminster and re-deploy with trained fighting men."

"I don't quite follow your logic, old chap. Go back tomorrow with your tail between your legs, you mean?" Lascelles purred indolently. "I thought you'd undertaken to do a job on a few Indian chaps, first."

"I beg your pardon?"

"My dear fellow. Why, tell me why you didn't send Waddington back to New Westminster in irons with the rest of those malcontents? That's what I'd have done."

Furious and red faced, Brew held his tongue.

As for Lascelles, he was thinking that Brew was a good sort with a fine record, but perhaps he lacked imagination, or some vital ingredient of character? He looked smart enough, mind you, quite a popinjay in that black uniform. But imagine, coming up here without checking to see that his supplies had been properly loaded!

Inwardly fuming, Brew had himself rowed ashore in one of the *Forward*'s longboats, which grounded on a mudbank ten feet offshore. Wading to the beach took the polish off Brew's topboots and rain was soon taking the starch out of his hatbrim. He had never seen such rain. Some of his ragtag volunteers were sitting on the beach, too hung over and disorganized to think for themselves. Others lugged gear ashore off longboats. Herrold and four courageous muleskinners were floundering about in viscous, grey, clam-beach silt, trying to catch their pack animals. Half a dozen cougar hounds barked and snuffled at deer scent along the shore.

One of Brew's men came up. Touching a finger to his cap he said, "Is this all there is to Waddy Flats? Just a few little cabins?"

"Right," Brew said. "It's a lot worse than I'd expected. And since those Indians ran off, there doesn't seem to be a soul about."

"It's mighty wet. Can't we stay on the ship, until we're ready to march?"

"Not practical," Brew replied tersely, and the man started to move away.

"Just a minute," said Brew. "What's your name?'

"Keogh, sir."

"Let me see your hands."

Grinning, Keogh held both of his hands up for inspection.

"Do you always keep your hands clean?"

"Generally."

"I need a cook. Somebody who understands basic hygiene."

"Suits me," Keogh said. "I'll want a couple of swampers, to peel the spuds and wash pans."

"Talk to Sergeant Herrold, he'll fix you up. Think you can manage tonight's dinner?"

"If I find a place out of the wet I'll give it a damn good try."

"Capital! You'll find our provisions in those wicker baskets over there." Looking towards Decker's barn Brew added, "That barn might serve as your cook-house for tonight."

Keogh marched off to have a look.

Brew looked about him. Waddington had gone huffing and puffing up the hill, to inspect the Slough. Buffalo hunters were lurching around all over.

Lascelles' steward came over and said, "Captain's compliments, sir. He'd be honoured if you could join him in his cabin, after supper."

The invitation took Brew by surprise. "Fine," he said after a pause. "My thanks to the captain. I'll be there as soon as my men are settled."

There was a loud cry. Brew reached for the revolver at his hip and started running. Keogh had found two dead men near the barn. The first was an old Indian, in a steeple hat and a dog-hair cloak. The other was a naked white man, about twenty-five. Brew had seen plenty of dead men during his work with the Irish Famine Board, in Dublin, and to his practised eye, the corpses had been lying in the mud for a couple of days.

This grim discovery focussed attentions sharply. Herrold organised a burial party. Brew had prepared a duty roster and now he posted a perimeter guard. By the time the unnamed corpses had been buried, side by side, and Brew had read the Church of England burial service over their graves, Waddington, distraught, was returning from the Slough.

"Dreadful news, Brew," Waddington gasped, short-winded from hurrying. "They've burned down my house, my sheds, everything. There's just one little bit of a turret left, that's all. What are we to do?"

"Do what you please," Brew said curtly. "I'm not here for your benefit."

Waddington's mouth dropped open and he stared in silence as Brew stalked off.

Keogh cooked dinner. The men didn't grumble, even though the salt-beef hadn't been rinsed enough and was slightly underdone. Brew ate with his men. With a raging thirst caused by beef-brine, he congratulated Keogh on an excellent job of work. The sentries were alert when he checked them, before going over to the *Forward* in the duty longboat.

Lascelles' steward showed Brew into the captain's stateroom.

"How would a spot of brandy do you?" Lascelles enquired politely. "Some cheese and biscuits?"

"Obliged," returned Brew, rather formally. He stood about with his hands in his pockets, frowning at the mahogany wainscotting until the steward reappeared with the refreshments on a silver tray.

"Well, down the hatch, old boy," Lascelles murmured, after pouring drinks and handing a glass to his guest.

Brew sniffed, raised his glass, and muttered his thanks in a very low voice.

"I say, old chap. You didn't take it amiss, what I said earlier, about the tents and so on?"

"I haven't given it a moment's thought," Brew lied.

"I took a poke about the ship's holds myself, just in case your feller missed 'em, but they're not aboard. I give you my solemn oath."

"C'est la vie," Brew said stiffly. "Can't be helped."

"No, it can't, but my sailmaker's got a few odd bits of canvas to spare, if that's any use to you."

"That's very decent, Lascelles."

"Not at all, have a biscuit. Try some of that cheddar," Lascelles said, sinking down onto a leather seatlocker. "Take the weight off your paws."

Brew sat down and tasted the brandy again. After a silence he said, "Not bad, this. I haven't had better cognac since I was in London."

"When were you last in London?"

"Ten years ago."

"You won't know the place since they strung those gaslamps along the embankment."

"Gaslamps, along the embankment?"

"Amazing things they are. Read a paper at midnight."

Brew discovered to his surprise that his glass was empty. Over a refill, he told Lascelles about Dublin. Lascelles told Brew about his hopes for a promotion and transfer to the Mediterranean squadron. Over a second decanter of brandy, more cheese and biscuits, and an apple, the two swore undying friendship.

"Good Lord!" Lascelles said, glancing through a porthole. "Miracles never cease. I do believe it's stopped raining. Let's toddle up on deck."

Lascelles and Brew carried their brandies and cigars up to the bridge, and were treated to a remarkable sight.

Three Indians were coming up the inlet in the dark, on four twenty-foot canoes lashed together with poles. They passed by less than fifty feet away, and Lascelles and Brew saw that the Indians had built a platform three feet above their canoes to carry a tepee. As they dragged their strange houseboat onto the beach, Brew said, "That's funny. There's a European fellow with them, a great, black-bearded brute."

"So there is," said Lascelles, with a gentle burp. "I'll swear that fellow is Randolph Schnurr. He used to be one of my ratings. When his enlistment expired, he took his discharge in Victoria, instead of England. Had a deuced bad character, as I recall. Sold one of my compasses to a ship chandler in Victoria, and squandered the money on liquor."

"Not squandered, old chap. Well spent, I'd say," Brew remarked jovially, until he noticed Lascelles' long face and added, "I imagine it cost the fellow dearly."

"Twenty of the best. He'll hate my bosun's rope-end and carry its scars to his deathbed."

"Well, goodnight, old chap," said Brew.

"Good night, old bean. I'll see you in ten days or so, will I?"

"Barring acts of God and Waddington's revenge," chortled Brew, as he was assisted into the duty longboat, and rowed ashore to rejoin his men.

CHAPTER TWENTY-THREE

An HOUR BEFORE dawn, wolves chased a deer along the shores of Waddy Flats and the expedition's half-wild tracking dogs went mad. With them barking and jumping at the ends of their tethers, the town woke up.

Keogh and two helpers cooked porridge and eggs. Groaning, cursing the dogs, the buffalo hunters emerged from the mudholes or tents or cabins where they had spent the night. A few volunteers stayed in their blankets too long. When they showed up at the grub tent late, Keogh said "Sorry lads, I'm not running a cafe. You weren't in my serving line until fifteen minutes after the gong went, so you're out of luck. Get up when the others do next time or you'll go without again."

There was some grumbling, but with Sergeant Herrold standing near, it died down and the latecomers dispersed. By nine in the morning, tents had been struck, loads were apportioned to the mules, and the expedition was ready to march.

Herrold assembled the troops and Brew climbed up on a stump to address them. "Men," he said, "this is the second speech you've heard from me. I made my first in New Westminster, and by the time I'd finished speaking, a few would-be volunteers dropped out. Well, it's too late to quit now. We sink or we swim together. This is going to be a weary and hazardous undertaking."

"I'll pay fifty gold guineas to the man who brings me the chaps who burned down my house!" Waddington shouted. "Fifty English guineas, dead or alive."

Brew reacted savagely. "Nobody will interrupt me again!" he barked. "If anybody else wants to speak, he'd better raise his hand first, and get my permission, savvy? Another bloody word from Mr.

bloody Waddington, and I'll have him carried aboard the *Forward* in irons, or my name isn't Chartres Brew."

Waddington ground his teeth, opened his mouth, thought better of it, and kept silent.

"We've found two dead men already," Brew said. "There'll be more casualties most likely, before we're done with this business. We've got rough country ahead, and hostile Indians, so pay attention," Brew waited for men to stop shuffling and coughing, and added. "Every man has his own weapon, and is responsible for keeping his powder and his personal gear dry. My advice is, look after your feet, keep your boots well greased. If you want to sleep comfortably at night, carry your own bedroll the whole way, and don't blame anybody else if you lose it."

Brew's gaze swung back and forth across the crowd as he assessed whether his words were being heeded. With a bit more emphasis he said, "You have all been sworn as constables and are subject to military discipline. As your commander, I have turned a blind eye to a few things, but from now on there will be no more slacking. I will not tolerate any rough-housing in camp. I will not tolerate insubordination. If any man is discovered asleep when he's supposed to be on parade, he will be punished. Everybody will treat me, Sergeant Herrold, and our cook, Mr. Keogh, with respect. You will obey Mr. Keogh's rules around the grub shack. Apart from the treats that you bring along in your own packs for your own consumption, your rations will be plain. If we run out of food and there are no hunters among us, rations may run short." Brew paused again, and added forcefully, "You've already heard my views about whisky..."

There was some low chuckling and Brew raised his hand. "Alright, I know that there's still a bit of liquor left in the odd backpack, here and there. Fine. I'm talking to men, not boys. Still, if any man here endangers the rest of us by drunken foolishness after we leave this camp, I'll shoot him with this gun." Brew touched the revolver at his hip. He looked around and said, "Any questions?"

There were no questions.

When Brew finished counting heads, he led the way out of town and up to the wagon road. Buffalo hunters and mules trailed in a long, straggling line behind. The sky grew narrower as they ascended from tidewater and entered the trees.

Big Smuts, an Australian, was the expedition's dog-handler. His six snarling, howling, half-wild hounds had been brought along to sniff out Indians, and they had picked up a good scent from around Decker's house. For the time being, distracted by wolf and bear scat, all except the lead dog — who stayed close to Smuts — ranged cease-lessly up and down the hillsides.

Brew, marching in front, turned around and a buffalo hunter caught his eye.

"Remember me, Mr. Brew? It's Harker."

"Sorry, Harker. I can't say I do."

"I was one of them fought alongside you at Snider's War on the Fraser, when them Injuns jumped our claims. I've grown a beard since them days, but I still got seven notches on old Betsy here," Harker said, grinning as he touched the stock of his rifle. "A notch for every Injun I put paid to."

"That was a bloody business, right enough. I hope we don't have a repeat of it."

"Wouldn't bother me none. Only good Injun's a dead Injun, and that goes for most of us."

Brew smiled thinly, and stepped off the trail to let Harker and others pass. He was finding out that hardly a man in the expeditionary outfit knew why normally friendly Indians had attacked Waddington's road-builders. What's more, they didn't want to know. As far as they were concerned, Injuns had killed white men, and an-eye-for-an-eye revenge was to be meted out. Well, he thought, a few days of roughing-it up the Homathko might dampen their warlike ardour. But that remained to be seen. The uncouth buffalo hunters were tough and, it seemed, immune to discomfort, pain, and cold. Many had hiked the Cariboo trails and carried their backpacks as if they were full of feathers. All except Waddington. Herrold reported that he was struggling, far behind the rest of the column.

"Experience might chasten his spirit, which is all to the good," Brew said. "I suppose it seemed like a jolly idea, back in New Westminster, for him to join us on an ocean voyage, settle the Chilcotins hash, and return to a hero's welcome."

Another hour's march up the gradually rising wagon road settled the ill-tempered men down, and they nursed all their energy for walking. The rain never stopped, and it was cold when they reached the site of the first massacre. Before Big Smuts could stop them, his cougar dogs were raking up human remains: red-flannel shirts, blue pants and boots. Smuts went after his dogs with a whip and got them tethered to a tree before they gnawed too many bones.

Brew helped to collect human skulls and other grisly reminders of the massacre, and shovel them into a common grave. He christened the site Murderers' Bar, and was reading his second burial service in as many days, when Alfred Waddington straggled in, exhausted.

Farther along, an immense slide had come down a mountain, creating a barrier high enough to bury trees. With mules and men floundering behind, Brew led the volunteers across the banked mud and snow to a decent campsite a mile on. Keogh's grub tent went up quickly and his cooking fire was the first one to be lit. Brew established a duty roster, assigned guards to watch the perimeter, and settled his troop in for the night.

Twenty separate fires were glowing in the darkness when Brew and Herrold went through the camp. Smuts, smoking a big, curving, yellow pipe, nodded as they went by. His cougar dogs, quiet for once, lay all around with their furry muzzles between their forepaws, listening to their wolf cousins out in the hills.

Brew stopped at Waddington's fire and warmed his hands, saying, "You're too old for this kind of thing."

"We'll see about that."

"How far is it from here to the crossing-keeper's house?"

"Another four hours or so. This is the first time I've had to walk it. In the past I rode."

"That house is as far as you are going to go. I won't have you delaying the march," Brew said firmly. "You can stay there and wait for us until we return, or you can go back to Waddy Flats by yourself."

"I don't accept your authority."

"Did you hear what he said, Herrold?"

"Yes sir."

"You are my witness. You may have to testify that on the seventh of May, 1864, Mr. Waddington received due notice. If he doesn't do exactly what I tell him to do, I'll have him shot, for treason."

"You wouldn't dare."

"Think so, Waddington? Try me."

At daybreak there was a loud rumbling, high up on the mountains ahead. Another enormous avalanche came thundering down and pine trees were swept along like match sticks. For several minutes, the earth trembled as vast quantities of snow and rock went crashing down into a valley. When the avalanche was finished, heat from the friction of colossal masses rubbing and grinding against each other created clouds of steam, which rose in the frigid air, condensed, and drifted onto the higher ground as snow.

Before the expedition got moving, two black bears, standing upright on the banks of the Homathko, were chased into the pines by Smuts' dogs. Out of sight in a ravine, crows were fighting over what was left of Davy Lemman.

With a final look at the distant mountains, one of which he had named after himself, Waddington, a broken man holding back tears, turned his back on the expeditionary force and started downhill for Waddy Flats alone.

CHAPTER TWENTY-FOUR

SCHNURR HAD WALKED the beach and now he was rummaging through MacCormack's old cabin. A few hundred yards away, lifeboats from HMS *Forward* dotted the harbour, and sailors with grappling irons were trying to snag the body of a rating who had fallen overboard, drunk, and was presumed drowned. In the meantime, Schnurr had absented himself in case Lieutenant Lascelles found out where that rating got his liquor from, and created a bother.

Schnurr found a pair of MacCormack's Sheffield-made scissors and shoved them into the pocket of his greatcoat — it was, after all, only prudent to collect MacCormack's things before somebody else beat him to it. Waste not, want not. Such homilies, Schnurr reflected, had stood him in good stead over the years. A stitch in time, et cetera. He was bundling up scraps of clothing when muffled cries interrupted his thoughts. Ah! Sailors had found the drunkard. Whisky and women had been the ruin of many a poor sailorman. Schnurr hefted a heavy chair. Could he carry that chair, plus the bundled clothing, back to his tepee at one go?

He was thinking, Young men and booze. Young men and sex. Booze booze booze. Sex sex sex. Booze and sex were all they ever thought about. And that ship over there was full of randy young drunkards. What a pity Isabel wasn't still here! With her looks, her dash, she was a born whore. She could have made a fortune last night, turning tricks while he supplied the sailors with whisky! He, Schnurr, would have been happy to cooperate with Isabel on such a venture, to bring fellows back and forth, and so on, whatever might be required, because busy whores needed a fellow to run errands, throw people out of the house if they got too boisterous, and look after such delicate matters as collecting the tariffs.

The trouble was, thought Schnurr, you never knew where you were with Isabel. In the old days, before the town burned, she'd had quite a reputation. Lots of fellows besides One-Ear Brown had tried to loosen her knickers, but nobody had, as far as he knew. But that didn't mean that she couldn't be made a whore. With One-Ear gone, without a husband, what else was she fit for? There was a trick to making whores, and the trick was to get them drunk. Booze, that was the ticket.

Sighing, Schnurr looked across the way at his little house and business. A floating tepee stocked with whisky, that's all it was, standing there on the mudflats. Well, as a house it wasn't much, but it was a start. Klymtedza, his Nuxalt wife, had died a violent death when the Indians burned the town (they were angry at her, he supposed, for having a white husband). He had a new wife now: a young Euclataw who spoke a bit of English. Tassie. Little Tassie. Tassie was helping him to start afresh. She and her cousins would him help to build a new lodging house here. Yes, a fellow had to begin somewhere, and one of these days that same lodging house might grow into a proper hotel. A hotel full of whores. And with One-Ear Brown out of the way, what was to stop a resourceful fellow from entering the bootleg trade in earnest? Nothing. Selling a few bottles of whisky to sailors was alright, but selling barrels of rotgut to Indians was a speedier way to riches!

There! Sailors were lifting a dripping corpse onto the deck of their ship.

***

Two days out of Waddy Flats, Decker, Bushrat and Isabel had passed the end of Waddington's road and were following Indian trails north through trees and across rockfields. Staring at the wild country, Isabel was glad to have Decker by her side. "Why are we going on?" she said. "There's no road at all now."

"The Palmer Trail is three or four days ahead. If we find it, we have to decide whether to head west, to Bella Coola and the coast, or east, to the Fraser River. Either way, we'll be in Chilcotin country for weeks."

With Decker on foot leading the chestnut and Isabel riding it, they came out of trees. There was no cloud and the sun was hot, but wind was lifting the hats off their heads when they started down a ridge. To the left, the Franklin Glacier filled a valley ten miles wide, from the mountaintops until it broke off at the edge of the Homathko in a perpendicular side of blue ice crested over with glistening white.

Four Stone sheep, their curving horns three feet across, danced across a high ledge as Decker followed the almost invisible trail down to the river again and upstream, where they crossed through a brake of pines. Overhead, trees thinned against the blue. The rocky terrain became too steep and broken for riding. They walked for hours, half dragging their horses and groggy with fatigue. The day grew steadily warmer and Bushrat, staggering along with his mouth open, was limping badly when Decker stopped on a height above the river, and looked back. There was no sign of pursuers. He had seen none since they left Waddy Flats.

Bushrat dropped the bay's reins. Leaning forward with his feet apart, clutching his knees and gasping, he raised his head and met Decker's eye. Bushrat grinned and wheezed jauntily, "What'sa matter, boss? Trail too tough you had to call it quits?"

"It sure is. If it doesn't improve soon, these horses aren't going to make it."

"This ain't nothin'," Bushrat boasted unconvincingly. "I feel like a champion, meself. Only complaints I got is, the trail's too smooth, the days is too short, and the grub we been eatin' is too rich and fillin'."

Nevertheless, Bushrat was content to sit and watch while Decker and Isabel staked the horses, lit a fire, and made tea and bannock. Two full hours passed before Decker resumed the march along deer trails and avalanche scars, hoping to travel another two or three miles before nightfall. The day wore on and grew even warmer until they reached a stand of magnificent cedar, hemlock, and Douglas firs. Some of the cedars were fifteen feet across at the butt. It was darker beneath the trees. The trail, running parallel with the river, was wide and well-trodden here. Cedars had been blazed where women had stripped bark for materials to make baskets and cloaks. The woods were completely silent as they went up a gentle rise and paused above a fifty-yard-wide clearing with two man-made hummocks in the middle of it. Thin puffs of smoke were rising from a hole in one of the hummocks and rolling up the trunks of three-hundred-foot firs. Decker pointed his rifle into the smoke hole, and shouted a few words in English. There was no reply. He fired two bullets into the roof.

"I'll take a look," Decker said, as the reverberations died away.

The pit-house was like the one near the upper camp, but smaller, only twelve feet across and six feet deep. Decker descended a notched log and inside, to his surprise, saw a small frightened dog, and then a woman, sitting on a sleeping platform. She was very old and shrivelled, her eyes blue-white and opaque from cataracts. Her face was the colour of mahogany and her hair was in stringy black locks matted with dirt and grease. When Bushrat came in and she got over her fright at almost being shot, she seemed pleased by the company. Chattering sociably, Bushrat took a chunk of tobacco from his pocket and gave it to her.

Delighted by both Bushrat's conversation and the tobacco, the old woman took a wooden dish off a shelf. Evidently the dish wasn't clean enough. She spat on it several times, wiped it with her hair, and filled it with the contents of a bentwood box. The smell, of fermented entrails, was too ripe for Decker's liking. She tasted a mouthful, smacked her lips, and offered him the dish. Grinning, he passed it to Bushrat, who put it down surreptitiously for her dog.

"She's mother to Cusshen The Scarface," Bushrat said after another jolly conversation. "She's been living here with two young girls and a couple of old men."

"Where are they now?"

"Either she don't know, or she ain't sayin'. Every other Chilcotin in the area has thrown in with Klatsassan, and is headed for Manning's ranch."

"God help Manning."

"Now what?" Bushrat asked.

"Do you want to leave her some bacon and a handful of tea leaves?"

"Sure."

"All right. We shouldn't linger though. Better move on out of these trees into open country."

A day short of the Palmer Trail, Decker was on guard at midnight. He raised his head and saw Cassiopeia and Polaris and the Ursas. With great Arcturus twinkling high above, Isabel, his lover, came out of her blankets and he watched without speaking as she glided by him in her nightclothes and stood for a moment in bare feet at the edge of a reed-dotted pond. Her clothing fell away to reveal another whiteness before she walked into the lake, her long legs so straight and beautiful, and lowered herself completely into the water and smiled at him. Not smiling he undressed and went across into the same water that lapped and bathed her body. With her blacker hair streaming long behind her head in black water they swam together and still without speaking went up through the reeds of the far bank together holding hands together and they lay together shivering and naked in the darkness with bats and nightbirds and the northern lights all about and they knew nothing about it.

CHAPTER TWENTY-FIVE

Chartres brew, tramping north along the wagon road, was brooding about Alfred Waddington. He was not sorry to be shut of the old man, but he was very sorry now to have humbled him so thoroughly. There ought to have been a gentler way to let him down; after all, his ruin was complete. All the same, it was becoming increasingly evident that his road was unbuildable — it would never supplant the routes already established and proven up the Fraser canyon from New Westminster, and Waddington had been deluded to think otherwise. A cry from one of the men brought Brew to reality. They had reached The Crossing.

Brew told Herrold to announce a smoke break. Men slipped off their backpacks and sat down to fill their pipes. Brew and Herrold went down to the water's edge to consider the situation where the ferry's endless rope passed through a pulley anchored to a Sampson post on the shore. Brew said, "Against my expectations, the ferry appears to be in workable condition. Unfortunately, it is banked on the opposite side of the river."

"I could ask a volunteer to fetch it."

"Of course, but it'll be damned dangerous, crossing this place."

Herrold stretched forward and touched the rope. It was actually a multi-strand steel cable, already showing signs of rust, with many protruding ends of jagged wire capable of ripping flesh. Herrold said, "I'm prepared to give it a try."

"Hand over hand?"

"Yes."

"Thanks, but you're too valuable. I won't have you risking it."

A broad-shouldered young man had been soaking his feet in the river. He came up and said, "I'll do it."

"What's your name?"

"'Arry Atkins, sir."

"Married, Atkins?" Brew said. "Tired of life? Take another look at that current and those sharp rocks downstream. Lose your grip and you'll be a goner. Strap yourself to the rope and you'll probably drown."

"I won't drown or lose my grip," Atkins said, with a widening grin. "I'm a hard-rock miner. Strong in the arm, weak in the 'ead."

"Do you know how these ferries work?"

"There's one on the Fraser, near Boston Bar," Atkins said. "I've seen the way it goes. There's a lever that you swing over."

"Alright, Atkins, you can have a go," Brew said. "But first, you'd better strip down to your shorts. And I've got a good pair of new leather gloves in my pack that you can wear. Wait a minute, I'll get them for you..."

With the buffalo hunters cheering and laying bets on the outcome of this daring escapade, Atkins grabbed the rope and waded into the river. The current soon swept him off his feet and the cable arced into a bow as Atkins lay horizontally on the surface with water breaking over his head. Halfway across, he was barely hanging on. With his eyes and ears full of water, unable to breathe properly, he kept going. Brew saw Atkins's face turning purple from lack of oxygen before his grip failed and he was swept underwater by the current. Thirty seconds passed before Brew saw him again, lying flat on his face on the opposite shore. There was a silence, followed by groans all around, until Atkins rolled over, sat up, and raised his arms. Cheering broke out anew when he moved upstream to the ferry.

The expedition overnighted at the crossing-keeper's house and the next morning, with the greatest difficulty, got their flighty mules along the chasm's boardwalks. Afterwards, they made good progress up the canyons. Men, perspiring and squinting in the sun, marched stripped to the waist, silent and bored, until they came out on a long vista and Smuts' dogs barked in unison. Two miles ahead, a band of natives was camped on a plateau. The dogs were given their heads. Baying, they rushed off. Dogs and Indians were soon lost to sight. By nightfall, with the Indians still out of sight Brew called off the chase. The men were setting up camp when five of the dogs came back. The last dog limped in on three legs with one paw dangling from a strip of fur.

The big Australian cocked his rifle, and held its muzzle to the dog's ear as it stood whimpering, trying to lick his hand. Moments passed.

"Here, I'll do that," one of the wranglers said, taking the rifle out of Smuts' hand.

***

Klatsassan's women were crying. In the battle for Waddy Flats, Decker had killed Cheddecki's number one son. Three slaves had been injured and were leaving their blood on the ground. Now The Creator had sent Fire Canoe men to pursue Klatsassan and his people.

What kind of men were these, who hunted other men with dogs? Seeing the hunting dogs for the first time, Klatsassan's people had been plunged into misery, thinking wolf packs were pursuing them, until Lowwa shot one, and the other dogs ran off with their tails between their legs.

Klatsassan and his people moved like dark ghosts across the land. Babies cried for milk as their enduring mothers bore them away from the Fire Canoe men through a landscape of evergreens. Here and there, snow mounds showed where, only two weeks ago, strong-necked elk had shouldered snow aside to reach dry grass.

Night came. A wounded warrior fell, then another, but Klatsassan did not stop. His people followed him even through the howling dark, stumbling and falling and getting up, with their feet sore and their bones aching, until mighty Klatsassan relented and allowed his people to rest.

For three hours, the Chilcotins bivouacked in a grove and ate cold salmon. Tahpitt The Magician was clever enough to make fire. By its heat, other fires were lit to warm their bodies and lighten their hearts.

Klatsassan called for Cusshen The Scarface and Chraychanuru and Lowwa and Tahpitt and Cheddecki and Squinteye and Hachis, and asked them what to do.

Cheddecki said, "Let us go to Puntzi Lake, and meet our brethren. Together, we will hunt for deer as in the olden days. At Rising Trout Moon, we will take fish out of the lake."

Chraychanuru said, "William Manning has made his ranch at Puntzi Lake. Now, our people must camp beyond William Manning's fence."

"There are other places where William Manning could have made his ranch," Tahpitt replied. "Why did he have to make a ranch on our ancient camp?"

Everybody pondered Tahpitt's words for many minutes.

"William Manning is another Trotter," Lowwa said finally. "Let us kill William Manning, and eat his cattle."

This sounded very dangerous.

Klatsassan asked Cusshen The Scarface what to do.

"Let us kill William Manning," said Cusshen The Scarface. "If dogs or wolves do not eat us, and if we do not die from the vengeance of Fire Canoe men, we will reach Puntzi Lake in three days."

Klatsassan said, "We have rested under these trees long enough. Now we will go to William Manning's ranch."

***

After dinner, Brew hiked up a crag in the twilight. Above, a goshawk with a slate-grey body and a black-topped head was perched on a stunted pine. Forests bathed in a deep velvet haze stretched all about and in the north, above a thin bank of clouds, mountain snow reflected the last golden rays of the sun. Below, expedition campfires glowed. The goshawk ruffled its white nape feathers and shook its white-tipped tail before settling down on its perch. Sighing, Brew filled his pipe. He was looking forward to seeing Lascelles again, because if he had a complaint, it was that he had nobody to talk to. These prospectors and hunters were all very well in their way, being rough, tough, and hearty fellows, but how could he talk to them about the way he felt when he saw a goshawk ruffle its white nape feathers? The trouble with these fellows was that long periods of isolation had sapped their ordinary social instincts. They swore, broke wind at Keogh's table without apology, and communicated with grunts, whistles, and monosyllables, instead of words. At night, they sat in silence by their fires, as darkness settled on the camp, only opening their mouths to burp, or spit on the flames. Brew wondered, What do these quiet fellows see in those glowing embers?

Brew heard plenty of derns! and damns! when the buffalo hunters reached the upper camp. The site had been littered with rags, bones, bits of human flesh. Brew wrote in his log:

Upper Camp:
The scene we discovered here was distressing beyond expression. All the tents had been cut up and were gone, and the whole camp gutted; or what was left, was smashed and destroyed — baking pans broken to pieces, cross-saws bent in two, books and papers torn up and scattered in the wind, with torn clothes and blood besmeared in every direction, but no bodies in the immediate vicinity. It was easy, however, to trace them, and see how they had been dragged down to the river, by certain marks which the scouts discovered. The body of Mr. Trotter was found, the head missing. There was a spear wound in the right breast. A large incision in the side showed that the body was empty and that the heart had been removed — to be cut up probably, and ate, as the greatest mark of

vengeance. The body was naked, a woman's shoe, and Mr. Trotter's pocket and time books, and several letters were found with the body.

A receipt from the Bank of North America for $15, and two $10 bank notes, belonging to C. McBeth, also a post-dated cheque for $1000, drawn on Mr. Trotter's account in favour of Mr. McEachren, plus a number of IOUs incurred by gaming, were found among the stray papers.

Motives for the massacre:

Plunder was certainly one of the chief incentives, there can be little doubt, however, that the main object in view was to put a stop to the road through Chilcoaten territory.

These murders are but a continuation of those earlier, which prove the aversion of the Chilcoatens to the opening up of their country by whites. The Bute Trail had lately entered their territory, and no compensation had been offered to them. Two years ago, Mr. Waddington succeeded in pacifying the natives down below with small presents. The Upper Chilcoatens only hated Mr. Trotter inasmuch as they hated this whole enterprise. The mutilation of Mr. Trotter's body was a well known act of warlike vengeance, and the natural consequence of being at the head of the enterprise in Mr. Waddington's absence. There is also the alleged business of Mr. Trotter's men ill-treating Indian women.

A third and last conjecture may be given, which is the removal of Governor Douglas, whom the Indians have known for 30 years and for whom they have had a profound respect. Nor can the Indians understand how a chief or governor can be removed except by death.

We have routed the Chilcoaten discovered at Waddy Flats, but I fear that we will not likely engage them on this ground, which is broken and desolate. Tomorrow, I will begin my return to New Westminster, and allow Governor Seymour to dictate what further measures may be undertaken to uphold the law.

When Herrold woke Inspector Brew the next morning, Brew polished his boots and whisked dust off his black uniform before doing his rounds, it being his entrenched belief that after valour, an officer's main duty was to set a good example in matters concerning dress and decorum. He chatted with the sentries, went to the grub tent, ate boiled flour and potatoes for breakfast and complimented Keogh on a job well done. Later, he settled a dispute between a Nova Scotian and a Canadian about the pronunciation of the word Newfoundland.

While striking his tent, Brew permitted himself a few moments of self-satisfied introspection. The buffalo hunters had acquitted themselves well under his command. Harry Atkins had proved heroic, and Brew made a mental note to put his name forward to Seymour, in case any honours might be forthcoming. Apart from a buffalo hunter who choked to death on a plug of chewing tobacco, and another who broke his neck falling off a cliff in the night while heeding a call of nature, no major casualties had attended the expedition. For the hundredth time, Brew wondered what had happened to Decker. Pity about Smuts' dog — the big Australian was still quite cut up about it. Funny, how sentimental some of these stolid-seeming chaps were, when you cut through all their nonsense and got down to brass tacks.

"Alright, Herrold," Brew said, as his sergeant came up. "Let's get these chaps together. It's back to Waddy Flats for us, now."

CHAPTER TWENTY-SIX

DECKER AND BUSHRAT and Isabel had left the tall cedars and pines and firs of the lowland forests behind. Stunted tamaracks and spruces grew between patches of muskeg and poor, sparse grass. Where soil had washed into hollows, strawberries and rattlesnake orchids and rein-orchids fought with plaintains and blackberries for a foothold. Cottonwoods and willows flourished along the banks of myriads of tiny streams. Wildfowl honked and croaked amid the bull-rushes and waterlilies, fattening themselves on dense floating banquets of flies and mosquitoes that were rising constantly from every drop of standing water. Four-legged animals were rare. Plagued by biting insects, Decker forged a path across bogs and rockfields until they came to a ravine down a slippery, hundred-yard zig-zag that was as steep as the roof of a house. Halfway down, two massive boulders came together in a vee the width of a man's shoulders. It was a terrible sight for men, and a worse one for horses. There was no way around it. The chestnut was blindfolded and with Decker holding its reins and both lawmen telling the horse how brave and smart and beautiful it was, they got it down. The bay was a thinner horse and it should have gone down too, but it lacked the chestnut's courage. With nothing else for it, Bushrat made a rawhide loop and passed it over the horse's muzzle, put a stick in the loop, and twisted until the rawhide bit into flesh. Unbearable pain drove fear out of the bay's mind and it made a sudden ungainly leap. Moving out of the way too late, Bushrat received a lightning kick which snapped his right femur and sliced open his wool pants from knee to crotch. The frenzied bay plunged down the ravine and fell head first, breaking its own legs. Bushrat's leg stuck out at an unnatural angle to his body; Decker dragged him down to a sphagnum bog below the ravine and found a dry patch to lay him on. Mosquitoes clouded visibility and any bare skin was black with them. Isabel scrambled down the ravine in a hurry. "What can I do?" she said.

"If we don't get smudge-fires lit, we'll go mad," Decker said, cutting Bushrat's pants away with a knife. "That leg's got to be attended to now, while he's in shock. When Bushrat comes round, he's going to hurt."

Sitting, Decker put his right leg between both of Bushrat's. With his foot against Bushrat's crotch, Decker yanked the broken leg until it straightened. Bushrat's eyes opened. He didn't moan overmuch, but Isabel stopped working on lighting a fire and held her hands over her ears when his noise became too loud. Bushrat's thigh was swollen but the ends of the femur seemed straight and true. Isabel went back to making smudge-fires while Decker splinted both of Bushrat's legs together with pine-wood and strips cut from a blanket. He looked like an Egyptian mummy from the crotch down when Decker got finished with him.

They made Bushrat comfortable on dry ground, brushed flies and mosquitoes away from his eyes, and Decker said, "I can do no better. If that thighbone's not lined up right, a sawbones can fix it later."

Decker wasn't talking to Bushrat, he was talking to Isabel, but Bushrat opened his eyes. "I be pure gone to hell," he said. "I'm a busted sonovabitch."

"You've been a busted sonovabitch all along," Decker said.

They spent two days being eaten by mosquitoes, while Decker, using nothing but his knife, built a travois out of lodgepole pines. He used the bay's straps and other leather to brace the cross-pieces and fix the travois to the chestnut's saddle. A harness passed around the trailing end of the travois and ended in a loop long enough to reach over Decker's shoulders. Then they had to get Bushrat out of the ravine up a route that was almost as bad as the one they'd come down. When they finally moved him, Bushrat could tolerate a travois ride across smooth ground. On rough ground, Isabel led or rode the chestnut while Decker walked behind with the weight of the travois' trailing end borne on his shoulders. He could keep going for ten or fifteen minutes at a stretch, sometimes, before he had to rest.

Decker and Bushrat and Isabel passed below a sandstone bluff and reached a plateau beyond Tatlayoko Lake where there were many small meadows covered in sweetgrass as high as horse bellies. Dotted with small lakes and jackpine forests, the view stretched to distant summits in the west as far as the eye could see. To the east it was mostly forests and lakes. Small birds were singing in the trees when they stopped at a crystal creek running across a mud bar and stared at each other. Decker wiped his sweating, fly-swollen face with the back of his hand and said, "That's pretty country."

"There ain't nothin' to touch it," Bushrat said with great solemnity from the travois. "Nothin' in this world."

Watched by a herd of mule deer bunched just beyond the range of Winchesters, Isabel filled their canteens at the creek. Bushrat, raised up on his elbow tasting the water, said with every evidence of satisfaction, "You can see every kind of animal print in God's creation on that creek mud, 'cept human."

The deer moved off unhurriedly. Decker lay down on the bare grass. When he opened his eyes, Isabel had built a fire and was frying what was left of the horse-meat they'd been eating for the last week. Decker finished eating, and climbed the sandstone bluff to check their backtrail. He liked everything about it, except for the Indians winding out of the broken hills they had recently traversed themselves.

Decker went back to Bushrat and said, "How many miles to Bella Coola?"

"You head north a few miles, and you reach the Palmer Trail. After that it's two hundred miles straight west. Maybe two-fifty. The going's a lot easier than what we've had. Head east, and it's eighty miles to the Fraser."

"It's only three miles to Indians," Decker said. "They're coming up on foot."

"Klatsassan's gang?"

"That's my guess."

"Go. Clear off," Bushrat said. "You and Isabel. Take the chestnut and they'll never catch you."

"I'm not leaving you on your own," Decker said. "It's taken me two years to get you trained to where you're halfway useful."

"You and me, we killed some of Klatsassan's people. It ain't likely he's forgot."

"We'll kill a lot more, if they come at us."

Isabel wouldn't leave Decker. "We'll die here," he said. "There's forty, fifty of 'em."

"I'm not going," she said.

They went up a hill, took Bushrat off the travois and, with him propped against a rock, loaded every gun. There was no point in trying to hide so they built another fire. Decker got water boiling. The Indians were a mile away.

Decker said, "One thing I can't figure. If this is the crowd that jumped us in Waddy Flats, they must have quit the place shortly after we did. Why?"

"Chilcotins ain't easy to figure," Bushrat said.

"Neither are we."

"Dern right. I'll never figure why you been wastin' your time packin' a busted-up one-legged jackass all over hell's half acre. Without me, you'd have been clear away, by now."

"You be quiet," Isabel said sharply. "Don't you know he loves you?"

Decker tended the fire.

Drinking hot water made slightly dirty by a few grounds of coffee, beneath the smoke of their campfire rising straight into the sky, Isabel and Decker sat on the ground together, cross-legged, waiting with rifles across their laps. With the Chilcotins five hundred yards away, Isabel reached out for Decker's hand. In silence, they watched the Chilcotins pass by along the trail below.

The great war chief went first in the full pride of manhood and majesty, his long hair beribboned and plaited and his hawkface chalked with stripes of red and yellow, carrying a yew-wood battle lance bound with eagle feathers. Lesser chiefs came on, not deigning to show their painted faces to the King George men watching them from above. Warriors armed with bows and muskets came on; boys followed with bows beside little girls holding flowers and dolls to their bosoms. You could hear footfalls and the rattle of knives and axes and bandoliers, and the sighs and groans of the walking slaves and women pitifully burdened in the rear of the caravan.

"Hellfire and damnation," Bushrat said. "I never seen the likes of it."

The Indians' chanted song had faded in the east when Decker made a foray on his belly in the long grass. He bagged a muley with one shot from his Winchester. After gutting and skinning it out, he sliced the meat into very thin strips. Isabel cut green-wood poles and set them on forked uprights above the fire. They watched the meat, hanging like laundry and turning brown in the smoke, the fat dripping and sizzling on the coals.

Three dots appeared on the western horizon and grew steadily bigger. The dots were horse Indians armed with bows, riding bareback on ponies shod with rawhide. Holding simple rope bridles instead of reins they rode straight and upright, their bare heels hooked underneath their ponies, and stopped a hundred yards short of the white men's camp, unsmiling, not talking, their eyes black as coals, staring mostly at Isabel. Decker nodded them in. Leaning forward, the Indians spat. Whipping their ponies with bridle-ends they wheeled off down to the creek. It was darker when they came back. With firelight darkening their copper faces they kept their distance, still unsmiling, holding onto their bridles.

Decker speared a generous amount of deer-meat strips with a pointed stick and carried it over to them. They would not meet his eye. Decker left the meat lying on the grass and went back to his fire. After a while, the Indians grunted, and reached for the meat. They ate it, fastidiously, one little piece at a time, and when it was all gone they came closer. Bushrat spoke to them in Chilcotin and listened to their halting, guttural replies. The Indians raised their right hands, swept them in wide circles, and rode away.

"Those boys are out of Whisky Creek," Bushrat said. "They been telling me that Ansanie Chilcotins attacked a wagon train, one or two days out of Bella Coola. The Ansansies killed the leader, a man called MacDonald, and twelve others. Three men escaped."

"When?"

"A month ago."

Alone with Bushrat later, Decker said, "What else did they say?"

"They'll pay twenty horses for Isabel."

"Not enough," Decker said, "I think I'll keep her."

CHAPTER TWENTY-SEVEN

THE WIND HAD been rising all day up at Hat Creek. Smelling of rain and rotten snow, it ruffled the tail of Henry Magwire's horse as he and his son, Duncan, herded fifty head of their cattle across the range. When they reached the creek, the Magwires got their cattle started across the knee-deep water. Henry Magwire, sitting motionless on his horse with one hand on the saddle horn, was a tall, quick, fearless man of fifty, with shoulder-length black hair. He took one last glance at the horizon. Jack Alexey, Magwire's Indian wrangler, was already far away across the creek, bringing in a couple of strays. Beyond, another horseman was galloping towards Magwire's house along the Hat Creek trail. Magwire touched his horse lightly with his spurs and went into the creek.

By the time Magwire reached his yard, a stranger was watering a foundered-looking horse at the trough beside the house.

"You Henry Magwire?"

Magwire nodded.

"I'm Herrold. One of Chartres Brew's policemen, from New Westminster. I got something for you."

Herrold took an envelope sealed with wax and a broadsheet out of his saddlebags. "You can read, I take it?" Herrold said.

"Why?"

"Because if you can't read, I'll read it for you."

"Then you'd know everything I know."

"I know what's in the letter already."

"That's good," Magwire said, "but I can read."

The broadsheet was a proclamation from Governor Seymour. Magwire's expression did not change when he read it:

$250 reward will be paid for the apprehension and conviction of every Indian or other person concerned as principal or accessory before the fact, to the murder of Europeans, who were cut off by Indians on or before the 29th or 30th days of April now past, in the valley of the Homathko River, in Bute Inlet.

Magwire folded the poster up and shoved it into a back pocket along with the envelope.

"I been riding my ass off for days, to bring you that letter. Ain't you going to open it?"

"I don't expect no surprises. Klatsassan has been killin' people, and I guess Brew wants me to do something about it," Magwire said, showing Herrold his dark eyes. He threw his reins over a hitching rail and added sarcastically, "If you knew anything about horses, Herrold, you'd know that animal of yours ain't gonna take you ten more miles. As for the letter, I'll read it when I'm good and ready. First, tell me what you think's going on."

"I've no time to waste. I've got letters for William Cox up north, in Quesnellemouth."

"Quesnellemouth is still frozen in."

Herrold shoved his hat back, folded his arms, and said, "The governor wants Cox to raise volunteers in Quesnellemouth, and ride to Chilko Creek. Chartres Brew is heading for Bella Coola on a navy ship with another force. Mr. Brew will strike east along the Palmer Trail."

"Where do I come in?"

"If you're willing, you've been appointed Cox's second in command. The governor's asking you to raise volunteers here, and rendezvous with Mr. Cox at Chilko Creek. The hope is that Brew's force and Cox's force will meet somewhere along the trail, and engage the renegades."

"This Seymour fellow. What the hell's he going to be doing?"

Herrold had run out of patience. "Tell you what, Magwire," he said, remounting his horse. "If you ever get off your ass and do something, you might actually run into Seymour on the trail. Then you can ask him yourself."

Herrold left Henry Magwire's ranch and changed horses in Hat Creek. Four days later, on May 29th, Herrold delivered his letter to the gold commissioner, Cox, at his office in Richfield.

William Cox, like Brew and Magwire, had no trouble recruiting good men. Cox's main difficulty was that there were no paddle steamers capable of moving them and their horses downstream because the Fraser was still jammed with ice. Inexplicably, instead of riding to Chilko Creek directly, Cox decided to build rafts to convey his volunteers and their horses a few miles downstream, first.

Henry Magwire's first recruit was his son, Duncan, and his second was Jack Alexey. Magwire raised another twenty-two horse volunteers and set a cracking pace out of Hat Creek, riding west from the Fraser into the eye of a storm.

Len Carruthers, a Californian, wondered out loud what the hell the hurry was. When Magwire didn't react, Stu Trotsky, a Canadian, ventured that Magwire might be deaf.

Magwire smiled.

Lightning had been lancing the rain out of black thunderheads for hours, when Magwire's party reached an unnamed creek. With huge raindrops pocking the waterlogged ground, Magwire reined in and dismounted. His men and their horses were worn out after three days hard riding, but they were deep in the Chilcotin. Magwire wasn't worried about night-warriors, he was worried about horse thieves, so he called it quits for the day. They all got their horses rubbed down and staked, and their tents up. After supper, Magwire didn't think twice about who his sentries would be. Carruthers and Trotsky had distinguished themselves as slackers and whiners, and Magwire figured he'd teach them to keep their mouths shut. He told Carruthers to get Duncan Magwire and another man to relieve them at midnight, then he turned in.

Carruthers felt aggrieved, because he had done as much riding as the others, and needed his bed. "Quit," said the night, as rain dripped off the trees and an owl hooted across the creek. Carruthers thought, I could clear off, go home to my gold claim, which is where I ought to be, instead of being out here under the thumb of a sorehead. The dark was as thick as a blanket though, and the rain was damnably cold in this uninhabited end of the earth. Carruthers slumped beneath a tree, his back to the wind, with thoughts of desertion warming his heart. Coyotes were yammering all around. Ten yards away, horses snuffled.

Trotsky came up out of the darkness and said, "You awake?"

"Yes, and I'm a porcupine if there's anything except them damned coyotes awake this side of Hat Creek."

Trotsky sat beside Carruthers and pulled out tobacco. "Put your head down," he said, "I'll cover for both of us."

"I'm too dern mad to sleep," Carruthers said. "Who the hell's Magwire think he is? Treats us like dirt, he does, as if we was common sojers. But my turn will come. We had a major like him. Jolly Jack Thorpe. Major Thorpe was a bully boy too, a regular terror. He died leading a charge at Valley Forge, with bullets in his back."

"One of 'em was yours, was it?"

"I ain't saying."

"Sure," said Trotsky, lighting his pipe. "There's more ways of killing a pig than tickling it to death."

"Damned right."

"Only thing is, Magwire ain't no soldier. He's an old Hudson's Bay trader. Had a falling-out with his bosses, they say, and quit to start that ranch of his. Married an Injun."

"That's obvious," Carruthers said. "His kid, Duncan, he don't look no different than Jack Alexey."

Carruthers and Trotsky were ending their watch when they heard a sound.

"It's wolves, out by the lake."

"Them ain't wolves," said Carruthers, his eyes glittering. "Wolves ain't so noisy. It'll be Magwire, trying to catch us out."

Trotsky emptied his pipe and moved with Carruthers to the edge of the grove. They saw nothing moving at first, because there was a dry ravine, deep enough to hide a walking man. Then, squinting into the darkness they noticed a fur cap, bobbing up and down as somebody marched along.

"It's Henry Magwire," Carruthers whispered. "We'll swing in behind, and give him the shock of his life."

Chief Klatsassan was tramping in the dark, navigating by instinct, hearing occasionally the stifled wail of a hungry child as weary Chilcotins followed the track of his moccasins. White men were camped in a grove nearby. Klatsassan thought, Their fires have burned down, but white men do have to worry about fire. White men carry engines of fire in their pockets. White men did not need old women to tend the flames while others sleep. Truly, white magic was as powerful as white wickedness.

When the trail became smooth, Klatsassan broke stride to sniff the air. Tobacco! White men were all around. Only old dogs who lived in pit-houses stank worse than white men. He went on, seeking a place uncontaminated by white men. Now his heart soared, because in this blinding darkness The Creator had guided his feet to the dry ravine he had been seeking. Soon his people would ascend without hindrance to William Manning's house. Then, Klatsassan's people would be warm and dry, with full bellies.

In that dead night, Klatsassan heard a sound. One of his comrades was making the warning cry! He spun on his heels, reaching for his knife.

Thin squeals, like the cries of stricken rabbits, echoed along the dry ravine, as Carruthers and Trotsky died.

Klatsassan was afraid. His people were wet and tired but there was no relief unless they robbed and killed more white men. Now, surely, Klatsassan's people would perish unless they found shelter. Bears and dogs would eat their bones.

Everybody said it was very wet, for Biting-Fly Moon.

"The Creator has turned his face away from us," said Tahpitt.

Klatsassan nodded. As a young man, Klatsassan had waded in icy lakes every day to harden his body. But he was a man. What about these little children? What about these old women?

Truly, this was a terrible journey. Only fools, or men chased by dogs, would endure such a thing. Even for men who had hardened their bodies by wading in icy water it was a very cold wetness. Klatsassan's people had never felt such misery in their lives.

Piell Who Was Burned In A Chimney said, "Who is sending this great misery?"

"White men are sending it," said Cusshen The Scarface. "This is white misery."

When they reached William Manning's ranch, Klatsassan asked Cusshen The Scarface what to do.

"Let us eat William Manning's food," said Cusshen The Scarface. "Let us sleep in William Manning's house."

William Manning was dozing by his fire when his Indian wife shook him awake.

"Run! Run! Klatsassan and Tahpitt are here," she cried. "His warriors are crossing the hayfields!"

"Calm yourself, Nancy. I've never hurt Klatsassan, or Tahpitt, and they won't hurt me," he said, laughing at her fears.

Nancy was cross-barring the ranch-house door when moccasined feet pounded along the porch. Battleaxes sundered the door battens and it burst open. Nancy was thrown to the floor. Manning was still fumbling in his pockets for the keys of his gun cabinet when he was overwhelmed. Nancy's sister was trying to hide inside a closet. Manning's Indian foreman appeared. Knocked to the floor, he was crawling blindly to escape the wrath of his kinsmen when he raised his eyes. A chief with a face like crumpled red metal towered above. The chief closed his eyes and spoke modestly, quietly, before he raised his battleaxe, and brought it down in a slashing arc.

CHAPTER TWENTY-EIGHT

HENRY MAGWIRE WOKE up with rain drumming against the taut canvas above his head. Fumbling in the dark he lit a candle and looked at his watch — it was five o'clock in the morning. "Damn! Why wasn't I called?" he said aloud. Reaching across the tent he shook his son's arm. Duncan came awake with a muffled cry.

"What are you doing in bed?" Magwire said. "You're supposed to be watching the horses."

"Jesus Christ! Nobody called me at midnight, like they was supposed to."

"Don't go blaspheming and taking the name of the Lord God in vain," the older man said righteously.

Heavy rain was flattening the grass as the Magwires went from tent to tent, rousing the camp. Fearing the worst, they counted the horses. None were missing. Nervous, jumping at every sound, the volunteers lit fires and cooked breakfasts of bacon and beans in the forbidding darkness of the woods.

It had been full daylight for two hours and the rain had stopped before Jack Alexey found Carruthers and Trotsky, lying together with their throats cut. Alexey, a Nechako Carrier, ranged on alone, grinning and muttering to himself as he passed up and down through the trees and along faint trails. He came back and said, "I don't see much, and I keep losing 'em."

"Who?" Magwire said. "Chilcotins?"

"How should I know?" Alexey grumbled, as steam rose from the waterlogged earth. "All I know is, they was wearing moccasins and there's mebbe forty, fifty of 'em. They're doin' what they can to throw us off their trail."

Henry Magwire insisted on giving the dead men a full Christian burial, with words and hymns, and the sun was at its maximum height when his troop mounted their horses and began a slow pursuit. Jack Alexey, walking in front, kept losing the trail and finding it again; progress was very slow and he lost the trail completely at Puntzi Lake. With night coming on and nothing else for it, Magwire made his camp in a mosquito-ridden swamp, three miles short of William Manning's ranch and eighteen miles from Alfred Jennings' place.

The sun was shining the next morning, and the humid air was thick with flies and mosquitoes when the sorely tried men left the lake and its marshes behind without stopping to eat breakfast. Alexey picked the trail up again near Manning's south fence line. Magwire made the mistake of leading his men within sight of William Manning's house, which overlooked a hundred acres of grazing land but was sheltered by trees at the back. Too late, he wheeled his horse around and led his hungry men back behind the trees — the men who killed Carruthers and Trotsky were inside the house, and they had spotted him.

Magwire told Duncan to take ten men in a wide circle around the grazing land, and position them on a hill overlooking the north side of the house. Magwire, Jack Alexey and the rest of his force left their horses picketed, and crawled on their bellies to a copse overlooking the south side of the house. A glint of polished rifle-steel showed at Manning's windows. "Take cover, men," Magwire shouted, as bullets started flying. "They're holed up!"

Chief Klatsassan's people and Chief Tahpitt's people were together in Manning's house. Most of them were asleep after slaughtering and feasting on Manning's beef. Klatsassan did not sleep. His mind was troubled. He thought, What will become of my people? They are tired of running; they are tired of being hungry; they are tired of being chased. What will become of these women and these little children? In anger we killed white men. Now, white men will pursue us to the ends of the earth. They will destroy our winter lodges. They will throw our winter food to the beasts of the forest.

Klatsassan was tired of killing. That was why he had stayed his hand, instead of killing Decker and Bushrat and their woman. Would The Creator now stay the white man's hand? If The Creator melted the white man's heart, the lives of Chilcotin women and children would be spared, as Decker had been spared.

Klatsassan slept, dreaming of The Creator, until a warrior burst into the house, crying, "White men have surrounded us! They are on the high ground!"

In a minute, Klatsassan's warriors were shooting at the harmless shadows moving on the hills.

"Do not waste your bullets shooting at shadows," Klatsassan said. "Now we will lay down our weapons and leave this house."

Magwire's men were busily shooting the siding off Manning's house with their hunting rifles, when Magwire shouted, "Cease fire! We're wasting ammunition."
That was true. The Chilcotins had dispersed like ghosts into the pines along trails impossible for horses.
Jack Alexey went hunting again and found William Manning's body in a well with three others, weighted down with stones.

***

Every night for three nights, Isabel went to Decker's bed. On the fourth day, two of the Whisky Creek Indians showed up, each leading a spare horse.
The Indians were shy and would not speak until they had drunk water from the creek and smoked two pipes of tobacco. Simon Twin Oaks rose to his feet and said to Bushrat, "In the olden days Mr. Manning needed men to drive stock from Williams Lake to his ranch at Puntzi Lake. I was such a man. In those same olden days, Klatsassan took my sister to wife. Now Klatsassan has killed Mr. Manning. Now, Henry Magwire is going to kill Klatsassan."
"What's Henry Magwire got to do with it?"
Simon Twin Oaks told him.
"It is the killing season," Bushrat said. "Klatsassan has killed more men than King Pox. Now the bill will come in."
"Klatsassan is tired of killing. Klatsassan has laid down his arms and is ready to talk," Simon Twin Oaks said. "Decker must tell Henry Magwire these things."
"Where is Magwire now?"
"At Mr. Manning's house with white men, now twenty-eight in number, and one Indian."
"What is Magwire waiting for?"
"He is waiting for William Cox to arrive from Quesnellemouth. When you are ready to mount the horses that we have brought for you, we will ride together to William Manning's ranch and you will speak to Henry Magwire. Henry Magwire must make an end to this killing."

Life was moving too fast for Decker. Sometimes walking, sometimes riding the Palmer Trail on the Indian pony that Simon Twin Oaks had brought him, he had become aware of a curious thing — he loved

Isabel more than she loved him. Last night he'd asked her to marry him and she had shaken her head. He was perplexed, but he knew this much: their lovemaking would come to an end soon, just as surely as the Chilcotin war would come to an end.

Decker had something else to worry about. The weather was turning hot and Bushrat's condition was much worse. He became delirious, raving to the point where they had to lash him to the travois. They took it in turns to walk alongside him, shading his face with their hats and trying to keep him cool with drinks of water. Decker had stopped looking at the broken leg. There was nothing he could do about it now, and the awful thing was, it was beginning to look worse than Henderson's fingers had before he lopped them off.

Henry Magwire was waiting for William Cox in Manning's house when Isabel and the lawmen showed up. They put Bushrat to bed, and while he was sleeping, Decker told Magwire what he'd heard about the MacDonald massacre.

"MacDonald couldn't have been murdered by Klatsassan," Magwire said. "According to you, he's been too busy walking here from Waddy Flats and killing Manning."

"That's right," Decker said. "Ansanie Indians killed MacDonald. We could be faced with a general uprising."

Magwire paced the room. "Dammit," he said. "I wish I knew what the hell Cox is up to. I've got a couple of men stationed at Chilko Creek, waiting to fetch him here if he ever shows up. He's supposed to be in charge of this outfit, not me."

"Klatsassan's ready to talk to you, now."

"I know. And where the devil is Governor Seymour?"

"He's probably two hundred miles away, and more."

"I've a good mind to take a small party, three or four men. We'll follow Klatsassan's tracks. He can't be far away. He and his people must be exhausted."

"Or as exhausted as your men appear to be," said Decker, gazing outside to where Magwire's men were sprawled in the long grass, enjoying the sunshine.

"They're still soft, but I'll toughen 'em up," Magwire said, making a move to go outside. "I'll go see if I can round up a couple of live ones. If Klatsassan wants to parley, I'm ready to parley with him."

"Count me in," said Decker. "Simon Twin Oaks, too."

"You look like hell. And I don't trust Simon Twin Oaks."

"I do. I've learned to trust him."

"Maybe so, but I'm in charge here. What I say, goes."

"Fine. but I'd still like to go along."

"Are you fit?"

"I'm fit enough."

"Oh no, really," Isabel said, appearing in the room. She touched Decker's arm. "Will you never be satisfied?"

"Don't worry."

"Of course I'll worry," Isabel snapped furiously. "Must you go on and on? What are you trying to prove, that you're fearless, a man of iron?"

"I won't be taking unnecessary chances," Decker said, as Magwire went outside, grinning. "I've got plenty to live for. How's Bushrat?"

"Resting comfortably, for once."

Decker was with Henry Magwire, Fred Harressen, and Jack Alexey when they left Manning's ranch on foot and followed Klatsassan's trail into the trees. The brush was thick enough to provide good cover and deaden sounds along the trail.

Anukatlk, guarding the trail to Klatsassan's bivouac, was full of rage. Klatsassan had now begun to speak of peace, instead of war. In years to come, Anukatlk's grandchildren would want to hear of his adventures during those glorious days when brave Chilcotins battled white men. He would have to turn his head away and admit that he had done nothing, that the war ended when he joined Klatsassan's lodge. His grandchildren would whisper behind his back and say, "Our grandfather is a coward. He did not join Klatsassan's lodge until the war was over."

Anukatlk came out of his bitter thoughts when a Carrier strode into view along the trail, followed by three white men. Anukatlk could not believe his good fortune — white men! They were sneaking up on Klatsassan's bivouac! He lay on his belly and rested his musket across a fallen tree, feeling a rush of exultation. The Creator had sent enemies into his sights. Anukatlk sent up thanks to The Creator, aimed his musket, and pulled the trigger.

Henry Magwire, two yards ahead of Decker, chose that moment to stop walking. He turned around to say something and was falling before Decker heard the crack of Anukatlk's rifle. Magwire wasn't dead; he was paralysed, with a bullet in his back.

Alexey and Harressen were shooting blind as Decker dragged Magwire off the trail. Magwire's mouth was forming words and he was making fluttery signals with the fingers of his right hand, until his eyes glazed over and he stopped breathing. Harressen was crashing about in the bushes ahead. When the noise stilled, he called out, "Anybody there?"

"It's me," Decker whispered.

"How's Magwire?"

"Shut the hell up, won't you?"

Ten slow minutes of silence passed. Flies were crawling over Magwire's eyes when Alexey came swinging back down the trail.

"Over here," Decker said.

Alexey came over, grinning. Not realizing that Magwire was dead, he said, "There was just one of 'em shooting at us, boss. I guess he was watching the trail alone. Klatsassan and the rest of his gang are camped right out in the open, less'n half a mile away."

"Magwire can't hear you," Decker said.

Alexey sank to the ground slowly and ended up sitting on his heels, staring at his boss, but he didn't say anything. Decker left him crying over Magwire's body and went back to Manning's ranch with Harressen. They returned with extra men and a pack mule and put Magwire across its saddle. Decker got back to Manning's just in time to see William Cox arriving over the skyline with his volunteers.

Klatsassan and his people were tired. When Anukatlk came in to say that he had killed Henry Magwire, Klatsassan was angry. He banished Anukatlk from his sight until Snow-Coming Moon and asked his people what to do.

"We are tired of killing. We are tired of running. Let us wave a white flag and talk to The Great Chief English," said Cusshen The Scarface.

"Wave a white flag," said Piell Who Was Burned In A Chimney.

"Wave a white flag," said Chessus, a slave.

A slave had no business telling a great chief what to do. Now, because of this slave's insolence, Klatsassan did not want to wave a white flag.

"For one more night, we will remain in this bivouac," said Klatsassan.

In the morning, Klatsassan told the people of his war lodge to listen to his words. "The Creator has spoken to me, and now, we will wave a white flag," he said. "Tahpitt will carry a white flag to The Great Chief English. The Great Chief English will tell us what to do."

Tahpitt walked under a white flag and cried, "Who is The Great Chief English?"

"I am Cox," answered a tall man. "I am the great chief here."

"Klatsassan and his people are tired," said Tahpitt. "Klatsassan and his people have no food. Klatsassan and his people have nowhere to lay their heads in peace."

Cox gave Tahpitt tobacco and said, "Give this tobacco to Chief Klatsassan."

When Klatsassan received the tobacco, his spirit was filled with joy. He and his fellow chiefs smoked the tobacco and Klatsassan said, "The Creator has softened the white man's heart. This tobacco is a peace-offering from The Great Chief English."

Klatsassan gave Tahpitt twenty gold pounds and said, "Take this money to Cox, The Great Chief English."

When Cox received the money from Tahpitt's hand, he said, "Tell me what Klatsassan wants."

Tahpitt said, "Klatsassan wants to live in peace on his own lands as he did in the olden days before the coming of white men. Klatsassan does not want his people to be hounded into the mountains by men from Fire Canoes. Klatsassan does not want to kill any more white men."

"Klatsassan must come to me," said Cox. "Tell Klatsassan that no harm shall befall him."

When Klatsassan heard that no harm would befall him, he brooded in silence for two days, sending for no one and speaking to no one. He then rose from his bivouac with seven of his warriors and went to Cox.

Klatsassan said, "I have brought seven murderers and I am one myself. I have given you twenty English pounds as a peace-offering. Here are twenty more gold pounds for The Great Chief English."

Cox smiled and took the money.

Klatsassan said, "The names of the men present are myself, Tellot, Chee-loot, Tahpitt, Piell, Chessus, Cheddecki and Sangtangi. Ten more are at large. Others are dead."

Cox said, "Who are the other murderers?"

"They are Quotanusky, Yeltenly, Ahass, Hachis, Cusshen, Seitah, Kalteth, Lutas, Yahooslas, and Anukatlk," said Klatsassan. "Anukatlk has been banished from my sight for killing Henry Magwire and cannot be brought in to you until Snow-Coming Moon."

Cox said, "Give up your arms."

When the words of Cox were understood, people were afraid. As for Klatsassan, he refused to give up his knife.

"Take Klatsassan's knife," cried Cox.

Klatsassan was disgusted, and he threw down his knife.

Irons were brought. The hands and ankles of Chief Klatsassan and his Chilcotin warriors were fettered.

Cox said, "I wish to inform you, in the name of the Queen, that I am placing you under arrest. You are my prisoners."

Klatsassan said, "But where is The Great Chief English?"

Piell said, "Mr. Cox must speak with two tongues."

Tellot said, "King George men are great liars."

***

It was Snow-Coming Moon, and ice was beginning to web the lakes and tributaries of the upper Fraser. Decker was with Isabel in their room in the Quesnellemouth Hotel. Bushrat was downstairs, drinking whisky and talking to a man about horses. Decker was lighting a cigar when somebody knocked on his door. It was Matthew Begbie.

Decker introduced the judge to Isabel. Isabel said hello, excused herself, and went out of the room.

"By God, you know how to pick 'em," Begbie said. "When are you going to make an honest woman out of her?"

"Never."

"You've no excuse. I'm authorized to perform marriages, I'll do it for nothing."

"It's not as if I haven't asked."

"What?"

"The institution of marriage no longer appeals to Isabel."

Begbie examined the room's brass andirons before saying, "Will you be attending the executions, tomorrow?"

"No, Judge, I won't."

"Why not?"

"I've got other plans."

"You were there at the beginning. Don't you want to see the end of it?"

"I wash my hands of it, and besides, it's not the end."

"Yes it is," Begbie replied testily.

"I wash my hands of it, Judge."

Begbie said, "Come with me, please."

Begbie took Decker across town to the makeshift cells that carpenters had built to incarcerate Klatsassan and his men. Sentries unlocked the door and Begbie led Decker inside. Klatsassan and the other prisoners were locked behind thick log walls in an unheated cell with earthen floors. A jailer opened a Judas hole before putting his key into the lock. "Christ, they stink in there," he said, wrinkling his face in disgust.

Klatsassan, chained to a wall, had eyes that were not black, but a deep, intense blue. He was tall, with a big nose and dark-brown hair. Now there was blood in his eyes because he had been beating his head against the wood and clawing his face with long fingernails. Other

chains rattled, where Klatsassan's four comrades, lying on pallets of
straw in the darkness, moved in their fetters.

Begbie reached out a hand to touch Klatsassan's wrist. When
Klatsassan calmed, Begbie said gently, "I am sorry to see you in such
a state."

"If I am miserable, it is because I have been tricked into betraying
the cause of my people."

"Do you understand the white man's law?"

"No," said Klatsassan, "I do not understand it."

"Do you understand Chilcotin law?"

"Yes," said Klatsassan. "That I understand."

"In Chilcotin law, what is the punishment for murder?"

"Murderers are put to death."

"You are guilty of murder. Why should I not pronounce death for you?"

"Yes. You have pronounced death for me. But we are proud, and
white men were lying with our women. A white man put our souls in
a box of papers, and told us we should all die, whose names were
down, of smallpox. A white man put fire to my son. Are Chilcotins
cowards, that they must tolerate such insults?"

Klatsassan had been looking at his feet. He raised his eyes, and in
that fraction of time when their glances joined, Begbie saw dark and
dangerous lights in them. Begbie said, "May I be allowed to pray
with you?"

"No."

"Such prayers are heard by the Almighty. Do you not fear death?"

"A man's life is the hoot of an owl in the night. It is the leap of a
fish in a lake. My soul is like a little cloud, nothing more. Today it
passes across the sky. Tomorrow, a wind will blow my soul away
beyond the high mountains. Whither, I do not know, it is true. But I
am not afraid of the Almighty. I am only afraid of white men."

Begbie had tears in his eyes when he and Decker shook hands with
Klatsassan, and with all the other prisoners, before going outside. A
new fall of snow lay sparkling in the sunlight.

"Noble. Noble," Begbie said. "I never met a nobler savage."

"Oh sure. Klatsassan, Tellot, Chessus, Tahpitt, and Piell. They all
hang tomorrow though," Decker said. "But that's not a bad
bargain, is it?"

Judge Begbie stared at Decker and said uncertainly, "I beg
your pardon?"

"Well, Seymour got an extra thousand pounds a year. Brew and Cox
will be presented with silver tea services to commemorate their valour.
Henry Magwire's widow gets a little pension."

Begbie looked at the sky. "Pensions and tea services. Those tea services are worth a thousand dollars apiece. Nevada silver, imported from San Francisco. I happen to know that Brew would prefer the money instead," Begbie cleared his throat and said, "How is Mr. Wright?"

"Pretty well. He still limps a bit, but he's ready to start riding again."

"An amazing recovery."

"He's made of strong metal."

"Look here, Decker. Why don't you come back to Victoria with me, eh? There's nothing for you in Waddy Flats. Everybody else has quit the place."

"Thanks, Judge," said Decker. "But there's plenty there to keep me busy."

"Don't be downcast, there's a good fellow. She's too young for you anyway, you know that."

"I know that. I've always known that."

Decker shook hands with Begbie and went back to the hotel. Halfway up the stairs to his room he turned around and went into the bar. He bought drinks for himself and for Bushrat, but did little talking. It was mid-afternoon when an ostler took them around to where a mixed lot of generally sad-looking paints and duns and chestnuts were bunched up together on the far side of a pole corral.

"There's a horse," Bushrat said.

"Which one?"

"That hammer-headed son of a bitch with white feet."

"That's not a lady's horse."

"Hell, no. Take that appaloosa over there, hit's a lady's horse. I'm talkin' about a seat for myself. That ugly hammer-headed bronc will run from hell to breakfast and back."

"That's a twenty-dollar horse," said Decker.

"That's a fifty-dollar horse," the ostler said. "He ain't never been rid by an old man."

"Not till now," Bushrat said. "Bring me a hull and throw it on him, cousin."

"You got your will writ out?"

"Whatsa matter, cousin? Scared we might kick yer fence down?"

Shaking his head, the ostler went over to the tack shed to get a saddle.

The next morning, one hour before daybreak, Klatsassan, Tellot, Chessus, Tahpitt, and Piell were wakened. The Reverend Lundin

Brown read from the English bible while the doomed men said their goodbyes to their wives and their children. Their wives and children were crying.

Settlers were waiting around a scaffold, shuffling their feet in the cold of the Snow-Coming Moon, and the Chilcotin chiefs were being led out of the barn when Decker and Bushrat and Isabel rode out of town.

Decker tried, but couldn't stop thinking about Klatsassan. A man who respected animals so much he prayed to their souls before he killed them for his supper. This was a fellow who hadn't hesitated to make war on the folks spreading smallpox to his people, but at the same time he went down on his knees, in the forest, before he took a tree-branch for his bow. Hell, Klatsassan used to throw valuables into the lakes, every year, because he thought that if he didn't, the sea would forget to send any salmon his way.

Bushrat, sweating fiercely, had been keeping the hammer-head on a short rein for a few hours when Decker took a glance at the sun. Its rays were at a low slant to the horizon. The hangman would have cut Klatsassan's body down, by now. There'd be some fuss about what to do with his corpse. Maybe they'd bury Klatsassan and his comrades in the woods, near Henry Magwire. Speculating about the topics their ghosts might discuss together, until Judgement Day rolled around, occupied Decker's mind nicely, for a while.

When he looked back, Bushrat was trying to remount the hammer-head.